HER NAME IS ANKA

HER NAME IS ANKA.

She used to have another name, but she can't remember what it was.

It is long gone from her mind.

There is no point even searching for it.

She has tried and tried but it is not there any more.

It doesn't matter.

Anka is her name now.

She is four years old and she has had many Mamas and Papas.

The Mama and Papa she has now are the worst she has ever had.

She hates them and they hate her.

THE ROOF SPACE

THE SMALL GIRL is sitting on an upright brown, wooden chair right in the centre of the bare wooden floor of the attic of a tall, narrow, terraced house.

She sits alone, silent and still.

She has pulled her feet up on to the seat of the chair and drawn her knees up to her chest. Her arms are wrapped around her lower legs and she is resting her forehead on the top of her knees. There is no way of knowing if her eyes are open or closed, as her whole face is concealed by a curtain of thick, dark hair, which has been hacked at by someone with no hairdressing skill or tools.

The chair has no cushion. It has no upholstery at all. It came from downstairs. It used to be one of four ordinary functional chairs that were placed around an ordinary functional table in the room where the people of the house take their meals. They don't need four chairs. They only need three. One chair has been brought up to the attic especially for the small girl to sit on.

Once in a while, she will turn her gaze upward and peer through the long fringe that flops over her eyes.

The roof tiles slope down on two sides from a peak just above

MAY THE PEOPLE KNOW I'M HERE?

S.J. PRIDMORE

Flat Island Publishing, Hong Kong

Book Layout ©2021 Flat Island Publishing

Cover Image by Fernand Hostyn

May the People Know I'm Here/S.J. Pridmore 1st ed.

ISBN -13: 979-8700603256

❀ Created with Vellum

CONTENTS

PART I
ANKA

her head. She is pleased by the pattern the tiles make with their overlapping edges and the way their flow is interrupted by the dark wooden beams that divide the roof into equal sections. There are 16 beams. She likes to count them, especially when she is agitated. It helps to make her calm again. She is a good counter.

Nothing at all is stored in the roof space. There is no bric-a-brac. No antique furniture gathers dust. No family heirlooms lie long lost. No once-loved toys await discovery. No abandoned, bizarre mechanical devices invite closer inspection.

Aside from the pattern made by the tiles and beams, there is nothing for the small girl to look at or wonder about.

She is the only thing of interest here and, if you ask, she will tell you that her name is Anka.

———

THE LIGHT in the roof space comes through a small single pane window high up on the wall. Although the window is square, there is a messy triangle of dirty beige mould in each corner of the glass, so the area that you look through is almost round.

Anka once had a book, which had a picture on the cover showing a boy in a boat looking out of a round window. The boy was smiling and, framed in the window, in a circle of dark blue sea and light blue sky, was a tall tree with large, spiky bright green leaves set on a small island of yellow sand.

To stare out of the roof space window, all Anka needs to do is turn her head a little and look up, but she can't be bothered. There's no point. She already knows exactly what there is to see. A circle of ugly grey, the colour of underwear and bed sheets, framing nothing.

There was a time, when she was first brought up here to sit quietly while her Mama and Papa went out, that the window would show a sky-scape of pale blue with patches of white fluffy cloud drifting past. This made Anka happy. Just like the boy in the book.

But the sky hasn't been blue for a long time and it is also a long time since Anka has been happy.

There may not be anything to see from Anka's perch, but there is plenty to hear. The streets around the house are usually quiet, but sharp sounds sometimes punctuate the silence. Dogs bark, bells ring, doors bang, boots stomp, engines roar. People shout or call back and forth to each other. Occasionally someone will scream or cry out. There is never any music though. Nobody ever sings or whistles and she has never heard anyone laughing either.

The most curious sound Anka hears used to frighten her, but now it is something she looks forward to.

It is a clattering, clanking noise, which appears first as a faint disturbance, then gets louder and louder and louder, before it fades away and eventually disappears completely. Only to return a while later.

The clanking follows a rhythm that has four distinctive beats you can tap your fingers to - ker-chunk, ker-chunk - and it's exactly the same every time. Anka's favourite bit is when, just as the noise gets as loud as it can get, there's a sharp screech, which sounds like a baby crying.

Anka knows it's not a baby. That's just the idea that comes into her head when she hears it.

Her excitement mounts as the noise builds up, but when it is already extremely loud, a little knot of doubt always forms in the pit of her stomach as she fears that the moment may have already passed and the screech is not going to come. But, then it arrives, piercing the air and attacking her little eardrums.

And she smiles.

The screech gives Anka satisfaction. It has never let her down, but she can't stop worrying that one day it will. There hasn't been much in her little life so far that she can rely on.

———

IN THE BEGINNING, her Papa had to carry her chair up four flights of stairs, with ten steps in each flight, and a stepladder with twelve rungs. Judging from the amount of puffing and panting and cursing and sweating that went on, it wasn't easy.

"She could just sit on the floor, you know," he called down, once he had finished.

Papa should have thought of that earlier, thought Anka.

"We can't do that. What would people think?" said her Mama.

Anka's ears pricked up at that.

People? What people?

IT IS NOT JUST WINDOWS

ANKA HAS holes in her socks. She can push the little toe on her right foot out of one of the holes, wiggle it around, then tuck it back in again, curling her toes up tight so that you can't even see the hole any more. She has been practicing.

When she sits on the chair properly, her legs don't reach the floor. Nowhere near. If she were to point her feet, stretch her legs, arch her back and move her bottom to the absolute edge of the seat, maybe then she could just touch the floor with her tippy toes.

But she won't even try to do that. This would not be a smart thing to do.

After Anka is already settled on her chair and before her Mama and Papa leave, they lay sheets of Papa's newspaper down all around her, lining the pages up with great care, so that there are no gaps.

Anka must not get off the chair before her Mama and Papa return.

She did it once.

She will never do that again.

———

SHE HAD BEEN SITTING on her chair perfectly still for a long time. Her back and shoulders were sore and stiff, but that was normal. Then, suddenly, an intense pain started building up inside her. It was coming from the middle of her back and spreading through her, up to her shoulders, along her arms and down her legs all the way to her feet. She was in agony and began to fear that something terrible was happening to her. Was she dying?

She found that waving her arms and moving her head around reduced the pain in her upper body a little. But her legs were on fire and the fire was coming from inside her bones. She wasn't supposed to get off the chair, but maybe if she just stood up and tried walking around a little, she would feel better. What else could she do? Just sit there? Unbearable! She might die! Her Mama and Papa wouldn't want her to die, would they? Surely, they would understand. Anyway, if she moved very, very carefully, they might never know. It would be a secret.

Anka likes secrets. Having a secret makes her feel strong. If only she had more.

Her legs didn't seem to want to obey her at first, but once she straightened them out and pointed them down with a little flex of each foot back and forth, the pain began to ease. As her toes touched the newspaper, it rustled and she stopped, holding her breath. She glanced down. It didn't look like the pages had moved.

So, she crept away from the chair, being sure to stay as quiet as a little mouse, just in case her Mama and Papa had come home without her noticing. They might have sneaked back into the house quietly while Anka's mind had been away in dream world, a place it tends to go to quite often.

She avoided going near the window, of course. Oh no, she never goes near a window, wherever it may be, even if it is high up on the wall at the top of a house like this one.

If she goes near a window, she gets beaten for sure.

———

IT IS NOT JUST WINDOWS. If she is noisy, she gets beaten. If her Mama and Papa hear an unusual sound somewhere in the house, she gets beaten. Even if she didn't make the sound. They just blame her for no reason, which is terribly unfair.

If she cries when she is beaten, she gets beaten some more, to stop her crying, which never works.

Now she has learned to swallow her crying. She has taught herself how to cry noiselessly inside, so that nobody knows.

She doesn't complain. This is for her own good, after all. At least, that is what they say. The beatings are so that she will remember.

But, she still forgets things. She will do something that she is not supposed to do and then she will remember too late that she is not supposed to do it. And then she cries because she has been stupid.

Never in her whole life will she forget these beatings though. Never, ever, ever.

They tell her she is a bad girl and that is why she gets beaten. If she wasn't a bad girl, the beatings wouldn't happen.

But, she is not a bad girl. She is a good girl.

———

So, that time, after she got down from the chair, she just stretched her legs a little. Then she climbed back up, feeling much better.

A little later, the sound of the key turning in the lock downstairs prompted her to assume her usual welcome home pose – spine straight, chin up, legs together, hands in lap, facing forward with her best smile ready.

Papa pushed open the hatch and popped his head through. He acknowledged her presence with a satisfied grunt - the same noise he always makes when he pushes his empty plate away at the end of a meal.

Then he knelt down in front of her and examined the paper on the floor, his nose almost touching it.

Anka began to get anxious. He was taking a long time over his examination. Whatever could he be looking for?

When Papa raised his head again, his face was red, his jaw was clenched and his eyes were cruel and terrifying.

"You ungrateful little kike brat."

His mouth was so close that his spittle flecked her cheeks and the smell of his breath went up her nose. She flinched and closed her eyes.

When she opened them again, she saw her Papa taking off his belt.

WHO IS THAT LITTLE GIRL?

THERE ARE no other children in this house. There are no games to play and no books to look at. Even when her Mama and Papa are home and Anka is allowed to be downstairs with them, there is no fun to be had at all. Anka has nothing to do but sleep or eat or sit and daydream or watch her Mama and Papa do whatever they do, which is never all that interesting.

Her Mama and Papa are frightened. Every grown-up she has ever known in her whole life has been frightened.

It's not that they tell her they are frightened. She just senses it. They speak in whispers. Sudden noises make them jump and then they rush to the nearest window and peer out through the net curtain to see what's going on.

Her Mama and Papa are allowed near the windows. It is only Anka who is forbidden.

So, Anka gets scared too. She doesn't know what there is to be scared of but, if the grown-ups around her are worried about something, she supposes she should be too.

———

THERE IS no heating in the roof space. She is wearing four layers of clothing on top, but she is still cold and she can hardly feel her toes. She reaches down to check they are still there. They are icy to the touch. It must be freezing outside.

Anka has not been outside for a long time. The few times she can remember being out, it was dark and the person carrying her or holding her by the hand was in a hurry.

Before she came to this house, she lived with a Mama and Papa who didn't make her hide when they had visitors. Then, one day, a stranger pointed at Anka and asked her Mama, "Who's that little girl?"

Her Mama replied that she was a little girl they had adopted in India.

Soon after that, she was moved on to another Mama and Papa.

India?

Is that true?

Anka doesn't think it is, but why would her Mama tell a lie?

Why wouldn't her Mama just say Anka was her Mama's daughter?

The stranger could have asked Anka. She knows exactly what to say.

Just as everyone always tells her, over and over and over again, when anyone asks Anka what her name is, she is to say, "My name is Anka".

And if they ask her who her Mama is, she is to point to her Mama and say, "this is my Mama".

Whoever her Mama is at that time.

A RAINY DAY

ANKA IS UNCOMFORTABLE. She has been on her chair for a while now. Her mouth is dry but there is nothing to drink. Even if she had something, she would not drink it, because if she did, she might then need to pee.

Normally, she is highly skilled at holding her pee in. After all, she has had a lot of practice.

However, quite recently, her Mama and Papa went out for a long time, much longer than usual. Anka felt the bottom of her tummy becoming fuller and fuller and the urge to pee becoming stronger and stronger.

It's OK, she thought, I can manage. I just won't think about it. They'll be back soon.

But they didn't come back and pain started to build up in her tummy. She wriggled around on her seat, kicked her feet up and down and leaned backwards and forwards and from side to side, but none of that helped. Thinking of something else was no longer possible. She now had only one thing on her mind. She was about to burst.

A few seconds later, she did burst.

She peed all over her clothes, all over her chair and all over the newspaper, which turned so thin that the floorboards beneath became visible. All the words got blurry, like when you look out through a window on a rainy day.

Anka had rained on the floor.

Tiny gaps between the boards let a little light through. It seemed they let water through as well. There was a gentle drip, drip, drip sound coming from beneath the chair.

Anka just sat, looked down at her hands and waited for it all to stop. Which it did, but it took a long time. Her bottom was wet and cold and she began to shiver.

When her Mama and Papa came home and saw what she had done, their faces turned bright red and they shouted a lot, but at each other, not at her.

Their loud voices echoed around the roof space. They kept yelling "Why?" and "How?" and calling each other stupid.

They seemed to have forgotten that Anka was there, but she was sure this would not last long. At some point, they would both turn their attention to her and no doubt, as usual, she would get the blame. To her astonishment, for once, this did not happen. And, for a change, she didn't get beaten.

The floor was cleaned up before she was, however. No surprises there.

IT'S JUST YOU, ANKA!

SINCE THEN, every time her Mama and Papa have gone out, they have not stayed away for long.

Anka is good at waiting, though. Time does not hang heavy on her small shoulders. She has had a lot of practice doing nothing.

Today, just as she thinks it's about time they were home, she hears movement downstairs.

She can't hear any talking. She likes to listen in on what her Mama and Papa say to each other, mainly because she wants to know more about who she is and where she came from. But, most of what they say is meaningless and boring and she learns nothing useful or interesting.

They never talk about her. Maybe because they are aware she is listening. Maybe because there is nothing to say.

There are slow footsteps on the stairs and the usual creaking and groaning as the metal stepladder is moved into position. Then light thuds and squeaks as somebody starts to climb up. The squeaking is louder than usual.

The hatch lifts, light pours through the hole and a face appears.

It's a woman's face, but it's not her Mama. It's someone new. Her face is round, her cheeks are red, her nose is tiny and she has short blond curly hair. She is a little out of breath and puffs as she pushes the hatch open.

She looks annoyed, as if she is doing something she doesn't want to do and it is a big inconvenience. A lot of people give Anka that look.

But, as soon as the woman notices that she is being watched, her smile switches on like a light and she says, "Hello Anka!"

————

ANKA JUST STARES BACK at her. She has learned that when a grown-up smiles at you, it is because they want you to do something you don't want to do and they are trying to trick you into doing it by pretending it is fun.

They know you don't want to do it because, if they were you, they wouldn't want to do it.

She has also learned that, even if they say, "WE" are going to do something, this is a lie.

They are not going to do it. Only you.

WE are going to bed now.

WE have to go to the basement now.

WE can't make any noise now.

WE mustn't cry.

WE have to wait in the cupboard / under the floorboards / in the back room / under the bed until the people go.

It's never WE.

It's just YOU, Anka.

Only YOU.

The other reason grown-ups smile is to make you return their smile.

They then interpret your smile to mean that you like them and that you actually want to do the thing they are about to tell you to do, even though you don't yet know what it is.

Smiling back at grown-ups makes them happy. However, judging from Anka's previous experiences, it doesn't do you much good.

———

ANKA USED to go along with the programme. She would smile back at everyone who smiled at her, in the hope that they would like her and care for her and play with her and love her in return. They rarely did any of these things, so now she has given up.

Grown-ups can smile as much as they like. Their ruse doesn't work any more.

Not that this seems to matter much to them. They still don't get the message.

"Oh she's so shy," they say.

"She's having one of her days."

"She's not too bright, is she?"

"She may be deaf."

None of which is true.

THIS CANNOT BE GOOD

THE NEW ARRIVAL pulls herself through the hole in the floor with difficulty. Kneeling on the newspaper, her face is level with Anka's. She is still panting a little, mopping her forehead with a white, lacy handkerchief and repeating, "oh my, oh my, oh my!"

She reveals that her name is Mrs K, she lives across the road and she has a little girl whose name is Kokki and who is just like Anka.

Anka is sorry for that little girl if she is just like her. If she is always sad, has no friends, no toys, no one to speak to and is always in pain.

It is no comfort to her at all to think that there may be other children like her. She would prefer to be the only one. She would not wish her life on anybody. She certainly does not wish it on herself.

But she likes Kokki's name. It should be an easy name for Kokki to remember. Like Anka.

———

A CHILL PASSES through her little body and she shudders as a frightening thought occurs to her.

In the old days, many Mamas and Papas ago, before she learned to be silent and not to ask so many questions, when they told her to come away from the window, she would ask why and they would tell her, "So that people don't know you're here."

Now, every time she has a new Mama and Papa, a new place to sleep, new walls to look at and new outside noises to listen to, she asks, "May the people know I'm here?"

The answer is usually a flat "No!"

Which is what Anka has come to expect.

She often wonders why she can't be seen or why nobody can know about her.

People often look scared when she is around, but, although, as she lies awake at night, she has often racked her brains for the reason, she has never worked out why this should be.

Is it because of her looks? Is there something about her that frightens people? Who would ever see her and be scared? She is so tiny and she couldn't hurt a fly even if she wanted to. Which she doesn't.

So, the problem can't be with her. It must be other people who are the problem.

And Mrs K certainly fits the definition of other people.

She knew Anka was in the roof space.

She even knows Anka's name!

This cannot be good.

THERE'S NOTHING TO YOU

Now Mrs K has seen Anka, what will she do? What does she want? Why is she here? Do Anka's Mama and Papa know she is here?

The woman is ahead of her.

"Your Mama and Papa are going to be out for a long time today and they asked me to come over and take you to the toilet, if you need to go. Do you want to go pee-pee?"

Anka does want to go pee-pee, but she shakes her head.

The woman suggests they go down to the toilet and try. Anka shakes her head again. The woman obviously doesn't know that Anka is not allowed to go anywhere. Or, she is quite aware of this and is trying to get Anka in trouble.

Anka is 100% certain that if they go downstairs and they get caught, then later someone gets beaten for disobedience, it won't be the woman.

Anka waits. The woman has a kind smile and doesn't look like she means any harm. But you can never tell.

There's a long silence.

Maybe the woman is deciding what to say next. Grown ups often say the most ridiculous things to try to get Anka to speak to them.

Or perhaps she is trying to work out what is in Anka's mind.

Good luck with that! Anka is an expert at hiding her thoughts. Unlike grown-ups. It is always completely obvious what they are thinking.

"It's OK, nobody will be angry if you come to the toilet with me."

Anka is amazed.

That's the second time that the woman has guessed what she's thinking. How is she doing this? Is she a mind reader? Or is she just much smarter than other grown-ups?

Then the woman surprises Anka again, this time with a question.

"May I pick you up?"

There seems to be no reason to object. At least, the woman was polite enough to ask.

Anka nods.

The woman stands, leans forward, grasps her under the arms and pulls her to her chest. She smells of soap. Anka's arms are around her neck before she has even thought about what to do with them.

"Oh, you poor little thing. There's nothing to you. What have..."

She has difficulty finishing what she wants to say. It's as if the words have got stuck in her throat.

Her hug turns into a squeeze and her fingers press down on one of the sore places on Anka's shoulder.

Anka cries out, although with her face buried in the woman's thick coat, all that emerges is a small squeak.

The woman, surprised, pushes her away a little.

"Oh, I'm so sorry. What's wrong? Are you sore?"

She pauses.

"Let me have a look. Is that OK?"

Anka doesn't want to let her have a look. This is not OK at all. She is ashamed. The woman will see the marks on her body and she will think that Anka must be a bad girl because she has so many.

But Anka is not a bad girl.

NO, NO, NO, NO, NO, NO, NO...

OF COURSE, the woman isn't really asking for Anka's permission. What was Anka thinking? As if she has control of anything in her sad little life.

The woman slips a hand under Anka's clothing and onto her thin, bony shoulder. She touches a place where the skin is broken and traces her finger back and forth along the line. Then she moves her hand a little further, behind Anka's neck and down her back.

She's looking for more, thinks Anka.

She'll find plenty.

Old ones, new ones, lumpy ones, itchy ones, crusty ones, very sore ones, not so sore ones, squishy bruises on bones, sharp scratches in flesh.

Anka knows them all. As she lies in bed, she runs her fingers over her body, tracing the patterns. She imagines that her wounds are like the stars in the sky and her fingertips draw lines connecting them to make shapes and patterns.

With her head turned to one side, she peers up at the woman through gaps in the dark curtain of her fringe.

The woman hasn't noticed that Anka is watching her. Her mouth is moving although hardly any sound is coming out. She is just saying one word, over and over again.

"No, no, no, no, no, no, no…"

Small ponds have formed in her eyes and are spilling over and drizzling down her plump, red cheeks. She just lets the drops fall.

Anka is horrified. No, don't cry! She wants to say. You might make me cry too. They don't like people crying. You get beaten if you cry. They may come home at any moment and catch us.

She doesn't say this. She just thinks it. Giving voice to the things she thinks is usually a bad idea. This she has learned over the years. It tends to make grown-ups either nervous or angry. So, these days she says as little as possible. It's for the best.

This is a curious new development, however. Anka doesn't believe this woman is saying no, no, no, no and crying because she finds her repulsive. On the contrary, at this precise moment, Anka is feeling more loved and cared for than at any time she can remember.

Finding her scars hasn't made the woman think Anka is a bad girl at all, but it has clearly affected her greatly in a very different way.

WHAT IS REAL AND WHAT IS NOT REAL

ANKA CLOSES her eyes and lets her mind wander. What would this woman think if she knew about everything? If she could see all Anka's wounds - the scars on her legs, on her arms, on her hands, even on her fingers.

The old marks on her hands and arms are from the days when she tried to stop the belt from hitting her. Before she realised that this was a stupid thing to do and that it was better just to let the belt hit you wherever it wanted to hit you and try to think about something else while it was happening.

During these times, Anka tries to escape by losing herself in daydreams of different places and different times.

In her favourite daydreams, she is playing with two other children. They are bigger than her and they like to hug her and hold her and kiss her. She makes them laugh and, when they laugh, Anka laughs too. This makes them laugh even more. These dreams are different from the dreams she has when she sleeps. They are crystal clear, the same things always happen and they are nice things. They never make her wake up shouting like her sleeping dreams often do.

She wonders if, in fact, these daydreams may be memories of

things that actually happened at an earlier time in her life. A time that she has otherwise forgotten. Although it's hard to believe that her life was ever different than it is now. She only remembers being alone and ignored.

Anka has decided that it is more likely that these are just memories of old sleeping dreams that she liked a lot and that she keeps alive by going back to them again and again and again whenever she feels the need.

Which is often.

Because that's all Anka wants. To be happy. To be with people she loves and who love her back. Is that too much to ask?

———

ANKA MAY SOMETIMES FIND it difficult to separate what is real and what is not real. But one thing is certain.

The pain is real and it comes in many forms. There is the pain of the belt hitting her and the different pain that comes and goes, rises and falls, long after the belt has stopped. There is also the pain in her legs and lower back when she has to stay in one position for a long time.

Then, of course, there is the special, particularly excruciating pain she has to go through when it is time for her to unfold her body after it has been curled up for a while in a space that nobody would ever think was big enough to hold a body.

She knows the pain of hunger. The pain of being thirsty. The pain of being alone. The pain of being ignored. The pain of being resented. The pain of catching people looking at her with hatred or fear in their eyes.

Finally, there is the pain of remembering. At the time that something bad is happening, she doesn't cry, of course. Oh no, that's a lesson she has learned the hard way. Instead, she tries her best to wish the pain away or escape into her dreams. But, later, when she's all alone, curled up in her bed in the darkness, she thinks back to what happened and the hurt returns along with the despair of how unfair this all is. Then, she doesn't have to stop herself from crying and she weeps and weeps and weeps. Although always in silence. Not only must she never be seen, she must also never be heard.

Oh yes, and there is one other pain. This is a dull, throbbing pain that sits deep inside her chest and never goes away. It's a constant companion. This pain is associated with the knowledge that she has lost something, but she has no idea where to look for it.

She doesn't even know what it is that she has lost.

THE BEST DAY EVER

THE WOMAN HOLDS her for a long time. Anka has no problem at all with this. It's wonderful.

The woman is saying things but Anka is not listening. She doesn't think the woman is talking to her anyway. She is repeating the same few phrases. It sounds like she is asking someone for something.

Anka is just enjoying the warmth, her smell, the sensation of safety.

Then a familiar urge starts to build inside her.

"Mrs K, I need to pee now."

The woman gives a little start, as if she is surprised that Anka can speak.

"Oh, my darling child. Of course you do. Do you know how to go down the ladder by yourself?"

She does.

"I'll be right behind you. Be careful now."

Anka steps off the last rung and looks up. A cloud of coat and skirt is descending towards her, accompanied by a few gasps and "ohs" and "ahs".

Arriving at last at floor level, Mrs K leans against the wall, pulls her handkerchief out of her sleeve and mops her forehead with it.

"Go on now. Do what you have to do. Call me if you need me. I'll be right here."

When Anka returns, Mrs K is sitting on the floor at the bottom of the ladder, feet tucked beneath her.

"You come over here and sit with me. We don't have to go back up there, do we?"

We certainly don't.

Anka squeezes in close. Mrs K wraps one plump, soft, warm arm around her shoulders and pulls her in even closer.

"Now, would you like to hear some stories?"

Anka nods. Her eyes are wide open, she doesn't even dare blink and her heart is beating so hard she can hear it.

This is turning out to be the best day ever.

Mrs K tells her stories about princes and princesses, about frogs and bears, about woods and mountains and, at the end of each story, the good people live happily ever after, while horrible things happen to the bad people.

Which is exactly how it should be.

Mrs K talks while Anka listens. Anka doesn't say anything for fear that Mrs K will stop talking.

Then she hears the door open downstairs and the spell is broken. That little girl in the house must have felt just like this when the bears came home.

"We're up here," Mrs K calls out, "coming down now."

She starts to stand up and has to let go of Anka's hand to steady herself against the wall as she gets to her feet.

"Oh," she cries out. "I've been holding your hand all this time. Made you all hot and sweaty, haven't I? What a disgusting old woman you must think I am."

Anka thinks nothing of the sort. She had been hoping the hand-holding would never end.

AS IF SHE EVER HAS A CHOICE!

ANKA HAS HAD many Mamas and Papas.

She had one Mama who gave her a glass of milk when she first arrived and stood there watching her as she drank it. The smile on her new Mama's face suggested that she expected Anka to be delighted.

Anka had never tasted milk before. She took a cautious sip. It was disgusting. She screwed up her face and tried to give the glass back to her new Mama.

Who then became angry and shouted at her. She told Anka not to be stupid and to drink it all.

Later, Anka overheard her telling someone the story, saying, "It is my job to keep her alive. How can I do this if she won't drink milk? Milk is what we have."

It was true. There were bottles of milk piled up in crates everywhere and, at almost any hour of the day and night, you could hear the sound of glass clinking as the crates were moved around. Many people would visit the house, probably because of the milk.

After that, Anka drank her milk without complaining, but she didn't stay there long.

In another place she lived, her Papa was always covered in black dust when he came home after work. Even after his daily bath, the dust was still ingrained in the lines on his face and hands and under his fingernails.

Even when he was clean, he didn't look clean.

Anka was afraid of him at first but, eventually, she got used to his appearance. The house was always warm and there was always plenty of coal for the fire and the stove. That was one thing she liked about that house.

But as always, after a while, just as she got used to being in a place, someone came and took her away to live with a new Mama and Papa.

She never wanted to leave any of the places she lived in, but, at some point the time would come and they would tell her she had to go. Her small case would be packed in a hurry and she would be sent on her way, often with hugs and tears.

The door would close behind her and she would be perched on a bicycle being pedalled by someone she had never met before, travelling fast through city streets in the dead of night, wrapped up in a coat and scarf and hat so you could hardly see that there was a person under all the clothing. Even if you were especially interested and looked closely and carefully, you still wouldn't even be able to tell the colour of her eyes or hair.

———

THIS TIME IT IS DIFFERENT. Anka doesn't want to stay in this house with this Mama and Papa. She has been unhappy before but here the unhappiness is on a whole different level. Even if she had to go to a home where they made her drink all the milk in the world every day, she would do it if it meant she could leave this house, right now.

But it is not up to her. Nothing is up to her. What she wants doesn't matter.

Sometimes people ask her:

"Do you want to do this?"

"Do you want to do that?"

"Do you want something to eat?"

"Would you like a glass of milk?"

Why do they ask? As if she EVER has a choice!

It makes her angry, although you wouldn't know it. She never lets on.

Every night, she dreams that Mrs K will take her away and she will get to meet Kokki at last. They will play together and tell each other stories. She will be happy and Kokki will also be happy.

They will be best friends forever.

A DELIGHTFUL CHILD

THEN, one evening, it appears that her dream may be about to come true.

There is a knock at the door. As always when there is an unexpected caller, Anka is ushered into the back room and pushed into her special space beneath the floor with the usual whispered threats.

"Don't move! Don't make a squeak! Don't cough!"

Anka hates this space. Things crawl over her, dust gets in her eyes and her nose and makes her itch, but she cannot fidget and she must certainly not sneeze – that would be an ENORMOUS crime.

But tonight, the dust and the creepy-crawlies don't bother her, because, between the shuffling, hanging up of coats and murmuring that always accompanies the arrival of visitors, Anka hears a voice that she knows intimately. It is a voice that she has been hearing every day recently, whenever she sits on her own, lost in thought, replaying wonderful, magical stories in her head.

It's Mrs K!

She gasps, then covers her mouth. Too late!

She's in luck. There's no reaction from above. The sound of her rapid intake of breath must have been lost in the thump of footsteps heading towards the front room.

There's a man's voice too, another man, not Papa.

The man speaks her name. At least, Anka thinks he does. She holds her breath and tells her heart to stop beating so hard, so that she can pick up as much of what is going on as possible.

Why is Mrs K here? Her Mama and Papa don't often have visitors.

Especially not unannounced visitors. They can't have been expecting Mrs K. If they had, there would have been no reason for Anka to hide.

Even though it's Mrs K and she knows all about Anka, still nobody comes to take her out of her hiding place. Yet another sign that this Mama and Papa really don't give much thought to Anka at all.

She's sure Mrs K is thinking about her, though. She probably imagines Anka is tucked up fast asleep in a soft, warm, comfortable bed, rather than lying with her knees folded up to her chest in a dirty hole under the floor.

The grown-ups are all chatting away. Anka gives up trying to follow the conversation. She just waits for her name to crop up again.

Which it does.

"We think it would be best for everyone if Anka were to go and live elsewhere," says Mrs K.

In the darkness, curled up, among the dust and the bugs, Anka deploys every fragment of energy and mental strength she possesses to draw the sound down through the cracks between the boards and into her ears.

She doesn't want to miss a single word.

Mrs K continues.

"You have given her so much for so long. She is so lucky to have had you to look after her. Especially given your position. You have been so brave."

Papa murmurs something inaudible. Mrs K goes on.

"You have taken huge risks. And as a leader of this community, we fear for your safety. We don't want to lose you. Your knowledge and your connections are so valuable for all of us. If we didn't have you, we would all be in much greater danger."

Anka is distraught. In danger? Mrs K? Oh no!

Papa speaks up, louder this time.

"You are right. It has been a long time. We sometimes do find her, um, how should I put it, a little troublesome."

Anka is not impressed with this.

Her Mama chimes in.

"We have had to make sacrifices. It has been a trial, as you can imagine. Sometimes I think we have been too good to her."

Anka doesn't agree with this either.

Papa again, intense and business-like.

"Can you help? Do you know people?"

The other man, who Anka guesses may be Mrs K's husband, says something that, once again, Anka can't make out, but she does hear him repeat the word troublesome.

Whatever he said, Mrs K takes exception.

"Not at all. She just has a strong personality. All children have their moments."

Papa murmurs again and Mrs K responds.

"Willingly. In a perfect world. I find her delightful."

The feeling's mutual, Mrs K.

Mrs K's husband, if that is who he is, butts in.

"It makes no difference. We have Kokki to think of. I am not an important guy like you. I don't have a sign in my window. They would not think twice about beating our door down."

Mrs K sounds irritated.

"Yes, yes, we have talked about all that. Anyway, there's a sister who lives in the north. She is quite happy to help, she has done this sort of thing before and she knows what she is doing. Anka will be in safe hands with her."

The conversation rambles on, but Anka is no longer listening. She has heard the news she was so desperate to hear.

At last, she is going to be getting out of this house.

She tries to get everything straight in her head.

First of all, Mrs K finds her delightful. That alone is enough to make Anka's day. No, that's wrong, not her day. Her whole week!

Second, Mrs K cares about Anka so much that she has come to save her. Anka loved Mrs K already. Now she loves her even more.

Third, Mama and Papa are quite happy for Anka to leave.

Finally, and most importantly, it sounds like she will be living with Mrs K's sister, which means she will see Mrs K again. She may even meet Kokki!

This is all such wonderful news that tears start to form in her eyes and she has to clench her fists and swallow hard to stop herself squeaking with happiness.

There's an increased bustle that suggests the meeting is winding up.

Her Mama says, "OK, Friday then."

Friday!

Friday can't come soon enough.

NO GOODBYE KISSES

As ALWAYS, they wait until it has already been dark for a long time.

Anka finds it hard to sit still. Her bag has been packed for hours. She did it herself this morning, although, of course, her Mama then went through it and repacked it.

Anka had put a few small bits of food in her bag. These her Mama removed.

"They will have plenty for you to eat where you are going."

No tears will flow at this departure. Anka won't be crying, that's for sure.

There's a soft knock at the door.

This time, she is not rushed into hiding. The knock is for her. She stands just behind her Papa as he opens the door. As usual for these outings, Anka is wrapped up in heavy clothing from head to foot. Even her woollen hat is pulled down below her eyes, so she has to lift her chin up to see anything.

She does this now, her heart set on seeing Mrs K's kind eyes and round face appear when the door is opened. But, it is not Mrs K. It is a young man. Once again, as with each move she has made in the past, the person who takes her is a total stranger. And, if things proceed as usual, she will never meet this boy again.

Doubts begin to enter her mind.

But she says nothing. She has to focus on the most important aspect of what is happening here. She is about to leave this awful house and these horrible people behind.

She must keep calm and not do or say anything that may change anyone's mind and prevent her departure. Of course, Mrs K would not come and get her in person. She and her sister must have many things to prepare. They will be waiting for her.

Anka's lips stay sealed.

The young man ties her bag to the rack on the back of his bicycle, then he swings his leg over and steadies the bike so that Papa can seat Anka on the crossbar. She holds on to the handlebar and the young man reaches past her on either side to grip the handles.

The process is fast and efficient. No words are exchanged and, as expected, there are no goodbyes or goodbye kisses. There are certain to be sighs of relief behind the door as soon as it is closed.

It slams shut even before they have set off.

The night air is cold against the small part of her face that remains exposed. It has been raining and the street is slick and shiny in the beam of the bicycle's front light. They move quickly.

Anka can't contain her excitement or her curiosity.

She turns her head as far as she can, although her neck movement is severely restricted by the heavy coat and thick scarf she is wearing.

"Where are we going?" She asks.

"You'll know when we get there."

"Will Mrs K be there?"

"Who?"

Hmm, that's not a good sign. Anka's tiny heart starts to break. Desperation wells up inside.

"Mrs K. I am to live with Mrs K or her sister in the north."

"Well, we are going to the north but I don't know no Mrs K."

Anka is later ashamed to admit that, at this point, she does indeed become what one might describe as "troublesome".

She starts wailing, wriggling and thrashing about. She screams, "Take me to her!"

The young man stammers.

"What? Who? Where?"

"I want to see Mrs K right now!"

Anka has reached the level of full tantrum. She is dimly aware that she shouldn't be behaving like this but she can't do anything about it.

The young man begins to lose control of the bicycle on the slippery road and the front wheel wobbles. The handlebar is shaken from Anka's grip and her heart leaps. The boy throws one arm around her and tries to steady the bicycle with the other.

Fear overrides her temper and she regrets her outburst at once.

But it's too late for remorse.

They slide.

She falls.

The boy is still holding onto her coat but the bicycle goes down and Anka and the boy go down with it. They hit the ground and skid along the road in a mess of boy, girl and machine. Something slices into Anka's left leg as they come to a halt.

She cries out in pain.

"Quiet! You are going to get us caught!" The boy shakes her, his face so close to hers that she can smell what he has been eating, even through her scarf.

She sobs. "My leg hurts."

"It's OK. Just stop yelling. I'll have a look at it. Where does it hurt?"

Anka is soothed by his solicitude. The boy is not unkind. Her anger is not for him. It was wrong of her to have made him crash. She stops sobbing and points. He runs his hand up and down her leg, squeezing gently here and there.

"OK, I don't think you've broken anything. You'll be fine."

It stings a lot. Anka doesn't agree that she'll be fine, but she doesn't want to argue. She has caused enough trouble already.

The boy picks the bicycle up, checks that nothing essential is damaged and lifts Anka with one arm back onto the crossbar. They set off again. At last, they reach a narrow street and slow down. The boy seems not to know which house he is looking for. Then a door opens a short distance away.

A woman appears. She calls out Anka's name softly, as if it's a secret she doesn't want anyone else to hear.

"Yes, ma'am, right here," answers the boy.

The light from the open door falls on them as they approach. The woman takes Anka from the boy's arms.

"She's tiny. And you are both wet through. Her trousers are torn and what's that dark patch? Is she bleeding?"

"We had a bit of an accident. Came off the bike. She said something about her leg."

"Let me have a look. Oh yes, there's quite a bit of blood, but it's all congealed. I can't see it clearly."

Catching the anxious expression on Anka's face, the woman laughs.

"Don't you worry, sweetie, you'll be just fine. You might have a bit of a scar though."

MAY THE PEOPLE KNOW?

No two houses are the same. No two sets of Mamas and Papas are the same.

The threadbare tapestry of Anka's sad little life rolls on.

Of course, nobody in this house has ever heard of a Mrs K. They look at Anka as if she is mad when she insists that they must know who Mrs K is.

In the end, she gives up asking.

In this new home, there are several other grown-ups, apart from her new Mama and Papa. What is even more unusual is that, although her new Mama and Papa go out all the time, the other grown-ups never leave the house. They stay inside, don't go near the windows and hide in a secret space behind a large upstairs cupboard when Mama and Papa have visitors.

———

In the early days in this house, Anka would go with the grown-ups when they went into the secret space, but now she doesn't. She is not at all unhappy about this as the secret space is small and smells bad.

There's not enough space for the grown-ups to sit, so they stand side by side, all pressed tightly together like matches in a box.

Anka would sit on the floor between their legs, but they found it awkward to have her there. She heard them complaining to her Mama and Papa.

So her Mama sat down with her one day and told her they needed to have a serious conversation.

It wasn't a proper conversation. Mama was the only one who said anything.

Mama told her she didn't have to go into the secret space any more. If they had visitors, Anka should just keep doing whatever it was she was doing - playing, eating, dreaming, dozing, whatever.

"If anyone speaks to you," Mama said, "just give them that stupid, blank look you give me all the time."

"And, if they ask who your Mama is, you just point at me. Got it?"

Anka nodded.

"Sure?"

Anka nodded again.

"Good girl!"

Anka had expected something more exciting, but instead it was the same old thing all her Mamas always told her.

HAS SHE BEEN TAKEN?

ONE DAY, Anka is with the people who hide in the secret space when they start talking about her. Like all grown-ups, they usually act as if Anka isn't there, but not today. This time they involve her in their discussion, at least briefly.

They ask her who her Mama is.

Anka replies that her Mama is downstairs.

"No, not her," they say, " your REAL Mama. What's her name? What's your family name? Maybe we know her."

Anka is perplexed. She has no idea what they are talking about.

"My name is Anka."

It's the best she can do.

The conversation moves on. Now, everyone is ignoring her again but Anka is still listening hard. This may be important. The people are talking about women they know, bouncing names off each other.

Anka thinks they are speculating as to who her "REAL Mama" is, whatever that means. All her Mamas are real. None of them is imaginary, although Anka does still daydream sometimes of how life would be if Mrs K were her Mama.

The people appear to have settled on an agreement as to the identity of one certain person. One of them asks, "Has she been taken?"

Another replies, "No, I think she's hiding somewhere."

As has often been the case with grown-up conversations Anka has eavesdropped on over the years, she is confused and frustrated. Why are grown-ups never clear? Why don't they say what they mean? Why do they never explain things thoroughly?

Taken?

Taken by whom?

Hiding?

Hiding like these people?

Hiding like me before?

Why do some people have to hide?

Who or what are they hiding from?

THINGS OF WONDER

SOME TIME LATER, they have visitors. Judging from her Mama's flustered reaction to the knock at the door, these are not ordinary visitors.

There is the usual wordless and almost soundless process of people moving to the secret space, covered by Mama and Papa calling out in a loud voice that they are just coming. Anka stays where she is, sitting on the floor in the front room, and waits. Maybe this will provide a little entertainment in what has so far been just another dull day.

The hubbub of voices suggests that there are several people outside, but at first, only one of them comes in. He is dressed entirely in black, he has a cap in one hand, a stick in the other and his trousers are tucked into the shiniest boots ever.

He strides into the room as if this is his house. Anka's Mama and Papa follow behind. The man sits in Papa's favourite chair and Anka expects that her Papa is going to tell him off, like he tells her off when she sits there. But her Papa says nothing. He and Mama just stand, side by side, facing the man. Papa looks grim, Mama has her face set in a polite smile. Her hands are clenched, knuckles white, gripping the front of her pinafore. Other people, strangers, most also wearing black, huddle in the doorway.

The man asks Mama and Papa some questions in a voice that booms and bounces off the walls. His presence makes the room feel much smaller. Papa in reply is quieter than usual. He stares at the floor as he speaks and calls the man "Sir".

Anka is not listening to what they are saying, though. Her attention is fixed on the new arrival's fascinating boots. She is sitting close to where he is reclining. He has crossed one long leg over the other and now one boot is hovering in mid-air not an arm's length away from Anka's head. The boots are truly things of wonder, dark mirrors that reflect the daylight entering through the curtained window. She is mesmerised by the shiny glow. She wants to reach out and run her fingers over the leather. It must be so smooth.

"Hello! What have we here?"

Anka looks up. The man in black is gazing down at her. He has pale skin, blue eyes, a sharp nose and flawless white teeth. His head is almost completely shaven, with just a thin crest of short tightly cropped hair in the centre.

Anka thinks he has a nice face and a nice smile. His eyes smile at the same time as his mouth, something that is not the case with all grown-ups.

"This is my daughter Anka," says Mama. "Say hello to the officer, Anka."

Anka says nothing.

"What a lovely child," he says, never taking his eyes off her, "you must be proud."

Most grown-ups pay little attention to Anka and never say anything nice about her. This man is different. It sounds as if he likes her and wants to be her friend. She is about to repay his kindness with a rare smile of her own and maybe even a small "hello", when he turns away.

She resumes her study of his boots.

Suddenly, he stands up, then crouches down in front of her, all in one quick movement. She is startled.

"Don't worry, child. There's nothing to be afraid of. Tell me, who is your Mama?"

She points over his shoulder to where her Mama is standing, eyes fixed on Anka. Her Mama mouths the words, "good girl".

The man in black is so close that Anka can smell his perfume. He is so wonderfully clean. There is no other word for it. His face, his hands, his clothes and especially his BOOTS are all immaculate and unblemished.

"No, no." He smiles. "Who is your REAL Mama?"

That concept again. So the man in black knows about this mysterious personality too.

Her Mama starts talking about something else. The man stands up and turns away.

Anka's Mama is asking if the man and his friends would like something to eat or drink.

It seems that they would. A short debate ensues over the details.

Anka is ignored, yet again. As always, it is as if she doesn't exist.

But, this time, for a change, she actually has something to contribute to the conversation.

So, from her position seated on the floor, forgotten at the feet of the grown-ups, she waits for a moment of silence and, when it arrives, she fills the empty space by saying,

"My real Mama is hiding somewhere."

In a flash, she becomes the centre of attention.

A GOOD GIRL

IT IS as if somebody has thrown a firework into the room.

Anka is the firework and she has just exploded.

Her Mama and Papa are staring at her in absolute horror.

The man in black smiles, reaches down and ruffles Anka's hair.

"You're a good girl," he says.

Just at this moment, judging from her Mama and Papa's reaction, Anka doesn't think that everyone would agree with this assessment. She is beginning to doubt it herself. She may, in fact, have just done something extremely bad.

The man in black barks out orders and the people who arrived with him start running. Some go outside, others head upstairs.

All hell breaks loose.

Anka starts crying. What else can she do?

Her Mama and Papa are now sitting on the floor with their hands behind their back. A man is standing over them and he is pointing what looks like a long metal pole at Papa's head. If Mama and Papa just turn their heads slightly, they can look straight at Anka, but they don't do that. They just focus their gaze on the floor. Anka has learned that sometimes if you stare at another person hard enough, they will sense it and look back at you.

Not this time.

The level of noise coming from upstairs is rising. It sounds as if people are fighting up there, although there are no voices. Not at first, anyway. Just the shattering of china or glass and a pounding sound that shakes the house like a succession of thunderclaps. This is followed by the cracking and creaking of splintering wood.

Then the shouting begins and a succession of hysterical screams builds to a crescendo. Anka covers her ears, but it doesn't help.

She closes her eyes and tries to find a safe place far away in her mind.

But there is too much going on. She has to look.

She opens her eyes a crack and watches as her Mama and Papa are pushed out of the front room. The man with the pole is poking them with it. Her Mama flinches. It must hurt.

The people who hide upstairs appear and stagger with difficulty past the doorway. Some are supporting others. A few are bleeding from the mouth or the head.

Then an engine starts up outside and its rumbling obliterates all other sound.

After a while, the rumbling fades away.

Anka sits alone in the silence that follows, immobile.

A woman, also dressed in black but with shiny shoes rather than boots, enters the room. Without a word, she picks Anka up, takes her out of the house and puts her in a car. The woman is not rough, but nor is she gentle. Anka is just an object to be moved from one place to another, like a houseplant.

Anka has never been in a car before. She knows about cars. She has always wanted to ride in one, but this is not at all how she pictured it.

It's not cold in the car, but she starts to shiver.

PART II
RACHEL

THE NET CLOSES

AT PRECISELY 9.30 in the morning on May 10, 1944, Rachel's luck
runs out.

And it's all because of her hair.

She wakes up late, rushes to the bathroom to clean her teeth,
glances at the mirror in mid-brush and freezes.

Her face forms a mask of horror. Toothpaste dribbles from her
lips. She turns her head first to one side then the other, then back
again. She can't believe it. Loose, bright tangerine ringlets decorate
her forehead. Her whole head is a mass of orange curls. Her eyebrows,
now raised as high as they will go, are the same colour.

She looks like a clown.

Maybe there was a problem with her new batch of hydrogen
peroxide or perhaps she messed up the dyeing process somehow. She
was so tired when she got home.

Anyway, there is nothing she can do about it. She has an appointment at 10 o'clock, a Bible study group. They will be waiting for her,
eager to start. She must not be late. She only recently summoned up
the courage to start running these sessions and she adores the work.

During her months of inactivity, she feared she was wasting her life away. Now, she is useful again. She has a purpose.

She peers out of the window. It's a beautiful day out there. One of those late spring days that tell you summer is around the corner.

Just what she doesn't need.

This is the sort of day when any self-respecting young Dutch lady will be out on her bicycle, whooshing along, hair trailing in the breeze, cheeks, pale from the long winter, flushed with a touch of morning sunshine.

Rachel doesn't have a bicycle any more. She was forced to hand it in. She is now well used to walking everywhere. That in itself does not attract undue attention. Lots of people walk by choice, even quite long distances. Not everyone rides a bicycle. Nor do people take the tram as much as they did before. The tram costs money and people don't have so much money these days.

With this untimely arrival of good weather and the even more untimely manifestation of her orange hair, Rachel is now highly likely to attract attention in the street. There's no way to avoid it. It is now a matter of choosing the lesser of two evils.

If she goes out with her head uncovered, the sunshine will make her hair glow as if it's on fire. She may as well be carrying a sign that says, "Look at me! I'm different!"

She can try wearing a hat, but that will still leave most of her hair uncovered and on display.

No, that certainly won't do. Far too dangerous.

She will have to take the other option and wear a headscarf, despite the fact that she will be the only person in the street under sixty wearing a scarf on this bright spring day.

Perhaps if she chooses some dowdy clothing, drags her feet a little, hunches her shoulders and keeps her eyes on the ground, then a casual observer might think she is more elderly and find nothing peculiar about her.

But, it isn't casual observers she is worried about.

She ties and pins her hair into the tightest bun she can manage and looks through her small collection of scarves. Most are perfect for winter but too wintry for today. She chooses her most summery scarf and wraps it so that it covers her hair and shades her eyes.

She'll be fine. She doesn't have that far to go. And it is mid-morning, hardly a time of day when those in hiding are likely to be venturing out, and therefore hardly a time of day when people will be looking for them.

She hopes.

———

SHE HAS BEEN STOPPED on the street in the past, although that was late at night, while she was moving from one safe house to another on the back of a friend's bicycle.

Two policemen on the prowl noticed that one of the bicycle's rear reflectors was missing. That's what they said anyway. It didn't matter if it was true or not. These days they don't need to have a reason to stop people.

One of them pointed his flashlight at Rachel's face, while his partner chatted with her friend. Although she couldn't see the man's face and he said nothing, she had the impression that he was studying her and her discomfort grew the longer he kept the light in her eyes.

She wanted to say something like, "Get that out of my face. You're blinding me!" but she didn't want to risk annoying him. Maybe an angry reaction was just what he was waiting for, to give him a reason to arrest them.

Not that they need an excuse to do that nowadays either.

She worried that he had worked out who she was and was thinking about what to do. Rachel might be able to dye her hair but she could not conceal her features.

Then, at last, the man flicked his light away from her. When her eyes readjusted to the darkness, she saw that he and his partner had moved away a little and had their heads together. There was a big discussion going on. From time to time, one of them would glance over, perhaps to check that Rachel and her friend were still there.

Of course they were still there. They had no option. If they ran, they'd be caught. Rachel was no runner. And to run was to be presumed guilty.

So they waited without speaking or even exchanging a glance. Rachel took encouragement from the fact that her friend appeared to be an oasis of calm. But, then again, Rachel probably seemed quite relaxed too.

She wasn't.

A scream was building up inside her. The tension was almost unbearable.

The police officers' debate concluded with a nod of agreement and one of them strolled over. His face told them nothing.

"OK, off you go. On your way. But walk, don't ride. Get that reflector fixed."

It took every ounce of self-control that Rachel possessed not to let the scream out, right there and then.

———

RACHEL LEAVES the house at 9.20 and sets off down the Zuider Amstellaan. The streets are almost empty. At first, she follows her strategy of shuffling along, her back slightly bent and eyes downcast, but after a while, she starts to worry that her slower pace might mean she will arrive late for her meeting.

She is never late. She takes pride in always being on time.

She increases her speed and, as she turns a corner, a gust of wind catches her scarf and it unravels. She reaches up to stop it flying away and catches it, but not before it has revealed her new crowning glory to the world.

Two men are riding past her on their bicycles as this happens and one turns, his attention drawn by the flurry of activity on the pavement.

Rachel stops, rearranges her scarf and tucks it in more securely this time, or so she hopes. When she looks up, she notices that the two men are cycling back towards her.

Her first inclination is to turn back, but what's the point? If they already have her in their sights, then it would serve no purpose. If they don't, then the change of direction might raise suspicion.

She keeps on walking towards them.

"Mevrouw!"

She doesn't stop.

"Mevrouw!"

A little louder this time.

Again she ignores them.

Finally, they draw in front of her and bring their bicycles to a halt, blocking her path.

She has to stop.

They dismount casually, kick their bike stands down and walk towards her, pulling out cards that identify them as members of the Dutch National Socialist Party.

NSB-ers! Utter bastards. A small band of freaks and outcasts before the Germans invaded, now the NSB is the only political party allowed and thousands have rushed to join its ranks, wanting to be on the winning side. The NSB-ers now rule the roost, at least locally. They are the Germans' lapdogs, but they think they are wolves.

Rachel wonders if the NSB-ers are still confident that they have chosen the winning side, given how things are going with the war.

Not that this is the moment to ask.

One of the men extends a hand.

"Your PB."

He is asking for her persoonsbewijs, the new identity card that the authorities brought in a few years ago, when they started dividing Dutch society into two types of citizen, Rachel's type and the other type.

Dutch people had never had identity cards before. They never needed them.

The man has a supercilious smile on his pointy, rat-like, little face. Rachel resists the instinctive urge to reach out and slap him. Instead, she just digs into her bag, pulls out her PB and hands it over without a word.

Then waits for the inevitable reaction.

It doesn't take long to come.

The men take one look at the PB and turn to each other in surprise. They were expecting to see a big, fat, black letter J on it.

But, her card has no J on it.

Instead, there is just quite a flattering picture of Rachel, which she picked out herself, looking much as she does now, except with light brown hair, rather than flaming orange, and some personal particulars including her name, which, of course, is not Rachel.

They look stumped. Typical NSB-ers. Never the sharpest knives in the drawer.

"Is this you?"

"Of course it's me."

"Wait."

They move away, out of earshot, taking the card with them. Rachel's mind is reeling but she concentrates on trying to look as if she doesn't have a care in the world.

An entire bureaucratic net has been set up just to catch her and others like her. Right now, she may be mere moments away from getting trapped in the net and losing everything.

She remembers how, after the Germans invaded, the government made them all fill in a form with their personal information. A clever Dutch man designed a technically advanced identity card, which included a fingerprint and a photograph. It was said to be impossible to forge. The same man also created a central registry containing all the data that was collected and linked it to the identity cards as a back up defence against forgeries, just in case anyone ever did manage to duplicate his design.

Dutch people were very proud that one of their own had invented such an advanced, foolproof system. They saw it as an example of typical Dutch ingenuity and efficiency.

The card Rachel is carrying, the one she just handed to the NSB-er, is a fake. It turned out that the PBs weren't so hard to reproduce after all. She destroyed her original PB, the one with the fat black J on it, the one with her real name on it, on the same day that she ripped the yellow six-pointed stars from her clothes and lightened her hair for the first time.

There are two ways this can go.

The men can insist that Rachel accompany them to a police station, so her identity can be checked via the famous central registry.

If the PB is proven to be false, they will be given a reward and be able to spend the rest of the day getting drunk and boasting of their success in a bar with their fellow NSB-ers.

If Rachel's PB is genuine, though, they will then have to spend hours filling in paperwork as a penance for wasting police time and upsetting an upstanding law-abiding Dutch citizen, there will be no reward and their whole day will have been wasted.

Do they want to try their luck?

Or will they just return Rachel's PB? Whereupon everyone will carry on with what they were doing before Rachel's scarf flew off.

Their discussion complete, the two men walk back over.

Rachel holds her breath.

"You need to come with us."

Although nobody understood this in the beginning, they all now know that the PB system was designed and implemented for one single purpose. That purpose is to facilitate the identification, location, segregation, apprehension and deportation of every Jewish person in Holland.

Today, the system has done its job.

The net has closed and Rachel is trapped inside.

She is not going to make her meeting. Indeed, she may not be attending any meetings for a long, long time.

FOOLISH, NAIVE AND TRUSTING

THE EUTERPESTRAAT STATION police will quickly discover that Rachel's PB is a fake. And, there is only one reason why anyone in Holland would carry a fake PB.

So they will also know she is Jewish.

There is no point in pretending otherwise. She has just got to stay strong and make sure she doesn't bring anyone else down with her. And stand up to them. Not that it will do anything to help get her released - there's no chance of that - but it at least will make her feel better.

They have no clue who they are dealing with here. To them, she is no more than a poor middle-aged woman with weird dress sense and bizarre hair. Not right in the head, is probably what they are thinking.

They'll soon find out. This isn't going to be the easy ride they are expecting.

———

As RACHEL SITS and waits for the inevitable verdict, she ponders over the events that have brought her to this moment. It is now almost four years to the day since Germany's surprise invasion, when they tore up the non-aggression pact supposed to guarantee Holland's neutrality.

Two weeks later, after German bombs had flattened the centre of Rotterdam, it was all over. The Royal family fled, the Government surrendered and the Germans took over.

For years, Rachel had seen on cinema newsreels what was happening to Jewish people in Germany, but like most people, she never imagined that the same thing could happen to her. She was Dutch, for goodness sake. Holland wasn't Germany. This was a peaceful, well-ordered, civilised country.

How foolish, naive and trusting she had been!

Changes in society were slow to be introduced in the beginning. Then one day they announced a ban on kosher food. Next, all Jewish civil servants, teachers and professors were fired and Jewish people were prohibited from entering public buildings, swimming pools, cinemas, cafés or restaurants. All their radios were confiscated and signs reading "Forbidden to Jews" started to appear in shop windows.

It was strange. Even as the restrictions and prohibitions increased, Rachel and her friends still held on to the illusion that things were not going too badly for them. They seized and clung on to straws of positive news wherever possible.

When her children were prohibited from attending public schools, Rachel took consolation in the fact that at least they could still attend Jewish schools.

When she was forbidden to shop in the market with other Dutch people, she told herself that she could still buy what she needed from the new stalls that Jewish traders had set up.

Even when the laws came into force stopping Jewish people from travelling outside their own town and barbed wire barriers went up around what came to be called the Jewish Quarter, Rachel wasn't particularly worried.

She didn't need to go far from home and, in her street, Jews and non-Jews still lived side by side, as they always had. Their non-Jewish neighbours would never tolerate anything serious happening to them.

Amsterdam-ers would stick together. They would always look after each other, wouldn't they?

———

EVEN THE IDENTITY card system appeared to be just a minor bureaucratic inconvenience when it was first brought in. So, Rachel's PB had a big letter J on it. Who cared? When it was tucked away in her handbag, who knew?

But, of course, as she should have guessed, marking Jewish people out in such a relatively subtle, invisible way was never going to be enough.

Shortly afterwards, they were ordered to sew a yellow Star of David onto all items of outer clothing.

Now, she was singled out. Now, she sensed eyes on her as she walked down the street. Now, she heard the comments. Now, her life was different. Now, she was vulnerable. Now, she knew fear.

The walls began to close in.

Jews were not allowed to marry non-Jews.

Jews had to sell their homes.

Jews had to put all their savings in a special German bank.

Jews were banned from public transport.

Jews had their bicycles taken away.

Jews could not go out after dark.

First, they removed them from society.

Then they removed their freedoms.

Then they stole their possessions.

Finally, the round ups began and they started to take them away.

———

THAT WAS TWO YEARS AGO.

On balance, Rachel can't complain. She has managed to stay free longer than most.

YOU'RE SUPPOSED TO PROTECT ME

OF COURSE, the registry has no record of Rachel's PB.

Two police officers, a man and a woman, take her into a small office. They say they have questions to ask her.

Oh do they? Well, Rachel has some questions to ask them too.

The officers ooze confidence. They are confident that they have her trapped and they are looking forward to their share of the beer money the Germans will give them for arresting one of the many Jewish people still hiding in Amsterdam.

They will need to give a commission to the NSB-ers who brought her in of course, but still, it's a nice bonus for doing very little.

The male officer speaks first.

"Who are you and what's your name?"

Without any further prompting, Rachel reels off her true name, age and birth date. She also gives him the address of her family home.

The officer's mouth drops open.

Rachel also detects a degree of disappointment. She guesses that this sort of information usually has to be dragged out of Jewish prisoners and that the officers quite enjoy the dragging-out process.

She looks him straight in the eye.

Hoping for a chance to bully me, were you?

Of course, Rachel has told him nothing that isn't easily available via the famous central registry and, anyway, she hasn't been back to that house for two years.

She has no idea who may be living there now, but it's highly unlikely that they are Jewish.

While the officer is momentarily flummoxed, she presses home her advantage.

"I am a Dutch citizen and a Christian, I was born in Amsterdam, I have lived here all my life and I have been unlawfully deprived of the freedom to walk on the streets of my own city. As police officers, you are supposed to protect me and all Dutch citizens. Yet, you have taken no action against the thugs who brought me here against my will. Instead, you have detained me and taken my belongings away. You have even taken my Bible. You have no grounds for doing this. I have committed no offence. You are contravening my rights. I demand that you return the things you have taken from me and release me at once."

Silence follows. Her final words, delivered in a confident tone that rings around the room, hang in the air.

Seeing that her partner has been struck dumb, the woman officer takes up the interrogation and tries changing the subject.

"Why do you have a false identity card?"

"Someone stole my old one and I found this one in an air raid shelter. The picture looked a bit like me, so I kept it."

"Who made it for you?"

"You tell me. It's just a normal PB. Who makes our PBs? I don't know. Who made your PB?"

"This is a picture of you."

"It's not me. It just looks like me. Look at the hair. It's completely different."

Which of course, on this particular day, is true.

This woman officer is getting nowhere. She tries a new tack.

"You are Jewish." It isn't a question.

"I am."

"Yet, you are a Christian."

"Yes, I am."

"If you were a real Christian, you wouldn't lie to us. Christians don't lie."

Rachel shoots back, her voice clear, calm and confident.

"Are YOU a Christian?"

The officer, taken by surprise, nods instinctively.

"I am."

"Yet you betray our country and its people by conniving with thugs and acting as a hand puppet for the Germans, who believe in nothing but their lunatic leader. How do you reconcile that with your faith?"

Rachel isn't finished. Her voice rises again. She thrusts an index finger towards the two officers. The change in her demeanour is so sudden that they jerk back in their seats.

"Traitors like you will never be permitted to enter the Kingdom of Heaven. Never!"

The woman officer raises an eyebrow. She and her colleague exchange a look that says this is all well beyond their pay grade.

They push their chairs back and stand up together, as if choreographed.

"We'll be back," says the woman.

Rachel is left alone again. Although she has so far succeeded in keeping her voice fairly even and tremor-free, adrenaline is flooding through her veins and inside she is shaking.

She watches the two officers disappear down the corridor.

Elation sweeps over her.

Haven't had a prisoner like me before, have you?

How long has she waited for a chance to say things like this out loud? How often has she railed privately in impotent frustration at the ease with which the Germans have convinced Dutch officials to obey their will?

How little effort did it take the invaders to persuade Dutch policemen, civil servants, railway workers, bankers and others to participate in the segregation, robbery and deportation of their fellow countrymen?

Most have showed no resistance at all. On the contrary, they have taken enormous pride in the efficiency with which they have executed their orders. The newspaper headlines scream self-congratulation.

And, look how greedily they accept the side benefits, whether it's a handful of guilders for a tip-off, a piece of abandoned land acquired in an under the table deal, a cheap price for a vacated house or the forced closure of a competing business.

Bastards!

SO, WHAT HAVE WE HERE?

AFTER A FEW MINUTES, the two police officers return, put Rachel in handcuffs and take her out. The male officer leads the way and his partner grips Rachel by the elbow as they navigate a maze of hallways, two flights of stairs, then more hallways.

All the corridors look the same, walls painted pale green on the lower half and dirty cream on the top. It's a design that oozes anonymity and functionality. The whole building lacks any trace of character or soul. There are no posters, no pictures, no banners, no decorations and precious little in the way of signage. How does anyone ever keep track of where anything is? It must be so easy to get lost. Maybe that's the whole idea.

Doors have frosted glass to confound the curious. Most are closed. People pass by, but nobody greets each other. They are busy people in busy times.

Eventually, they arrive at an open door. The male officer stands to one side. The woman stops and gives Rachel a gentle shove through the doorway. Neither of them follows her in.

Rachel finds herself in a much larger room. A dozen or so uniformed men lounge against the wall at the far end. In front of them is an enormous desk made from heavy, dark wood, behind which sits an extremely fat man, also in uniform.

The fat man has his elbows planted in front of him on the desk and is resting several of his chins on the back of his hands, which are clasped together, pudgy fingers interlaced. His eyes are already on the doorway as Rachel steps in.

Not just him - everyone in the room is looking at her as she enters. There's an air of anticipation.

So, I am this morning's big news, she thinks. A Jewess with a fake PB, who turns out to be a Christian, talks like a preacher and isn't afraid of policemen. Quite a catch. Maybe it's a dull day in the cop shop and I'm here to offer a little entertainment. Is that what this is all about?

She catches the fat man's eye. This is the cue he has been waiting for. He juts his chins in her direction.

"So," he declares, "what have we here?"

He unwraps one fat finger and points to the single chair placed in front of his desk.

"Sit."

She walks over, head held high, and sits.

His chair must be on some sort of plinth as she is now looking up at him. Her chair is uncomfortable, un-cushioned and one leg must be shorter than the others, as she has to shift her weight to stop it wobbling.

Rachel emits a gentle sigh. Such an obvious ploy. So transparent. He must think she was born yesterday.

With Rachel's arrival, the stage is evidently set. She and the fat man are to be the players. The others are merely their audience. Her part in this drama is to elevate the fat man's stature and reputation - to make him look good. He is to dominate her. She is to quail before the force of his personality. The broken chair is just part of the theatre. It is designed to make her feel awkward and keep her off balance, literally.

Rachel is unperturbed. She can handle this.

The fat man is sweating despite the open windows and a slight breeze. Dark pools have formed in his armpits and have spread out over his rib cage. Moisture is collecting in tiny beads between the lines on his forehead. Clearly, the warmer weather doesn't agree with him.

He fixes her with what he probably thinks is an intimidating glare. It isn't.

"So, they tell me you are some sort of prophet." The last word drips with disdain.

"I am simply trying to be a good servant of Christ," Rachel replies.

He opens a desk drawer and takes out a Bible. He raises it in the air and delivers a short rant about how precious his Bible is to him.

Rachel just stares at him as he rambles on, a small smile playing across her lips. So this is his strategy. Guessing that Rachel's adoption of Christianity is just a self-preservation ruse, the fat man has decided to challenge her credentials with his own.

She is on solid ground here.

When he sees he is not impressing her or inducing any sign of fear, he stops in mid-flow and puts the Bible down.

"I think you're a fake. Are you even baptised?"

"I am," Rachel replies.

He leans forward, eyes narrowing, like a chess player sensing an opening.

"Where were you baptised?"

Is the fat man trying to get her to betray somebody? Perhaps he imagines that he will uncover the tip of an underground organisation secretly converting Jews to Christianity in an attempt to protect them. What a coup it would be for him to lead the round up of a bunch of treasonous priests. How that would burnish his reputation as a top detective.

If that's the way his train of thought is moving, Rachel is going to push it off its tracks.

"At home in my bathtub," she answers.

"By whom?"

"By a friend."

"Which friend?

"Nobody you know."

The fat man is bewildered. This is not at all how his interrogation was supposed to proceed.

A huge portrait of Adolf Hitler hangs on the wall to Rachel's left. The fat man gestures towards it. Rachel turns her head.

"God has appointed the Führer to rule the world." He announces.

"You say you know the Bible well?" says Rachel.

The fat man blusters.

"I certainly do."

"In that case, tell me which verse in the Bible you are quoting from. Because, what you have just said is completely untrue."

The fat man's face turns the colour of Rachel's hair. What was previously a thin sheen of sweat is now a series of rivulets, which he is trying, though failing, to mop up with an enormous beige hand-kerchief.

He starts quoting from the Bible, choosing verses apparently at random, as they come into his head.

When he pauses, Rachel calmly and patiently corrects a couple of mistakes he has made.

This infuriates him. He fumes.

"You may not correct ME!"

Rachel is ready for him.

"When pride comes, then comes disgrace, but with the humble is wisdom. Proverbs 11, verse 2."

The fat man flinches. His voice rises in fury and frustration as he continues to fire unconnected verses at her.

Then he stops again, puffing through pursed lips. He seems to be tiring fast.

And Rachel pounces.

"Be not quick in your spirit to become angry, for anger lodges in the bosom of fools. Ecclesiastes 7:9."

Rachel suppresses a smile. It's a smile, which, if revealed, is likely to get her shot. This is a war of words that the fat man will never win. It is simply a question now of how much humiliation he is willing to bear.

Not much, is the answer.

He gasps, lets out a strangled cry and slams his palm flat on the desk. This produces a sound like a rifle shot and it startles Rachel, as well as everybody else in the room. Some of the men along the rear wall duck. One throws himself to the floor.

"What faith do you have, woman?" asks the fat man.

"I am just a humble Bibelforscher," she tells him.

She deliberately uses the derogatory term used by the Germans, well aware that, by doing so, she is placing the fat man in league with the invaders.

His confusion is total. He throws up his arms in exasperation. A murmur runs around the room.

Rachel would bet on her baby's life - a baby she is not going to tell any of them about - that none of them has ever encountered a Jewish Jehovah's Witness before. She is quite a rarity. There aren't too many like her.

"Get her out of my sight!"

The two escorting officers appear on either side and lift Rachel to her feet. The fat man throws them a vicious, venomous look.

Someone's head is going to roll for this, thinks Rachel.

When she is taken back to the downstairs office, the woman officer removes the handcuffs. As she does so, she bends and whispers in Rachel's ear, asking if she has any non-Jewish relatives.

The officer's demeanour has changed. Her tone is now that of a supplicant rather than an interrogator.

Rachel guesses she and her partner want to find some kind of exit route from this mess they have got themselves embroiled in.

The Germans' complex race rules legislate for certain degrees of Jewishness and that, if she has sufficient non-Jewishness in her blood-line, she may go free. A notion she finds ridiculous and offensive.

"I have none!" she replies.

"Not even one?"

"Not even one."

"In that case, I can't help you. I'm sorry."

"Did I ask for your help? I have Jehovah with me. He will protect me."

Rachel is on top of the world. It is a particularly good feeling. She is long overdue a winning moment, although she's aware it may be fleeting.

THE NEIGHBOURHOOD ICE
CREAM MAN

As Rachel expected, her euphoria doesn't last long.

Time passes. People walk by the office. The door is open but nobody even glances in. There is an ebb and flow of activity, but none of it involves her.

It's as if she has become invisible.

The officers are probably under orders to punish Rachel by ignoring her and keeping her waiting. This is the fat man's attempt at revenge.

"Let her stew," he will have told them, thinking that this will sap her confidence, bring her down a peg or two, maybe cause her to regret being so difficult, even induce an apology.

Well, that isn't going to happen.

Unhappily, however, by chance the fat man has stumbled upon the most effective form of punishment possible.

Because Rachel is left alone with her thoughts.

This is not something she is ever comfortable with.

In her daily life, Rachel works hard to make sure it rarely happens. She stays busy, lives day to day, focuses on the present and makes sure that she exhausts herself in the daytime so she sleeps well at night.

Because she fears where creating a vacuum in her mind and allowing time for reflection may lead.

Her memories can and often do seize upon any opportunity they are given to wander in and occupy the empty space. Once they arrive, they tend to settle in. They are weighted with sadness, doubt, regret and loss and thus hard to shift.

She expends every possible effort to keep them out because, more than anything, they represent a serious threat to the shield that she has erected to protect her from a descent into despair. This carapace is fragile and she fears it may be easily shattered.

Four years ago, she was so happy.

———

IT'S the 10th of February 1940 and Rachel is lying in bed holding Johanna, still warm from the womb. Louis is standing over her with an encouraging smile on his face, but residual terror in his eyes. This is his first time and he is still in shock. For Rachel, this is the third time she has given birth. Serious Sylvain, her first-born, and sweet, placid Carry are kneeling on the bed at her feet, agitated, eager arms outstretched, wanting to hold their brand new sister, smell her smell and feel how her tiny chest rises and falls gently with each baby breath.

There is so much love in the room.

So much blindness and arrogance too.

As always, memories of scenes from this period in her life - the last time she was genuinely, unreservedly happy - are warped by the curse of hindsight.

At the same time as her little family is gathered to celebrate the new arrival, elsewhere in Europe, Jewish people are being tormented and brutalised. They are trying to flee their enemies but their enemies' reach is expanding. The refugees are pursued and consumed if they don't flee fast or far enough.

Yet, she and Louis act as if they are immune, as if they have nothing to fear from the hellishness taking place just across the border.

They do not for one moment consider the foolishness of bringing a child into a world that anyone with an ounce of sense could tell is on the verge of being torn apart. A child who, even as she opens her eyes for the first time, is already an object of murderous hatred for millions, just by virtue of her ancestry.

———

Now, four years later, Louis is gone and their children are scattered to the winds.

Might things have been otherwise if Rachel had made different choices?

She tortures herself again and again by running through the time-line, looking for cause and effect, interrogating the decisive moments. Did she go wrong? If so, where? Was there something else she could have done? Would this have changed anything? She searches for mistakes and mis-steps, even as she dreads the guilt that will over-whelm her if she uncovers any.

———

RACHEL'S FATHER died when she was still a child and her grandfather came to live with them. He was highly devout and made sure that Rachel and her two sisters were brought up in accordance with Jewish traditions. The annual round of celebrations thrilled and enthralled them.

Louis was not at all religious, however, and after they were married, Rachel stopped practising her religion, although she still held on to her beliefs.

From the age of 14, Rachel had been a diamond cutter, following in her father's footsteps. Louis was a diamond polisher. They were colleagues and friends. When Rachel's first marriage broke down, they became a couple.

Employment in the diamond industry was sporadic. Sometimes there was plenty of work available. Sometimes there was none. Many diamond workers had part-time occupations. Rachel would find work in textile factories. Louis was the neighbourhood ice cream man.

Rachel can still picture her beloved husband, dark of complexion from spending so much time out in the sun, standing with his ice cream cart on the Afrikanenplein in north Amsterdam on a summer evening, when the shadows were long, the colours were bright and the light was golden.

Such a handsome man.

Such a kind man too. The neighbourhood children would always scream with delight when he appeared and rush to gather around him. He would always give them extra ice cream - and not just a little extra.

Good looking and generous. What a fine combination! She was a lucky girl.

———

AFTER JOHANNA WAS BORN, Rachel stayed at home. From time to time, she would answer a knock on the door and there would be a person standing there, usually a man wearing a collar and tie, a smart suit and a big smile.

They always said the same thing.

"Would you like to talk about Jesus and the Bible?"

Rachel would decline, although always politely and with what she hoped sounded like a genuine excuse. After all, they were nice people and she didn't want to hurt their feelings.

They never insisted. They just offered her some pamphlets.

"For you to read, but only if you have time."

Rachel took the literature out of courtesy, but it went straight into the trash. She never even looked at it. She wasn't interested in Jesus. In the synagogue, they just called him a false prophet.

The callers never gave up, though. One day, Rachel had just returned from a trip to the shops. She had been chatting with a neighbour and, as usual, the conversation had revolved around stories of death, destruction and deprivation.

Rachel always came home following these exchanges feeling immensely depressed, with the problems of the world weighing heavy in her heart.

There was a knock at the door.

"Would you like to talk about Jesus and the Bible?"

Rachel hesitated, on the verge of declining, then, on the spur of the moment, decided instead to share with her visitor the thoughts that were whirling around in her head.

What did she have to lose by asking?

"What I would like to talk about is why God allows so much hatred, misery and suffering in this world."

She took a breath. There was more on her mind.

"Why do men wage war and why did God not create different people after Adam and Eve sinned."

Her caller was taken by surprise, but swiftly recovered his poise.

"Maybe we can arrange a home Bible study session some time?" he asked. "Then we can discuss all these things and perhaps you will find some of the answers you are looking for."

And that's how it all began.

———

LOUIS WAS NOT at all interested in Rachel's new friends nor the things she was learning, but he didn't object when, after a while, Rachel told him she wanted to become a Jehovah's Witness.

Soon, Rachel was one of them, knocking on doors and talking to people about the Bible.

She loved it. She was bringing hope to people in bleak times. Soon, she was spending at least a couple of hours each day going door to door, preaching and telling others of her newfound faith.

She wasn't bothered by the rejection, the insults, the threats or the general hostility she was confronted with. It was all just part of the job. When it was clear she wasn't wanted, she would just move on and knock at the next door. Coming across one new person with a receptive heart and mind, someone like the person she had been, would make her whole week.

She was content and fulfilled.

It didn't last long. Soon, the round ups began and the illusion that somehow life could go on with some semblance of normality, however tenuous, was shattered.

Jewish people all over Holland started receiving letters telling them to show up at designated assembly points to be transported to labour camps in Eastern Europe. Some dutifully obeyed and arrived at the appointed place and time, laden with luggage and food for the journey.

Others ignored the summons, but it was not as if this was an invitation that they could choose to decline. The letters were supplemented by raids to sweep up the reluctant. Thanks to their wonderful new registration system, the authorities knew exactly where to find everyone.

Then, one evening, Louis didn't come home.

PAPA? PAPA? PAPA? PAPA?

Just like that, he disappeared from her life.

One moment he was there, by her side, sharing her problems, her decisions, her fears, her victories, everything.

The next, she was alone.

For a while, she held onto hope and prayed that somehow he would be returned to her.

In their home, Louis was still present in the form of his clothes, his things, his newspapers and his favourite chair. At night, in the complete darkness of their bedroom, he was still with her. All she had to do was turn her head to one side to smell his hair oil on the pillow. She didn't change the pillowcase until long after the last trace had faded.

That was the decisive moment. There was no point waiting for a miracle. She packed away or threw out all the things that were reminding her of him, distracting her from her daily tasks and causing her to spend hours immobilised by grief and self-pity.

Not that she wanted to forget him. She just had to focus on what mattered. He was gone and she had three children to look after.

All of whom, of course, were entirely confused by what had happened.

Most evenings, around bedtime, when Louis would usually be the one to take her up and tuck her in, Johanna would toddle around the house looking for him, then go to find Rachel and ask:

"Papa?"

"Papa?"

"Papa?"

"Papa?"

Johanna's high-pitched squeak would rise in intensity and anxiety until Rachel could stand it no longer. Then she would sweep her baby into her arms, hold her tight, cradle her head in the pillow of her shoulder and rub her back to calm her, while she wept in silence and unseen for her lost love.

As for Carry and Silvain, Rachel just told them that Louis had gone to work in Germany for a while.

"But, why didn't he say goodbye?" they complained.

Rachel hated to keep the whole truth from them. Although she didn't think either of them fully believed her anyway. It wasn't as if they were the only children at school who had suddenly lost a parent. Rachel was sure they and their friends shared stories. They might not understand the reasons, but they knew what was going on.

It wasn't long before they stopped asking.

————

RACHEL NOW THINKS the children had it all figured out before the adults did. Now, everyone knows that nobody comes back. For a long time, she and her Jewish friends found this difficult to accept. But, like Louis, none of the thousands upon thousands of Jewish people who have been taken away over the last two years have ever returned.

Stories abound, but nobody can tell what is true or what is just baseless rumour or propaganda. The only undeniable fact is that, once you are picked up, you are never seen again.

Today, it is Rachel's turn. Now she'll find out for herself what happens to the deported.

A quiver of anxiety runs through her like an electric shock. What if the truth is as appalling as some have suggested?

She fends away the thought. No time for that. No point worrying about something she has absolutely no control over.

Her host sister will be arriving home about now, expecting Rachel to be there as usual, although she won't be completely surprised not to find her at home. In the past, Rachel has often stayed over with brothers and sisters in other parts of the city, on nights when there has been a lot of police activity and it has been too dangerous for her to walk home.

So, it may be a day or two before her friend realises Rachel is gone for good.

Rachel wishes she could send word to her, to relieve her from doubt and worry, but of course she must not even try. She cannot risk revealing any connections. Just a hint of an association is enough to get someone arrested.

Perhaps news of her absence from that morning's Bible study meeting will circulate quickly through their community and, when it turns out that nobody has seen her all day, they will assume the worst.

"Our sister Rachel has finally taken one risk too many," they may say. "We should have looked after her better."

But, it's not their fault. Not one little bit. In fact, it is only because of their courage and care that she has managed to remain free as long as she has.

WE DON'T WANT TO LOSE YOU

AFTER LOUIS DISAPPEARED, Rachel continued to knock on doors and preach, dressed in her coat with the yellow star, although now she could not devote as much time to her work as before.

One afternoon, a small group of her brothers and sisters arrived at her home unannounced. The moment Rachel opened the door and saw their serious faces, her heart sank.

Was she in trouble? Had she done something wrong?

She invited them in, sat them down and went to make coffee. She told Sylvain and Carry to take Johanna and go and play upstairs. If this was a telling off, she didn't want them listening in.

By the time she returned to her visitors, she had prepared her excuses.

"I'm sorry I haven't been able to put in as many hours recently…"

A raised hand stopped her in mid-flow.

"It's not that, Rachel. We actually wish you wouldn't do so much. In fact, we don't think you should be doing anything."

"You're far too visible," another person chimed in, "it's so dangerous. You can't go on like this."

Rachel was dismayed. "But it's my duty, this is what we do."

Her eyes moved from face to face, looking for affirmation, seeking an ally.

To no avail.

"We have all discussed this and we are agreed. It's for your own good."

Rachel tried a different approach.

"But, it's not just me. Each one of us is at risk. The Germans hate Jehovah's Witnesses. You can be arrested too."

Which was true. The Germans did hate them. They represented an American church, they were against the war and they were scornful of Hitler. They had been banned in Germany for many years and a lot of them had ended up in prison camps. Now they were banned in Holland too.

However, Rachel was all too aware she was clutching at straws.

As one of her sisters swiftly pointed out.

"Forgive me, Rachel, but you know quite well that it is not the same for us. They don't call us vermin and sub-human or threaten to exterminate us. If we are arrested, they don't seize our houses and everything we own. They don't make our whole families disappear."

Which, of course, was true.

"When you say we all take certain risks for our faith, you're right. But the danger for you is far greater than it is for us. And we don't want to lose you."

The others all nodded, murmured their agreement, spoke her name and declared their love, anxiety in their eyes as they gauged her reaction.

This visit had not been made on a whim. Rachel could just imagine the debate that had led them to intervene. Some would have worried that it was not their place to speak up. Others would have guessed at Rachel's confusion and concluded that she might need help.

"It is time you left this house. They have Louis and they will come for you. They know where you are. It is just a matter of time. You must move to another part of the city. You should even consider adopting a new identity. We have heard this can be done. There is an artist."

The sister who had been leading the conversation looked around at her colleagues, as if searching for someone to share her burden. It was as if they all knew what was coming next, but none of them wanted to be the one to say it.

A brother sitting close to Rachel leaned forward and gripped her forearm. Their eyes met.

His expression put her in mind of a doctor giving a patient bad news or a judge about to deliver a death sentence.

A frisson of fear ran through her.

"Going away and adopting a disguise only solves part of the problem," he said. "We have to think of the children. It wouldn't be fair to ask them to play-act. They wouldn't be able to keep up the pretence forever. They are still very young, even Silvain. One wrong word, one false step, one casual remark - the whole house of cards would collapse!"

Rachel wanted to put her hands to her ears. It was almost unbearable. And not because what he was saying was wrong.

"All it will take is one nosey neighbour or a local NSB-er who wants to earn a little money and you will all be picked up and taken away. If you stay together, you will be in extreme danger."

Rachel's eyes widened. Her hand flew to her mouth as if to stop the words that were forming in her mind from being uttered.

"You mean..."

A door inside her head that she had kept slammed shut had just flown open, exposing a clear, dreadful vision of a future she had not even dared contemplate.

Of course, every Jewish person in Amsterdam was dealing with the same dilemma. Do I wait until I'm called up or arrested? Or do I run or hide?

And, for Rachel and other Jewish parents, a second, even more impossible question nagged at them constantly.

How do I protect my children?

She and Louis had talked about this a lot but had never done anything more than list all the options, go through them and reject every one. And now, with Louis gone...

She thought of her sister Lina, smart, sharp, wealthy, well connected and married to Jaap, an antiques dealer. They were always a step ahead and sure of themselves. Early on, even before the deportations began, they foresaw the impending danger and came up with a clever way of saving themselves and their daughter Netty.

They decided to flee in disguise to neutral Switzerland, taking only a couple of weekend bags with them, leaving their house and everything they owned in the care of life-long non-Jewish friends, who lived in the same street.

As soon as they had set off, their supposed friends reported their escape plans to the authorities.

Lina, Jaap and Netty were caught at the French border with fake identity cards and shot dead. The story had been reported in the newspapers. It was a message for all Jewish people. Try and make a run for it and this is what will happen.

If Lina couldn't find a way of getting her family out of this alive, what hope was there for Rachel?

———

HER BROTHERS and sisters waited patiently, seated in silence around her. They could only guess at the turmoil in her mind.

However, they had not come just to present their friend and sister with a problem, then abandon her to find a solution for herself.

One of the women got to her feet. Three quick steps took her across the room to where Rachel was sitting hunched over, head bowed, elbows resting on her thighs, fists clenched against her forehead. Dark, dangling ringlets concealed her face from view.

Kneeling before her, the woman gently touched Rachel on the knee.

Rachel started as if roused from a dream, raised her head, swept the hair away from her face and looked around the room.

She had quite forgotten that they were there.

"Forgive me…" she began.

Her friend stopped her.

"There is nothing to forgive. Now, if you would allow, we would like to help you."

THE BRUTAL TRUTH

AFTER HER BRETHREN had departed with hugs, kisses and not a few tears, Rachel went upstairs.

Right now, more than ever, she needed to be among her children.

Later, after putting them to bed, she stayed in their room, sitting on the floor with her back to the wall and her knees drawn up to her chest, listening to three overlapping sets of soft, rhythmic breathing, punctuated by occasional sighs and squeaks and murmurs. This was always her favourite time of the day. The symphony of happy children sleeping peacefully was the best section of the soundtrack to her life.

The blackout curtains taped to the walls closed off all light from outside and ensured that the faint glow of Johanna's bedside lamp, so essential to a quiet night for them all, did not escape the confines of the room.

After the last of the children had drifted off and there was no longer any point in continuing with the story she was reading to them, Rachel moved among them, tucking a blanket in here, pulling up a bed sheet there.

Silvain, as always, was frowning, forehead furrowed, dark eyebrows drawn together, studious and serious even in sleep. He had one arm flung across the pillow, hand extended, fingers splayed - the long fingers inherited from his father that helped him play difficult piano parts with ease.

Carry lay serene as always, entirely at peace with the world, a slight smile playing on her lips, as if, even in dreams, she was charming everyone she encountered.

And Johanna, restless, twitching, murmuring, never able to settle, still crackling with energy while she slept. She was just a baby, but she was already showing a curious intelligence beyond her years.

How could she ever leave them? She loved them all so much, yet it was the extent of this love that was the clinching factor in the decision she had reached.

It was her only option. Her friends had opened her eyes and she now saw the brutal truth confronting her and her little family. Together, they would not survive.

Apart, they might - just might - stand a chance.

———

BEFORE THE WAR, at the cinema, Rachel watched newsreel footage of vulnerable Jewish children being taken out of Germany to safety in Great Britain and elsewhere as part of an emergency scheme called the Kindertransport.

There were tragic scenes at German train stations, mothers and grandmothers holding weeping children in their arms as they said their goodbyes. Then the scene switched to London, showing the children, now alone, standing on the platform next to the single tiny suitcase they were allowed to bring. Some had no luggage. They had nothing but the clothes they stood up in and a cardboard tag on a string with a number on one side and their name on the other.

They looked lost and utterly forlorn.

"The poor, poor things, whatever will become of them?" she had asked Louis, her eyes welling with tears. It wasn't a question with an answer and he had not replied. He just held her tight until her sobbing subsided.

Reliving the memory, her eyes begin to prickle and there is a lump in her throat. How she wished Louis were here with her now.

Then, she could not fathom how any parent would ever abandon their children to the care of others. Surely, as a parent, your job was to protect your children and keep them close, not send them away.

Now, she understands all too clearly that sometimes, when events are far beyond your means of controlling them, there may be better ways of keeping your children safe.

Sometimes, you have to accept that you are not their best option and you have to assign the role of protector to others.

However much that hurts.

As far as Johanna was concerned, the decision was Rachel's alone.

But, for Silvain and Carry, she would have to consult their father.

She wasn't looking forward to that.

RIPPED ASUNDER

"No, absolutely not!"

"Total strangers?"

"No, never!"

Rachel's ex-husband had quickly worked himself up into a fury. She had found him at his parents' house and she was now sitting facing the three of them across the kitchen table, him and his mother and father. The mother was in tears. The father's mouth was drawn in a tight stubborn line, his arms folded across his broad chest.

She was out-numbered and out-gunned.

As she had expected, he was taking her plan as a personal insult.

"I will take care of them. They are my children too, you know," he said, petulant as usual.

"I do know. That's why I'm here talking to you," said Rachel. "But, can you look after them? What about when you get the call-up letter. You know it will come. What will you do then? Will you go?"

"No, I'll hide and I'll take the children with me."

"And if you are found?" Rachel pressed on.

The father interrupted her. He turned towards his son.

"It is said that those who go into hiding are treated more harshly when they are discovered than those who volunteer."

"Bah," replied Rachel's ex-husband. "So many theories. So much nonsense. Nobody knows anything for sure."

The father went on.

"Perhaps we should look after the children here. Keep them with us. Your mother and I are too old to be called up for the labour camps. After all, what work could we do for the Germans? Peel potatoes?"

He slapped his wife on the thigh and laughed with forced exuberance.

Rachel felt an eye roll coming on, but she managed to contain it.

Peel potatoes.

Every elderly Jewish man always came up with the same argument when the topic of the deportations was raised. In fact, they always used exactly this phrase. She guessed it was something they had all read in Het Joods Weekblad. She had long suspected that, rather than keeping Jewish people informed, many of the articles in this paper were designed instead to confuse and deceive them. Nobody had ever heard of this rag before the Germans arrived. Now it was their only source of information.

However, her former father-in-law now had the bit between his teeth and was managing to convince himself of the validity of his hastily formed plan with every successive thought that occurred to him.

"Why would they ever raid the homes of old poor people like us anyway? We have nothing of value. Yes, Silvain and Carry will be safe with us. We'll make sure of it. We'll keep them indoors. Out of sight and out of mind. Bring them over with their things one night after dark. Nobody will even know they're here."

Placing one hand on his wife's knee and throwing his other arm around his son's shoulders, he declared, "and best of all, they'll be with family. Nobody better than family!"

He beamed, first at one, then at the other, and finally at Rachel. There, that was the clincher. Who could ever argue with that?

Rachel just stared at the three of them. They were united and she was defeated. What could she say? They looked so confident and sure of themselves. Who knew what was actually the best thing to do? Maybe they would be proven right, after all.

Sylvain and Carry would have no objection. They loved their father and their grandparents, so this would be an easier plan to sell to them than the idea of being separated from each other and going to live with strangers.

What her friends had proposed was that Rachel place herself and her children individually in the care of the city's Jehovah's Witness community, which now numbered several thousand.

Rachel would adopt a new identity and maybe one day she could even preach again, as, in her case, hiding in plain view might well be the best strategy. Who would ever guess that a Jehovah's Witness was a Jew?

————

So, it was done. Her perfect family was ripped asunder.

One dark night, her ex-husband turned up to escort Sylvain and Carry to their grandparents place. He had been a frequent visitor over the previous few days as, bit by bit, he moved all the children's clothes and toys to their new home in an assortment of anonymous boxes and bags, delivering them to the house empty and taking them away full.

They had conjured up a flimsy story for the children about Rachel having to go to work in another town, where she would have to live in a tiny apartment with just enough room for her and Johanna. They had tried to make sure the children focussed on the positives of the move - the big house, a bedroom of their own, Grandma's cooking.

Fortunately, Johanna was too young to take in what was going on. Even, earlier that evening, when Sylvain and Carry had hugged their baby sister tight and told her they loved her and would miss her, she didn't react as if anything special was happening. She just yawned, held her arms out wide to Rachel and asked, "Mama, bed? Hanna sleep?"

So far, over the past week or so, Rachel had succeeded in distracting herself with managing the practical aspects of the move, but now the much-feared moment had arrived.

The two children had welcomed their father's arrival with great enthusiasm and he had played along, promising them all sorts of treats and telling them how thrilled their grandparents were that they were coming to stay.

"Oma is so excited, it's like she's sitting on hot coals!" he told them. They laughed.

"Does Oma have a hot bum?" shrieked Sylvain.

Rachel bent down and picked Carry up for a final hug.

"Mama, why can't you come with us? You'll miss all the fun."

"I know, sweetie," said Rachel. "But, you will be fine. You will have Papa and Opa and Oma and you are all going to have a great time together."

"When will you come and visit?"

"When I can. But, you know how difficult things are these days. It may be hard for us to come. It's a long way."

Tears began to form in her little girl's eyes and her upper lip was starting to quiver. Sylvain stood nearby, now silent, no longer laughing, but watchful and taking in every word.

"There's no need to be sad. You just have to be brave. We all do. Even if I can't be with you, I'll be thinking of you every day."

"Every day?"

"Yes."

"Every hour of every day."

"Yes."

"Every minute of every hour of every day?"

"Every single minute!"

Rachel turned her face away. She was close to cracking and she couldn't allow that. Not now. Not until the door had closed behind them. She caught her ex-husband's eye and grimaced.

He got the message.

"Right, come on. It's getting late. Your Mama has a lot to do and she can't do it with you two under her feet. Let's get going."

He took Carry from Rachel's arms and Rachel turned to hug her son. She held him and whispered in his ear.

"Love you. Don't forget."

Sylvain whispered back, "bye - bye, Mama".

And then they were out, in a scurry of coats and scarves and boots and satchels.

Even though she was invisible to them, Rachel stood in the darkened doorway and watched and waved until the night swallowed up the last faint glimmer of the small torch her ex-husband was using to guide the way.

Then she closed the door, sank to the floor like a discarded rag doll and wept.

———

A FEW DAYS LATER, while Johanna was having her routine afternoon nap, Rachel scooped her up, kissed her forehead softly so she wouldn't wake up and placed her gently in the arms of a girl she did not know and would never meet again.

Johanna would wake to a new home, a new name and a new Mama.

Rachel had not been told where Johanna would be taken, what her name would be or who her new Mama was. She didn't want to know. If she didn't have the information, she could never be forced to reveal it.

Shortly after her baby had left, another knock came at the door. A young man was standing there with a bicycle. He addressed Rachel by her own new name. She had practiced using it in front of the mirror a hundred times. This was the first time she had heard it used by someone else.

Rachel handed the man her small bag of clothing and photographs, then turned and closed the door on the person she had been.

There was no yellow star on her coat. Her hair was light brown instead of black, she was wearing foundation to lighten her skin and, in her pocket, she had a brand new PB, which was not adorned with a black letter J.

The night before, she had lit the gas ring and held her old PB to the flame, watching as the brown burn line inched across the card, first obscuring then consuming the words before curling and blackening her photograph.

Finally, nothing remained but ashes on the stovetop. Rachel pursed her lips and, as if she was blowing out candles on a birthday cake, scattered them to the floor.

SHE MADE herself comfortable on the back of the bicycle and tapped the young man on the shoulder.

Off they went. A new life was waiting.

Rachel had done the best she could do for her children. Their fate was now out of her hands. Now, she had to take care of herself, so that when this was all over, they could be reunited.

No, that was the wrong way to look at it.

When what was all over? The Germans' stated aim was to rid themselves of all the Jewish people in Europe. If they won this war or if the war continued long enough, then one thing was certain, there would be no Jewish people left in Holland at all.

By giving her children into the care of others, she might not be saving them so much as giving them time. By adopting a new identity, she was giving herself time.

Who knew how much time?

She would use her time well. She would focus on the present, rather than dwell on the past or waste time fantasising about a rosy future that might never arrive.

As they sped down an alley, they spooked a small ginger cat that was rooting in a rubbish bin. It scuttled up and over the wall and out of sight.

That's what she would have to do from now on, keep her wits about her, duck and dive, lie low.

They reached a canal, turned and sped along the waterside. Grey, heavy clouds were scudding across the sky and the tips of the weeping willows were almost touching the foamy rim of the wind chop. Few other people were out and about. Only a few hardy folk scuttled along the footpath, bent against the breeze, heading home fast.

Wherever they were going, she hoped they would get there soon.

A storm was coming.

THAT MAKES NO SENSE

SHE HAD ACTED JUST in time. The intensity of the police action against Jewish citizens escalated and, during her first few months in hiding, Rachel didn't dare leave the house.

Her host sister would always return home with news and it was never good.

Jewish homes were raided and it didn't matter if you were young, old, rich, poor, male, female, healthy or sick. If you were Jewish, you were hauled away. Then your house was looted.

So much for the confidence of Rachel's former father-in-law and his fellow optimists that the old folk would be spared.

Why had she let that arrogant, opinionated old man push her around?

When they found that they were often raiding empty houses, the authorities worked out that Jews must be sheltering with non-Jews, so they started raiding their homes too, either acting on tip-offs or just at random. They would descend upon a street and start knocking on doors. If nobody answered, they just forced their way in and ransacked the house, looking for hiding places.

Anyone found harbouring Jews was arrested.

Rachel had to move several times. She got used to packing fast and making sure she remembered to take everything with her when she left, never leaving any trace of her presence behind.

Once, she forgot a bottle of blond hair dye in a house where only blond-haired people lived and panicked for days that this might have led to awkward questions or worse.

Then word came that they had found the bottle and got rid of it before the police turned up.

It was getting harder and harder to hide.

The few houses that remained immune from the onslaught were those where there was a card placed in a downstairs window, signifying that the occupants were police or NSB and therefore above suspicion.

Rachel hoped that, once her ex-husband saw that his father's theories had no substance, he might have come up with a better plan to protect Carry and Sylvain, but she was doubtful. He wasn't a fool, but she had never known him go against his father's wishes and his father wasn't the sort of man who'd ever admit when he was wrong.

And, how were the people looking after Johanna explaining away her dark hair and complexion? They would have to keep her out of sight all the time. She couldn't imagine her inquisitive, lively baby girl responding at all well to being trapped and confined.

———

RARE POINTS of light punctuated the darkness of those days.

One of Rachel's host sisters told her about a courageous policeman who worked in the station on Jonas Daniel Meierplein. Apparently, when this officer learned that a raid was being scheduled, he would find a way to pass the information on to local children who had taken to hanging around near the station. They would then zip off on their bikes and scooters and give people in the targeted streets advance warning.

Her friend had told her the story because she wanted to let Rachel know that there were people out there who cared, even among the police, but Rachel was far from reassured. In fact, this made her even more anxious about her children's safety.

If her friend knew all about it, then it must be the talk of the town and that meant that the Germans would certainly soon find out too. The story would eventually find the ear of the wrong person, the station would be raided and the guilty officer identified.

She'd be much happier if nobody talked about anything.

But Rachel was equally to blame. She was as hungry for news as anyone. Every evening, wherever she was staying and whomever she was staying with, as soon as they returned home, Rachel would quiz them on what was going on.

One particular evening, as usual, as soon as her host sister poked her head around the door, Rachel jumped up.

"So, what's the news?"

"Nothing special," came the reply.

Now, it was the case that some days were quieter and less dramatic than others. But, even so, it was never the case that there was nothing to report. Besides, her friends knew how frustrating it was for her to sit alone, day after day, with nobody to talk and no radio or newspapers. So they always made sure they had some snippets of gossip to pass on.

Not today though.

She decided to let it go for now, but, as the evening wore on, it became obvious that her friend was avoiding her. She cornered her in the kitchen.

"What's going on? Are you keeping something from me? Is it one of the children? Has something happened?"

"Me? No, nothing. There's nothing going on. I'm just tired. Long day, you know."

She was looking shifty. It was obvious she wanted to be left alone but Rachel would not be put off.

"This isn't like you. What is it? You're hiding something."

Her friend sighed.

"Well, yes, you're right. I do have news. Something terrifying. But I wasn't sure if I should tell you. It is just rumours. Nobody knows if it's true."

She caught Rachel's expression.

"Don't worry. It's not one of the children. Well, not directly, anyway."

"Come with me," said Rachel, leading her back to the sitting room. "Whatever it is, I can handle it. You have to let me decide what to believe. I'm not a child."

Her friend sat down on the sofa next to her. At first, she just stared at the floor. When she at last summoned up the will to speak, her voice was so soft that Rachel had to lean in to hear.

"My friend has a hidden radio and she listens in to the English stations, the ones the Queen talks to us on. They are saying that the whole labour camp story is a lie."

"Well, we guessed that already, didn't we?" said Rachel, interrupting her. "Especially when they started deporting even babies, old people and sick people. Are they putting them in prison camps? Like the ones they sent all our German brothers and sisters to?"

Her friend shook her head.

"No, they are saying it's worse than that."

She hesitated.

"Tell me!"

Rachel's voice was louder than she had intended. Her friend flinched, glanced at her, afraid.

Rachel raised both hands in apology.

"I'm sorry, I'm sorry. I know it's hard. I'm sorry. Please..."

When her friend continued, she spoke in not much more than a murmur. As if she thought the walls might be listening.

"They say the Germans are killing all the Jews they take away. Every single one. Murdering them, just like that, for no reason. It's too terrible to imagine."

A succession of horrifying images flashed through Rachel's mind - Louis, the children, so many people - it was impossible. Yes, that was it. It WAS impossible. How could that be correct? Think of the numbers, the thousands, the tens of thousands.

It made her angry.

"This makes no sense at all. Why would the Germans kill everyone? They are not stupid. Why wouldn't they be doing exactly what they say they are doing? Sending all the people they arrest away to work to help them win the war? I know they hate us but we are free manpower, slave labour, call it what you will. Why wouldn't they take full advantage? They are too practical to waste such a valuable resource. We are worth nothing if we're dead. They may talk about exterminating us, but they don't mean it. Or at least, they might mean it but not until they have wrung every drop of use they can get out of us."

Her friend just stared at her. The look on her face said, "You see? This is why I didn't want to tell you."

Rachel closed her eyes and shook her head. It was better to be aware that stories like this were doing the rounds, but she couldn't let herself be sidetracked by this sort of talk. It would either send her crazy or drive her to despair. Some people said one thing. Some said another. It was all just gossip. How could you ever tell what was true and what were just vicious lies? The Germans were always spreading propaganda. Everyone knew that. But now, the propaganda was coming from all sides and Rachel and those like her were caught in the middle.

She reached out a hand and laid it gently on her friend's arm.

"I can see what you're thinking, but thank you for letting me know. You did the right thing. I'd rather know than be kept in the dark. And, forgive me. I can't help over - reacting. I just can't believe it. They have arrested so many people. They can't have killed them all? I mean, think about it. Practically, how is it even feasible? It's ridiculous. It has to be an exaggeration. The Queen and the rest of them are safe over there in England or in Canada or wherever they are. Why do they try to scare us like this? What's the point? What good does it do?"

LOST WITHOUT HIS MUSIC

THE CODED KNOCK told Rachel she had a friendly visitor.

She sprang to her feet. A much needed distraction on a dull day.

She drew back the double bolts and pulled open the front door, a welcoming smile already in place.

And froze.

Two friends from the old days stood side-by-side, so close it was as if each was holding the other up. Their faces were pale, eyes anxious. They looked like they wished they could be somewhere else. Anywhere else. Just not there.

Rachel's smile faded.

This was no social call.

So that meant…

She ushered them in, secured the door and turned.

Tears were already streaming down their cheeks. Rachel abandoned any attempt to hold herself together and collapsed into their outstretched arms.

———

IT WAS a while before she summoned up the strength to pull herself away. One of her visitors cleared her throat.

But Rachel wasn't ready. She raised both hands and shook her head.

"Not now, please. Not yet."

She showed them into the living room, muttered "a little coffee maybe", then escaped to the kitchen.

———

SHE FUSSED OVER THE COFFEE. For her visitors, she took two spoonfuls from the small tin at the back of the cupboard. There was precious little left. For herself, the tasteless brown fake coffee powder, made of God-knows-what, which was all you could get in the shops now, would have to do.

The cups and saucers came from the display cabinet. Her host sister wouldn't mind. On an impulse, she lifted out the old pewter tray too. It needed a little polish. Special occasions were rare these days.

Into each saucer, she placed a small biscuit. Thank goodness they still had some left that were not too old and hard.

She was well aware that, in occupying herself in such detail with the preparations, she was merely postponing the inevitable, but she needed the breathing space. She was ashamed of her earlier outburst.

What a way to act!

She had anticipated this moment for so long. She thought she had steeled herself well. She thought she was ready for it.

Apparently not.

———

RACHEL HAD SERVED her guests and they were all seated on the sofas in the front room. So far, they had only exchanged light pleasantries, about the crockery, the weather, how difficult it was to find real coffee.

There was a long awkward pause in the conversation. This was the moment. They couldn't continue to avoid discussing the reason for the visit forever.

It was up to Rachel to take the initiative.

"OK, out with it. What's happened?"

Despite her efforts to compose herself, she still found it hard to get the words out. Her voice betrayed her emotion. The final syllable was just an expulsion of air.

Again, she was embarrassed at her lack of self-control.

Her friends were anxious.

"Are you sure?"

Rachel tried to sound more assured.

"I'm OK. It's just… you know."

She caught the eye of the older of the two women. She had been one of Rachel's mentors. They had been close. Rachel trusted her.

"Tell me," she said again, softly.

"Well, we only just heard about it. Apparently, a few days ago, your ex's parents' house was raided and they took them all away. It was early afternoon. There had been no warning. The neighbours heard piano music coming from the house as usual, then the music stopped and they saw the police outside. Later, after everyone had been taken away, they watched the piano being loaded into a truck along with all the other furniture."

Rachel sighed. She was struck by how commonplace it all was. How easy it was to use mundane phrases like "taken away" to describe such a barbarous, callous act. Their country was destroying the lives of thousands upon thousands of its own people, separating them from those they loved, depriving them of their freedom and for what? Their sole offence was that they existed.

The scenario her friend had described was being played out dozens of times a day, every day, all over the city. In any sane society, this would be exceptional and rejected as an intolerable deprivation of citizens' rights.

Yet, if you were not directly affected, it wasn't a much more noteworthy event than the arrival of the postman. There would have been no drama, no pitched street battle with protesters, no angry mob defending the innocent, not even raised voices.

How could it be otherwise? When the perpetrators of the crime were salaried employees of the state - just following orders - and the victims had been brainwashed into passively accepting their fate - oh well, it must be our turn now - what should witnesses do? Fight for those who won't fight for themselves? Report the crime to the very people who are committing it and risk becoming victims themselves, merely by association?

The mention of the piano playing revealed the identity of at least one of those who had been arrested, as her friends knew it would.

"Poor Sylvain. He will be lost without his music. And Carry too? Were they still together?"

Her friends both shrugged and shook their heads.

"We did ask around, as much as we could without arousing suspicion, but nobody has seen Carry for a long time. Some of the neighbours think she was picked up last year, but no one has a clear idea of how or where."

Rachel slumped back in her chair.

"I failed."

"You didn't fail. You were in an impossible situation. What else could you have done? You tried your best."

Her friends meant well. But she could have done better. She should never have trusted her ex. In retrospect, it was a mistake to have even consulted him.

A horrifying thought suddenly crossed her mind. She remembered the rumours that had been flying around.

"Do you think they will be killed? Are the stories true? Are they really murdering all of us?"

She didn't wait for an answer. It had just occurred to her that there WAS something else she could do.

"What if I just turn myself in? They might take me to the same place they have taken Sylvain. He might need me."

Her friends were horrified.

"That's crazy talk. You can't do that. Anyway, Sylvain has people around him. He wasn't taken alone. And what about Johanna? You have to be strong. She needs you to stay alive. She needs you to still be around when the war is over."

Rachel hardly dared ask.

"Have you had any news of Johanna?"

The last thing Rachel had heard was that Johanna had been moved from one family to another, and then another, and so on, until they had lost all trace of her. This was somewhat encouraging. If her friends in the community couldn't track her baby down, then maybe the authorities wouldn't be able to find her either.

Her visitors shook their heads.

"Still nothing."

———

NOTHING.

This is how it is today too.

Rachel has had no news of Johanna for a long time.

It's a good sign that her baby is safe and well hidden.

She hopes she's happy, surrounded by kind people and that she has found a Mama and Papa she loves and who love her.

As for Carry and Silvain, although there is little chance that she will ever see them again, nevertheless, in her heart she still carries a spark of hope.

As she sits in the Euterpestraat police station, waiting to begin her own journey into the unknown, her thoughts return to the wild notion she had before, when she learned that they had been picked up.

Maybe they are still out there somewhere along this road she is about to travel.

Maybe they are still alive and being cared for by her ex and his family.

Maybe they followed the path that Louis took and somewhere, somehow, they have all found each other.

Yes, she is being optimistic, almost to an insane degree, but at this moment, when all appears to be lost, hope is the only thing she has to keep her from falling apart.

THIS IS HOW WE DISAPPEAR

THE WAGON STINKS OF PISS.

Rachel stands with dozens of people. Like her, they are all sporting yellow stars on their outer clothing.

They are packed solid inside a windowless, unlit train car with walls made up of wooden slats.

It's the sort of wagon normally used to transport animals to their death.

This is not a thought she should dwell on for long.

The women around her, mostly older, are wearing dark scarves knotted under the chin. The men have wide-brimmed hats. Many are smartly dressed. In other circumstances, they might be city folk heading out for a day in the country.

As the wagon lurches from side to side, they hold on to each other to keep from falling. Stranger supports stranger. Nobody speaks. Nobody catches anyone else's eye.

Nobody wants to perceive their own humiliation reflected in the ashamed glance of another.

The urine that sloshes underfoot, soaking the straw on the wagon floor, may be animal or human. What does it matter? This is where yellow star people currently stand in the hierarchy of things. Her fellow travellers may have dressed for their journey with dignity, but every last shred was stripped away the moment they were herded on board.

They should not be surprised. Why would those who say they are sub-human treat them as people?

————

RACHEL WAS in prison in Amsterdam for about ten days, or so she guessed. She was told only that she was being held pending transportation. Nothing more. No charge. No interrogation. No communication of any kind. On her own. Fed sporadically. Ignored.

All she had to wear was the light clothing she was arrested in. Her windowless cell was damp and the chill penetrated her to the core of her being. Bouts of shivering would overtake her and, once she started to shake, it took a long time to stop. The thin blanket on her wooden bunk offered no warmth.

She would only sleep when she could no longer keep her eyes open, but then she would wake with a start, feeling that no time at all had elapsed.

What if she died right there? She might fall asleep and just not wake up. They would find her, dispose of her body and she would be gone.

Like so many others.

Who would they tell? There was nobody to tell.

This is how we disappear.

Every time a meal was delivered by an anonymous hand through the hatch, she would shout out with as much energy as she could muster, complaining about the cold, asking for blankets, clothing, something - anything to keep her warm.

With no response.

There she sat, hour after hour, huddled on the bunk, knees folded beneath her, the useless blanket draped over her shoulders, pulled down and tucked around her legs.

Then, without any warning at all, her cell door was unlocked and opened a crack. An arm appeared and dropped what looked like a small pile of blankets onto the floor. Then, the door was slammed shut again.

Rachel crept aching from her huddle and crawled over to investigate this unexpected bounty.

Which turned out not to be blankets at all. It was a single winter coat, dark grey, thick, expensive, full length, with buttons all the way up to the neck and a wide false-fur collar. And, of course, a yellow star.

She slipped an arm into one sleeve, shrugged the coat on and wrapped it around her. It still held the distinctive odours of face powder and good quality scent.

At once, her shivering ceased. In a hurry, with cold, clumsy fingers, she did up the buttons from neck to thigh. There was a pocket on each side, angled at the waist.

She thrust her hands inside.

The coat enveloped her, shrouded her, held her in its embrace like a living thing.

Where did it come from? Whose was it? Why did this person no longer need it? Was the owner dead?

She mulled over the last of these questions for some time and concluded that it was unlikely. The coat looked, felt and smelt recently used. There was no trace of mould or damp. It wasn't creased or moth-eaten. There was nothing to indicate that it came from, for example, a pile of abandoned clothing in a closet.

So what was the story?

Had the owner just been moved on? Had she left it behind by accident? It was not the sort of thing one forgets. But, then again, who would deliberately abandon such a beautiful coat?

Or was the owner still here? Was she in a neighbouring cell? Had she heard Rachel's cries? Had she been better prepared for her own imprisonment? Was the coat surplus to her immediate needs?

If so, perhaps this was a deliberate act. A decision taken on a whim, a gesture of goodwill to a fellow sufferer. A spark of humanity in an increasingly inhumane world.

A bribe offered to a guard and the good deed was done.

Rachel would never be sure but she wanted desperately to believe that this was how it was. That someone had chosen to donate her coat so that a stranger might live.

In which case, Rachel therefore had a duty to perform in return. She had a responsibility to accept, a promise to make.

She had to survive. She had to make it through the challenges ahead. She must not give up.

She could do that.

Her new coat would sustain her. It would not only keep her warm. It would lift her up. Her spirits would rise and stay risen, buoyed by the generosity of her unseen, unknown benefactor.

She would not die in this place.

And from that moment on, all the time she was in that cell, she never took her coat off.

———

SHE IS WEARING IT NOW. She buries her nose in its soft, furry collar and inhales. It smells much, much better than the train.

NEXT!

After many hours and countless stops and starts, the train judders to a final halt. A side panel is unbolted and pulled open. Light floods in.

Rachel closes her eyes. Turns her face away.

"Out!"

"All of you."

"Out now!"

Dutch voices.

Still in Holland then.

She peers out. It is quite a drop from the wagon to the platform and there are no steps. Rachel's legs ache from the effort of remaining upright, keeping her balance against the movement of the train and trying not to bump too often into her neighbours.

During the trip, some had abandoned the fight to stay on their feet and collapsed into the sodden, stinking straw or tried to stay dry by sitting on their bundles, bags or suitcases.

A strong gust of chill wind whips in through the open door and catches the tail of Rachel's unbuttoned coat, blowing it open. She shivers, wraps the coat back around her and gazes out onto a desolate landscape. Leafless sprigs of trees and low, straggly shrubs struggle for life on a bare, brown heath that stretches to an indeterminate horizon.

The Dutch voices belong to a crew of men and women who are assisting the new arrivals in getting down from the wagons and directing them where they should go.

They have no yellow stars and they are acting like they work here, but Rachel is pretty sure they are all as Jewish as she is.

Who on earth are these people?

They are wearing some sort of uniform consisting of a loose-fitting hessian-bag tunic with a white armband attached to one sleeve by two safety pins. Stencilled on the armband are the letters FK. A narrow black belt completes the ensemble.

They look like children playing soldiers. All that's missing are the toy guns.

There are some real guns on the platform though, slung over the shoulders of a few disinterested German soldiers, who are hanging back, keeping their distance, not getting involved. They stand smoking and chatting in small groups, cigarettes pinched between thumb and forefinger. Their exaggerated outbursts of laughter draw frightened glances from those passing by, heads bowed, hoping they don't get singled out.

Boys, thinks Rachel. They're just stupid boys. Stupid boys who rule the world. Stupid boys who have the power of life and death over her and everyone like her.

———

SHE JOINS a long queue that snakes around an enormous shed.

The person in front of her is an older man, who appears to be on his own. He is fidgeting, hopping from foot to foot, peering over the crowd, glancing this way and that. With his height, slim build and long neck, he looks like an agitated wading bird.

Watching his antics, Rachel makes the mistake of catching his eye.

He touches the brim of his hat and raises his chin in greeting.

"Cold enough for you?"

Good grief! Rachel gives him a thin smile and looks away.

"You know where we are, don't you?"

Rachel has a good idea, but the man doesn't need a reply.

"Fucking Westerbork! Pardon my language. Who would ever believe it?"

He ducks his head a little and lowers his voice, as if trying to draw her into a conspiracy.

"We built this for Germans. That crowd who ran for their lives to the border after Kristallnacht. There were so many, we had to let them in. Didn't want to though, did we? Now who's it for? It's for us. The bloody irony."

This is uncomfortable. Nobody else in the line is talking. Maybe he'll stop if she ignores him.

No such luck.

"I thought I'd got away with it, I did. Had a bunch of NSB pals. Did them favours. Did favours for the mof too." He cocks his head towards a group of German soldiers gathered some distance away.

His voice rises. "Arrogant, ungrateful bastards!"

Rachel cringes. The man turns back.

"Then the letter came. Called up. All those favours? Waste of time. How about you?"

Rachel refuses to bite.

But he is not waiting for an answer. He just ploughs on.

"Do you remember all that fuss when they were deciding where to build it? Do you? When the Queen decided it was too close to her precious summerhouse. Didn't want Germans in her backyard. Ha ha! Now they're in everyone's bloody backyard, aren't they? And where is she? Buggered off with all the rest of the toffs, leaving us to it…Ha!"

He almost bellows the word out. Heads turn. There's a shout.

"Quiet in the line."

The man mutters.

"Not that we'll be staying here. Look at it. No labour camp, this."

He falls silent.

Relieved, Rachel looks around. It's all so bleak, unappealing and miserable. Double strands of grey, metal fencing form a rough circle around row upon row of thin, long, grey single-storey huts couched under a low, grey sky. Around the huts, people mill like disturbed ants. The man is right. There's no sign of industry, no factories, no fields, nothing at all but barren land.

Years ago, the radio was full of gossip about Queen Wilhelmina's objection to the original site chosen for a Jewish refugee camp and then the controversial decision to build it on a sparsely inhabited, windswept plain in the northern province of Drenthe instead.

At that time, the notion that one day Rachel would be held in Westerbork was unthinkable.

Yet here she is.

The world has been turned upside down.

————

INSIDE THE SHED, twenty or thirty women are sitting behind a row of desks lined up along one wall. Most of the women are around Rachel's age and each has a typewriter in front of her. They all have large yellow stars sewn onto their blouses. Rachel's queue curls first one way, then the other, doubling back on itself a couple of times before dividing into a series of shorter lines in front of each typewriter.

The organisation is impeccable. There is a buzz of calm conversation and an air of quiet efficiency. It is like a factory floor, where each person understands who they are and what they have to do. This is a place where things are getting done and done well.

Rachel imagines she is on a conveyor belt, being drawn into the gaping maw of a well-oiled machine. She wonders where the machine will spit her out, or if it will ever spit her out. Maybe spitting people out is not the purpose of this machine.

When she gets to the head of her mini-line, the woman in front of her pulls a white card out of her typewriter and slides it with care into a box to her left. She then picks a new card from the pile on the desk to her right, inserts it behind the roller and cranks the knob to bring it around to face her. She leans forward to examine it, then, satisfied, looks up, smiles at Rachel and invites her to sit.

She asks for her name, birthdate and home address, then begins to type. She continues for some time after Rachel has stopped speaking. There must be other details to note down, things she doesn't need any help with.

The tapping of the keys is almost hypnotic and Rachel's thoughts drift as she waits. She doesn't notice when the noise stops.

"Occupation?"

Rachel starts.

"What? Excuse me. I'm sorry. What did you say?"

The woman is the very model of patience.

"Your occupation, my dear. What do you do for a living?"

Rachel's first thought is to say that she is a preacher. Which is true, but it's an answer that may invite further questioning and put other people in trouble. Why take the risk?

Perhaps she should just say housewife and mother. But she hasn't been asked about her family. Why offer the information when she doesn't have to? The others may be gone, but she still has Johanna to protect.

The woman is now staring hard at Rachel. Her smile is fading fast. She probably has a quota to fulfil and Rachel's hesitation is having an adverse effect on her processing rate.

Rachel picks the easy option. It has been a while but it is still true.

"Diamond worker. I'm a diamond worker."

The woman does a little more tapping.

"All done. Thank you."

With a brusque wave of the hand, Rachel is dismissed.

"Next!"

YES, LUCKY ME!

RACHEL IS ASSIGNED to one of the barrack rooms, a long concrete bunker with bare wooden rafters supporting a tin roof and planks on the floor that you can see daylight through.

"It's your lucky day," says the woman with the FK armband who has been tasked to show her to her new living space.

Rachel raises an eyebrow.

The woman catches her expression.

"Think you're too good for us, do you? Well, never mind, you won't be here long. You'll be moved on before you know it. I bet you're a hider. Usually, we send people like you straight to the punishment block, but it's full now. We can't squeeze anyone else in. So, as I said, you're lucky."

She points.

"Right, this is you."

It's clear that the small single bed space is already in use, although the occupant is absent. Rachel is going to have to share.

She turns away. Her gaze takes in the ranks of narrow three tier bunks, so closely packed that you have to pass between them in single file. Piles of belongings are packed beneath, thin, worn, filthy mattresses, covered with skimpy bedclothes. The floor is decorated with piles of animal droppings and termite dust.

Under her breath, she murmurs, "yes, lucky me!"

And instantly regrets opening her mouth.

Even almost empty of inhabitants in the middle of the day, the atmosphere in the room is so thick with the residue of unwashed humanity that she can taste it on her tongue.

————

AT NIGHT, it's worse - much worse. The stifling odour emanating from several hundred bodies and the breath of several hundred sleeping souls exhaled into a closed space almost makes her gag.

It is obvious that Rachel's bunk partner is unhappy with the new arrangements. She's an older lady and has not spoken a word to her. She did not even respond when Rachel introduced herself. Now, they are lying back to back, each pretending the other doesn't exist. A single blanket covers them both equally ineffectively.

Rachel pulls her half of the blanket over her head to try and escape the stench. Her face starts to itch.

Bad idea.

————

WESTERBORK IS A BIZARRE PLACE. Yes, it's a prison and the inmates are confined by tall fences and barbed wire but already, not even halfway through her first full day, Rachel has spotted some peculiar aspects to camp life.

She expected that there would be two categories of people, guards and prisoners, the first group controlling the second, as in the prison in Amsterdam.

But, the situation in Westerbork is much more complex and ambiguous. It is hard to work out what is going on here.

First, there aren't many actual guards at all.

She has spotted the occasional German officer, dressed in the standard long dark coat and high black boots, striding through the camp like royalty, deferred to by every person he passes. And there are armed soldiers at the sentry posts and in the guard towers dotted around the fence line, all facing inwards.

After all, who on Earth would want to break in here?

But, the military personnel all exude a remarkable lack of tension. Just as Rachel remarked on the train platform, the camp masters are relaxed. Westerbork must be a cushy posting.

The prisoners are free to move about inside the camp. They don't have to stay cooped up in their barrack rooms - thank God! At least not during the day. There's a dusk to dawn curfew, though, so there will be no way of escaping the hell of the barrack room in the evenings.

The bitter wind blowing across the heath and funnelling at pace along the avenues between the blocks does not make her want to seek shelter. On the contrary, it is cool and refreshing after the still, humid pestilence of the night.

As Rachel explores her new surroundings, she starts to discern patterns and distinctions in the prison population.

First there are the obvious newbies, like her, wide-eyed and clueless, wandering around, trying to answer the multitude of questions on their mind. Where are they? What is this place? What are they supposed to do here? What will happen to them? How long will they be here?

At the other extreme, there is a group of prisoners, whose situation, judging from their behaviour, could not be more different.

They gather in pockets of sunlight, seated on a mishmash of chairs or repurposed crates placed against a wall. The men smoke and stare. The women knit and gossip. Just as they would back in the Jewish Quarter, ensconced on the pavement in front of their homes, warming their bones, greeting passers-by, scolding children or spouses, exchanging titbits of news, watching the world go by.

They are all completely at ease. Each acts as if they were in their assigned place in the scheme of things. Their eyes don't dart around anxiously. Unlike the recent arrivals, they show no sign of fear, confusion or agitation.

In fact, the absence of tension among the soldiers is mirrored by the total lack of rebellious zeal or vocal discontent among the prisoners. Maybe the one is a consequence of the other?

It is impossible that every prisoner should be so passive and tolerant. Is that why there is no space in the punishment blocks? Do they lock away the bad apples? But, if so, who puts them there? Who deals with troublemakers? Not the solitary officers. They wouldn't demean themselves to manhandle the sub-human masses. They might get their soft leather gloves and shiny boots dirty.

Nor will the soldiers be leaving their perimeter posts to deal with the inmates. Not for nothing are they armed with rifles. No close-quarter work for them.

Her mind turns to the platform assistants, the team of typists and the woman who showed her to her room. All are as Jewish as she is. Yet there is a definite sense of us and them in their attitude.

"YOU won't be here long," the woman had said. "WE send people like YOU…"

Her stay here is temporary. She's just passing through. This is nowhere near the end of the line for her.

Yet, Westerbork bears all the signs of a permanent establishment. There are shops, a hairdresser, a clinic, and blocks with signs saying office of this and bureau of that. Peeking through the doorways, she detects the same atmosphere of calm bustle as in the reception block.

Something's going on. For many of the Jewish people here, this actually is the end of the line and has been for a while. They are settled. This is their home.

Westerbork is not so much a prison as a community of Jewish people. But it is clear that membership is not open to all. Some are on the inside. Others are on the outside.

Rachel is definitely an outsider.

NOT COMPLETELY GREEN

AN FK SQUAD is lined up in ranks on an open patch of dried mud. This patch is distinguished from the many other open patches of mud by a rusted climbing frame and a set of old swings with chains hanging from the bar but no seats.

The squad marches up and down and back and forth, calling changes of direction, clattering to a halt every now and then. None of this does anything to convince Rachel to revise her first impression of children playing soldiers. Their formation and time keeping are as loose as their clothing.

Two older women sit facing each other on a pair of wooden stools nearby. They are wearing matching dark green pinafore dresses with the sleeves rolled up and there is a child's tin bathtub in between them. They are peeling potatoes.

Maybe Rachel's former father-in-law and his cronies were not entirely wrong in their predictions after all.

The women have a sunny little corner at the back of one of the huts all to themselves. A stubble of grass struggles for life and some twigs planted in a neat row along the wall are showing green shoots. Another indication that not everyone is just passing through.

As Rachel approaches, the women lift their heads simultaneously, like startled deer at the scent of a hunter. They neither greet her nor smile in welcome, but Rachel decides nevertheless to take advantage of their acknowledgement of her existence to attempt a conversation.

So far, every other person she has crossed paths with during this miserable morning has completely ignored her. It's as if she doesn't exist. She understands. Everyone has their own problems to deal with and talking to other people risks getting you involved in their problems too. Still, you've got to have some human interaction or you'll go insane.

In an attempt to break the ice, Rachel gestures at the marchers.

"What's this all about? The toy soldiers in their flour sacks."

"It's the FK," one of the women replies, "my husband's one of them. There he is, that one, over there, on the right."

Good start! It sounds as if Rachel has put her foot in her mouth already.

She tries to make amends.

"Are they the camp police or something?"

The women laugh.

"They wish! They fancy themselves as policemen, but they are just grunts. Come here, do this, go there, do that - they just do what the real police tell them to do."

"What does FK stand for?"

The women laugh again. An encouraging sign. Rachel's first remark may not have been a mis-step after all. Instead, she has given the women a welcome opportunity to have a little fun at the expense of their menfolk.

"It stands for Fliegende Kolonne! Would you believe it? The flying brigade. This lot aren't flyers, they're crawlers!"

They crack up again as if it's the most hilarious thing they've ever heard. Rachel joins in, although she's not sure if she should.

"Fancy name isn't it? For - what did you call them? Flour sack soldiers? But, they are so proud of it. My God, when they first came up with the name, my husband wouldn't shut up about it. Strutting about as if he was some kind of commando, talking about missions and training and exercises and deployment. Ridiculous! And how they love their little armbands!"

"So, who are the real police, then?" Rachel asks.

"Oh, you haven't yet had the pleasure? You're lucky. Make sure it stays that way."

Her famous luck strikes again!

"The real police, my dear," one of the women explains, "are the OD, the Ordnungsdienst. They're easy to spot. Peaked caps and dark overalls with a leather belt. All men. No women in the OD. And them, we don't laugh at. Them, we don't even look at, if we can help it. Their job is to keep the peace and they are never happier than when this involves beating someone up or carting them off to the punishment block. They are mean and most of them are stupid. The worst combination. You'd best steer well clear."

She beckons Rachel closer. Announces in a stage whisper.

"We call them the Jewish SS. But, shh, don't let them hear you say that."

"They are Jewish?"

"Oh yes, they are Jewish. We are all Jewish here."

"And they are Dutch?"

"No, not Dutch. Well, most of them aren't Dutch. They're German Jews, like the camp bosses. That's why they are so powerful."

"The camp bosses are German Jews? How…"

Rachel can't get the question out. She finds all of this difficult to compute.

"My dear, you have so much to learn. Come here. Sit with us a while."

———

THE POTATO PEELING has been set aside. Gossip takes priority over preparing lunch. Rachel sits down on the little tended patch of grass and pulls her legs up beneath her. She collects her coat tails as she does so and folds them neatly into her lap.

The women watch her closely. They catch the fastidious care with which she protects her coat and exchange a glance.

Rachel is aware that they are appraising her and is conscious for the first time in many days of how she must look. She hasn't passed a mirror since she was arrested, nor has she had access to a hairbrush. Her bizarre failed dye job will be growing out by now and her dark roots will be showing at the base of her messy, tangled orange curls.

"Nice coat."

Rachel can read their thoughts. She may have just arrived but she is not completely green. She has spent her entire life being judged by women like these two.

They have processed her unkempt appearance, her relative youth and her lack of awareness and they have concluded that the only way someone like her could have got hold of a coat like this is by stealing it.

Becoming offended will get Rachel nowhere. She doesn't give a toss what they think of her, anyway. She wants to learn what's going on in Westerbork and keeping this pair on side for as long as possible might give her at least some of the answers she's looking for.

"Yes, isn't it lovely? It was a gift from my mother. I was so lucky to be wearing it when they arrested me."

She doesn't want to talk about her coat.

"So, how come German Jews are in charge? Where did they come from?"

"My dear, they were already here! They've been here for years! They are the ones we let in to the country after Kristallnacht. So the story goes, when the German Army arrived and expanded this place to make room for all of us, they came to an understanding. The German Jews had the language and they had the experience. They knew how to make themselves indispensable. They promised to ensure the camp ran smoothly, so those in charge could have a quiet life and so the Army would not have to deploy many soldiers to watch over us."

"So," Rachel says slowly, "what you're saying is, in this camp, prisoners are ruling prisoners. Jews are ruling Jews"

"Well, yes, you can put it that way."

"Jews are running the place and it doesn't cost the Germans a thing. In fact, they are doing the Germans a favour."

"That's right."

"But why would they do that? The Germans detest Jewish people. Why would any Jew help them? They must be getting something in return. What's the deal?"

The women are delighted with her reaction. One claps her hands and rocks backwards on her stool, almost falling off in her excitement.

The other leans forward with the air of a comedian delivering a punch line.

"Well, that's the clever bit, isn't it? In return, they have favoured status. They can all stay here. They don't have to leave."

Rachel stares at them.

"That's amazing!"

"Isn't it just? Weren't they smart?"

Smart isn't the adjective Rachel would have chosen. But her lips stay sealed tight while her mind whirls. The women turn to each other to celebrate their coup.

"Did you see the look on her face?"

"I thought her eyes were going to pop out of her head!"

They cackle in glee. This has made their morning. Much more entertaining than peeling potatoes.

They are right. Rachel is indeed stunned by their revelations. But the two women might not be so pleased with themselves if they could see inside her mind and read the thoughts that they have managed to plant there, in their misguided enthusiasm and careless desire to impress a young newcomer.

The simple question Rachel began with has now multiplied into a whole host of lines of enquiry, leading her down a path, which might have big trouble lying at the end of it if she is not careful.

IT'S THE HOPE

THE QUESTIONS JOSTLING for prominence in Rachel's head are these, listed in the order in which they crossed her mind.

What aspects of life in Westerbork camp are so wonderful that they would persuade Jewish people, who fled for their lives from Germany, to sell their souls to their persecutors?

Or should this query perhaps be phrased differently? Should it focus instead on the alternatives to staying in Westerbork? If so, why do the German Jews fear these alternative fates so much?

How is it that Dutch Jews like these women have also managed to become so comfortable here in Westerbork?

What deal have they made with the authorities? The women have revealed the German Jews' secret. But, what secret are they hiding themselves?

Rachel is pretty sure that if she turns this into an interrogation, there is a good chance that her new friends will clam up. They may even get angry with her.

And, in this new world, where there are multiple levels of society and where she occupies the bottom rung, the last thing she needs is to make enemies.

But she has no choice.

Because it has occurred to her that, if there are Dutch Jews who have been in Westerbork for a long time, then there is a possibility that people close to her heart may still be here too.

If that's the case, then the chance that she may be able to find them justifies almost any risk.

Of course, in the sort of situation she is in right now, it's crucial to have allies. Having friends in the right places may even have a bearing on her survival.

But the spectres of her husband and children, long banished from her mind in all but her weakest moments, have just risen before her. What if they are here?

It's illogical and, statistically, the chances are slim. Although there may be thousands of people in Westerbork right now, their number is tiny compared with the huge mass of Jewish people who have been transported out of Dutch cities in the past two years.

But, she must ask, or forever regret that she didn't. Even if, by doing so, she ends up ruining her chances of coming in from the cold, being accepted by this protected community and becoming an insider.

It's the hope. However faint, hope always betrays wise counsel. Where had she read that?

———

"I AM SO IMPRESSED. You ladies have managed to work it all out. How clever you are! I am delighted to have stumbled upon you. I was incredibly confused and you have explained everything so clearly."

She worries that she may be overdoing it, but the two women beam at her with satisfaction.

"Well, you have to keep up, don't you?" says one. "Otherwise, life would be so dull."

"Yes," says the other, "they may not think we old folk are very smart, and maybe we aren't the brightest, but we have a good idea what's going on. They think we've just got sharp tongues, but we've got sharp eyes too."

"And sharp ears, my dear," her friend reminds her.

Cue a further outburst of cackling.

Rachel takes a deep breath. Here goes nothing.

"But, how about the two of you? You have obviously been here a long time too."

The cackling stops.

Rachel keeps going.

"So, I wonder if you ever met my husband. He was arrested a couple of years ago. I'm sure he would have been brought to Wester-bork. What I mean is, everyone comes through here at some point, don't they?"

The women are listening but their smiles have vanished, replaced by the mask of suspicion that greeted Rachel when she first encountered them.

"His name is Louis and he's a good guy. Strong, clever with his hands, hardworking. Does that ring a bell at all?"

"No, we have never heard of this person."

The woman's reply is automatic. There's no pretence at reflection, just a bland statement of fact. Her friend just stares at Rachel, as if challenging her to contradict them.

Rachel won't let up though. In for a penny...

"If he was here, I am sure you would recognise him. Such a fine-looking man. Not a face you quickly forget. You know what I mean?"

She forces a smile, hoping she looks excited and positive, but afraid she may just appear desperate and pitiful.

They are not falling for her feeble attempt to recreate the bond between them. The mood has soured. The embers of their brief moment of mutual understanding are beyond rekindling. They are as stony cold as the look on the women's faces.

They will not be charmed. The spell has been broken.

Rachel tries a new tack.

"Well, if he's no longer here, do you have any idea where he may have gone?"

"On the train," comes the reply.

"Where does the train go?"

A shrug.

"Somewhere. Nowhere. Who knows?"

A long pause.

Rachel has nothing to lose by continuing to plug away.

"Maybe you have met my children? They were arrested more recently."

"We know nothing about children. Neither yours nor anybody else's."

The women are no longer willing parties to this conversation. So much is clear. They just wish Rachel would get up, walk away and leave them alone.

The urge to prod them, to throw a stone in their pond in order to provoke a reaction, to draw some sort of response from them, is too strong to resist.

"Then I wonder if you can help me with just one more thing."

Their expressions could not be more disinterested.

"Could you tell me if there are any Jehovah's Witnesses here?"

"We told you, this place is only for Jewish people."

"Yes, I heard you. But, although I am Jewish, I am also a Jehovah's Witness. I wondered if there are any others like me here."

This piques their curiosity.

"You? You are a Bibelforscher?"

The disparaging German word seems to have become universal.

"That's not possible. A Jewish Bibelforscher? Never heard of such a thing."

The women look at each other. Their faces radiate complete astonishment.

Rachel just nods and opens her arms towards them, palms raised.

"Yet, here I am!"

"But you look so normal. Such a nice girl. We thought…"

Another long pause.

"Oh well."

They return to their potatoes. Rachel is no longer worthy of their attention. The Jehovah's Witness thing was the last straw.

Well, at least she's given them something to think about. They must even now be reviewing what they have told her and wondering if perhaps they have said too much.

Too bad! Old gossipers!

She gets to her feet, brushes her coat down and wanders away. She has no idea where to go next.

"Hey, Bibelforscher!"

One of the women is pointing with a raised arm at a building on the other side of the FK parade ground.

"If you're looking for children, ask in the school."

A school? What sort of prison camp has a school?

NO FRIENDS

CLASSES ARE NOT IN SESSION. Rachel steps through an open doorway into a deserted corridor. The walls are decorated with notices in Dutch and German, interspersed with drawings and paintings of what look like camp scenes.

From the far end of the corridor come sounds of squeaking and scraping. She passes several closed doors but the final door on the left is ajar and she pokes her head in.

A woman a little older than Rachel, smart in a fitted skirt, jacket and heels, is busy rearranging chairs and tables. The furniture is not uniform in colour, shape or style, nor is it all child-sized.

Rachel clears her throat. The woman looks up and her eyes take Rachel in at a glance - early thirties - young mother - just arrived - potential new customer - worth interrupting her labours for.

She straightens, smoothes her skirt down and marches over, hand outstretched. She presents herself as the head teacher. No names at this point. Her status is sufficient introduction.

She speaks Dutch with a strong German accent.

"You have children?"

Rachel nods. Not a good time to try to be more specific.

"Excellent!"

The head teacher proceeds to whisk Rachel around the building, opening each door, ushering her in, pointing out features and ushering her out again. The rooms are all similar, sparsely furnished and in sore need of a little paint.

Eventually, they arrive in an office.

"Staff room," the head teacher announces.

There are just two desks. A young girl sits behind one, writing in an exercise book, head down, concentrating hard. She does not look up as they enter.

"My daughter, excellent student!"

It's time for Rachel to speak up.

"I think I may have misled you."

The woman stops. Glares at her, suddenly suspicious.

"You have children, no?"

"I do, but they are not with me now. In fact, I believe they may have been here some time ago. I can't say exactly when. I wonder if you may remember them."

The head teacher purses her lips.

"Perhaps they may even still be here," Rachel adds.

"They are not here."

"I haven't given you their names yet."

"They are not here."

"Perhaps if I…"

"When did they come?"

"Over a year ago."

"They are not here. Children pass through. They come. They stay a short time, then they go."

Irritated, Rachel changes tack.

"How long have you and your daughter been here?"

The woman gives her a sharp look. She has guessed where this is leading.

"I am different. I am a teacher. I am a necessary person."

"Perhaps my children arrived with other necessary people?"

"I can assure you they are not here now."

The conversation is going nowhere. But, maybe that's because there's nowhere it can go. This head teacher is being abrupt, but that may just be because she doesn't want to fill Rachel with false hope. Rachel may not be the first desperate mother she has had to deal with.

An idea pops into her head.

"How do you become a necessary person? I am also a teacher of sorts. Maybe I can help you here? Do you need more teachers?"

Where did that idea come from? Is some sort of survival instinct kicking in? Would she even want to work here? What could she teach anyone about, anyway? Her Bible classes would probably not go down well.

Or, is she just subconsciously trying to get under the skin of someone who is being difficult and unhelpful?

If that's the case, it has worked. Flustered, the head teacher decides it's time to retreat.

"We have no vacancies. I'm sorry I can't help you find your children and I'm afraid I have to leave you now. I have important work to do."

She turns and stalks briskly out.

Rachel watches her leave. That's it. Another dead end. She heads for the door.

"What are their names?"

Surprised, she turns back.

The excellent student has lifted her head from her studies and is gazing at Rachel. The girl's face looks so sad, it makes Rachel want to take her in her arms and console her.

She resists the urge. The head teacher may return and that would be very awkward.

Instead, she forces what she hopes is a sympathetic smile.

"Hello there. I'm sorry. What did you say?"

"Your children? What are their names?"

The girl's Dutch is perfect, with no trace of a German accent.

"My daughter's name is Carry. She's about your age, I suppose. My son, Sylvain, is a little older. I'm sorry, I don't have pictures to show you."

She should explain. What kind of mother doesn't carry pictures of her children? How much does the girl know of life outside the camp? Probably very little. Would she understand that families have had to separate and go into hiding, that there is always a chance of being stopped and searched and that pictures can place the people they show in great danger?

It is as if the girl has sensed her dilemma.

"That's OK. My mother has a picture of me that she shows everyone, but it's from when I was a baby. It looks nothing like me now. It's embarrassing. I hate it. I don't know why she even keeps it."

She shakes her head.

"Your children have nice names. I'm sure I would remember them if I'd met them, but I don't. I'm so sorry."

Rachel tries to hide her disappointment.

"Oh, well thank you any…"

The girl cuts her off.

"I wish I had met them. I wish they were my friends. I have no friends. So many children come and they stay here just long enough to become my friend, but then they all go away and they never come back."

The girl's eyes begin to well up. She returns to her book and begins to write again, forming each letter with great care. A tear falls on to the page, causing the ink to run.

Rachel is on the verge of crying too. It is as if there is a small dark cloud that follows her everywhere she goes and brings sadness to every person she encounters.

But it's not just her. And it's not just here. There is no happiness anywhere in the world these days.

IMMUNITY

THE LINE of supplicants at the administration office snakes out of the door and continues past several neighbouring blocks. Everybody in the camp has questions, requests, demands or complaints. Rachel cannot imagine that she will learn anything that will justify waiting hours in a queue.

Instead, she continues her rounds of the camp. She is crossing an open space full of people milling about or sitting together in small groups, when she hears a high-pitched shout.

Of course, it can't be anything to do with her.

Then she hears what the voice is calling out.

"Tante Rachel! Tante Rachel! Tante Rachel!"

It is a long time since anyone has called her that.

A small boy flying towards her, his feet hardly touching the ground, waving one arm wildly in the air as he comes.

She waits, conflicting emotions tying her heart in knots.

The boy arrives, skidding to a halt.

"Tante Rachel, it is you, isn't it?"

All she can offer is a sad smile. She dare not say a word for fear of choking and tearing up.

"It's me! Joseph!"

Rachel squats, opens her arms.

He falls into her and she wraps herself around him.

"Oh, Joseph, how you've grown."

The boy allows her to hold him, but not for long. He's far too excited for hugs. He breaks away and points.

"Papa's here too. Look, here he comes. Guess what? I went on a train! And soon, we're going to take another train. Will you come with us? Will you? Please!"

Rachel stands to greet the young man striding towards her.

"Maurice…"

"I'm sorry about Joseph. I couldn't hold him back. As soon as he spotted you, he was off and running. I wasn't sure… we thought, well, you know…"

"It's been so long. I'm sorry I didn't tell you all. I thought…"

"It's OK. We understand…"

Suddenly, his expression changes. His eyes widen in horror. He reaches out and clutches her arm.

"What about Johanna? Is she OK? My God, she's not here with you, is she?"

"No." Rachel reassures him. "She's not here. As far as I am aware, she's safe. But who can tell… you understand…it's not possible."

Now, it's her turn to have a flash of concern.

"And Louis, I don't suppose…"

Maurice shrugs his shoulders. Shakes his head.

Rachel looks behind him, in the direction he came from.

"You and Joseph are here alone? What about…"

Maurice cuts her off.

"She was out shopping when they came to get us. She's not here. I hope to God she is well hidden now. And you? I suppose you went into hiding as well? After Louis was picked up and then you disappeared too, we all feared the worst."

They move away from the crowd to find a place where they can sit and swap stories in private.

Rachel is conflicted. She is happy to find them but distraught that they are sharing her fate. It must be over two years since they were last together. She can't recall the occasion. Must have been some family event. In a different world.

As they walk, Joseph slips his small hand into hers and she thinks of Carry and Sylvain. They thought the world of their little half-cousin. She remembers the story Louis's sister used to tell of the day she brought this little packet of energy into the world.

"What a fireball." She would say. "He screamed the house down."

Rachel glances at the boy walking by her side, his face now solemn and serious. Despite his excitement when he found her, he is more subdued than she remembers.

He hasn't mentioned Carry and Sylvain. He must know.

She turns to Maurice.

"When did you arrive?"

"A few weeks ago. We'll probably be leaving soon."

"Is that what happens to most people?"

Maurice nods.

"Another train?"

"Yes, but nobody knows where to."

"But not everybody leaves, right?" Rachel whispers.

She then goes on to tell him of her conversations with the potato-peelers and the schoolteacher.

He is attentive as she speaks. Louis always used to tell her that his sister married a thinker.

"He doesn't say much." Louis would say. "But there's plenty going on in that head."

Maurice hesitates for a moment after Rachel has finished her story. He taps Joseph on the shoulder.

"Would you mind getting us all some water to drink?"

The boy looks troubled.

"Don't worry. We aren't going anywhere. Tante Rachel and I will stay here until you get back."

Joseph leaps to his feet and runs off. Rachel watches him go. He's like a clockwork toy with the spring released.

"That's unusual, the long-termers aren't normally so talkative," says Maurice. "How on earth did you get them to open up? Usually they are highly evasive when they talk to people like us."

"What is it with them?" Rachel asks. She is happy to have someone to share her indignation with. "They act as if we are not all on the same side, as if we are beneath them, like a lower class. So snooty!"

Maurice has a quick look around. There's no one nearby, but nevertheless he drops his voice to little more than a whisper. Rachel cranes her neck forward to make sure she catches every word.

"A train leaves for the East every Tuesday. Well, most Tuesdays. And that's the day when you find out if you are on the passenger list."

He pauses. Rachel waits. She can sense that he is trying to find the right words, that these are ideas that have hitherto lived only in his brain and he is having difficulty giving voice to them.

Maurice takes the plunge.

"While they are waiting for the names to be announced, most people are nervous. Anxiety is written all over their faces. There is a lot of talk about whose turn it will be this time and endless speculation about what is in store at the end of the line for those whose names are called out."

"Right, I can understand that." Rachel says, encouraging him to continue.

"But, not the long-termers. They act as if they don't have a care in the world. It's as if they are sure they are not going anywhere. None of the German Jews is ever called and there's a whole group of Dutch people who have been here a very long time too. And they are never called either. Some come along to hear the roll call, but they just laugh and joke around while the names are being read out. Others can't be bothered even to turn up. They just stay around their barracks, which, by the way, are in a different zone. The rest of us aren't supposed to go in there."

Rachel thinks of her encounters that morning. Maybe she had just wandered by chance into one of these restricted areas.

"I had no idea," she tells Maurice. "You'd never think a prison camp would have a VIP zone. How do you know who's who?"

"It's not hard," he replies. "Usually, with the so-called elite prisoners, it's just their attitude. Strutting around like they own the place. Also, most of them look pretty well off. In fact, I recognise a few of the faces, the men in particular. I used to see their pictures in Het Joods Weekblad. You remember, celebrities, dignitaries, company bosses, that sort of thing."

Rachel scoffs.

"That stupid rag. I never could understand whose side it was on. Did you notice it never criticised the Germans for anything? And, long after we all started getting picked up or went in to hiding, somehow it still kept operating. I always thought there was something creepy about that."

Maurice nods and returns to his theme.

"It's not the same deal for everyone. That's for sure. You want to know what I think?"

Again he lowers his voice.

"I think what those women told you is true. The SS have made a deal with the German Jews to run the camp in return for no deportation. And, as for our Dutch VIPs, I think they are paying through the nose for their immunity. Gold, diamonds, hard cash - whatever it takes."

He goes on.

"I've even heard rumours that it's the German Jews who actually choose who goes on the transports. Anyone who crosses them finds themselves on the next train out. Even long-termers have been known to get packed off. The OD is always on the lookout for potential troublemakers. The administration puts together a list, gives it to the Camp Commandant and he signs off on it. Much less work than making his own list. That's how the German Jews make doubly sure they don't go anywhere."

He sees the look of disgust that crosses Rachel's face.

"Don't worry. They will get their comeuppance. They will go in the end. You wait till you see how many people they cram into the wagons. With a train leaving every week, it won't be long until there are no Jews left here, in fact, none left in Holland at all. Dutch, German, whatever - we'll all be gone."

Rachel notices Joseph walking slowly back towards them, his usual inclination to dash around blunted by his concern not to spill the pan he is carrying before him in both hands as if it is the most precious thing in the world.

She has time for one last question.

"Where DO they take us? Where do YOU think the trains go?"

Maurice shakes his head.

"I don't know, but, wherever it is, it must be awful. The German Jews are well connected. They will have a good idea of what awaits at the other end of the line. Look how carefully they have engineered the system to make sure they stay here as long as they can. I don't think the rich Dutch Jews have the same inside knowledge, but I'm pretty sure they've figured out that what's good for the German Jews must be good for them too."

Just as he says this, Rachel looks up and notices the head teacher walk past. She raises a hand in greeting. The look she receives in return is one of pure venom.

SELECTION

IT'S TUESDAY, it's selection day and the camp is in a state of high tension.

Rachel sits with Maurice and Joseph to await the announcement. She has only been in the camp for a few days, so her interest is intellectual rather than involved. It will be a few weeks before she and the other people who arrived with her will be sent east.

Rachel is concerned for Maurice and Joseph though. Maurice has made his calculations and is expecting that this will be their time.

The reading out of names begins and continues for what seems like hours, but is probably no more than 30 minutes or so. The calling of a name is usually followed by a loud sigh or sob somewhere in the crowd.

Maurice's expectations are realised. When he hears their names read out one after the other, he turns to Rachel and shrugs his shoulders, trying to stay casual with an I-told-you-so look on his face, but there is anxiety in his eyes. He pulls his son closer and squeezes his shoulder hard. Sensing the change in his father's mood, the boy looks up at him with enquiring eyes.

Then, Rachel hears her own name called out.

And the announcement ends.

———

WELL, she wasn't expecting that.

Questions swirl in her mind. Why has she been pushed up the queue? Is Maurice right? Are they selecting some people just to get rid of them? It's hard to believe that the innocuous questions she has been asking would have marked her out as a potential troublemaker. Is it something else then?

The initial shock wears off quickly, though, and, to her surprise, she feels remarkably calm.

What does it matter? The die is cast. The page turns.

It would have happened some day. Might as well be today.

After all, she has no reason to stay in Westerbork.

Louis, Sylvain and Carry are not here. Maybe she will find them at her next stop along the way? And, by leaving today, at least she will have some family by her side. They can support each other, whatever the journey has in store for them.

She glances down at Joseph. Catches his eye. Ruffles his hair.

"Hey, cheer up, it looks like we're all going to be taking that train ride together!"

———

THEY ARE GIVEN no time to reflect on their fate. They have to move and move fast.

Rachel, Maurice, Joseph and hundreds upon hundreds of other prisoners make their way towards the waiting train.

The sign reads Westerbork – Auschwitz – Westerbork.

One platform, one place - Auschwitz - wherever that is. It sounds German. A village, a town, a province? Is it their destination? Or just the end of the line? Or both?

And what's with the suggestion implicit in the sign that there are people who travel from there to Westerbork? Is this someone's sick idea of a joke?

Who do they think they are kidding? Nobody comes back. Everyone knows that.

The members of the FK team chivvy the prisoners along, helping with bags, keeping spirits up, shaking hands and wishing the departing prisoners "auf wiedersehen".

Bastards! They must know they are never going to see these people again.

Not for the first time, she has the sense of being an actor playing a role in some evil-minded playwright's tragic black comedy.

ONE WAY JOURNEY

THERE IS LITTLE FUSS. Nobody forces them aboard or pokes them in at gunpoint. No rifle butts crack the heads of the recalcitrant. There is no shouting and no crying. No vain attempts at escape. No screams of resistance fill the air. No volleys of gunfire send them sprawling.

Goats - that's all they are. Goats on their way to market. And they aren't even bleating. Just dumb, docile, obedient domestic animals, meekly accepting their lot.

No wonder the soldiers just stand around, rifles slung, laughing and joking, almost ignoring the prisoners. They represent no threat at all.

The conditioning, the calm messaging, the sense of normality and the numbing mundanity. All have combined to deaden emotion, quash fear, quieten nerves.

Rachel should not have directed her anger at the FK. She has fallen for one of the many devices that the Germans use to blind the prisoners to what is really going on.

The FK guys aren't their tormentors. They are just the sheep dogs. When sheep are being herded, they only see the dogs. They don't notice the shepherd giving the dogs their instructions. They think the dogs are the enemy. They don't understand that the dogs are only marginally freer than they are.

If the FK workers are guilty of anything, it is of having the will to survive. The "auf wiedersehens" may not be callous and vindictive, as she first assumed. Instead, they may just be an expression of support, intended to encourage the anxious deportees. Like the kiss for the soldier on his way to the battlefront or the banging of tin mugs on bars for the death row inmate en route to the electric chair.

Rachel has seen too many movies. But she can't help drawing the parallels.

Even the German Jews working in the camp administration and the elite Dutch prisoners paying for special treatment are only reacting to an impossible situation that they have been forced into. None of them asked for this. It is the Germans who are demanding the bribes, offering immunity from deportation in return for loyalty, cash or slave labour.

Who can blame them for accepting the deal? You would have to be either very brave - or very foolish - to decline. Your survival and the survival of those you love in return for swallowing your pride and your principles or handing over your life savings? Who would say no?

The ultimate tragedy, as Maurice says, is that the immunity they earn can only be temporary. One day, their time will run out and the train will be waiting for them.

The conveyor belt moves them along. Each stage of the process leads inexorably to the next. The technology has been perfectly tweaked and the parts meticulously oiled. It runs so smoothly, silently and surreptitiously that not even those carried along by the machine are squeaking.

———

AGAIN, the train consists of a line of closed cattle wagons, stretching into the distance. Each wagon has a single sliding door. They spy one that appears to be relatively sparsely populated and stop. Willing hands reach down to help them aboard.

Rachel expects her nostrils to be assaulted by the odour of animal effluent and is not disappointed. At least the straw-matted floor is dry. For now. That won't last long. She sits, drawing the lower section of her coat up and folding it carefully in her lap. Funny how quickly this has become a habit.

She looks around. Women and children cocoon themselves among their bags and food supplies. Tight, pinched faces peer out from dark headscarves. Nobody speaks. What is there to say?

The men, most of them, are still on their feet. Some stand at the open door. They wave to fellow travellers in neighbouring cars, assist new arrivals, then, when the wagon is full, encourage late-comers on the platform to try to find a place further down the train.

"All full here. No room for you lot. Have you got a first class ticket?" Just a little light banter among friends. They're all in this together. Voices crack and strain, though. Any laughter is forced, brief, humourless.

Rachel watches them with deep sadness. These men carry a burden shared by her father, her grandfather, Louis, every male she has ever known. The constant need to put up a front. To show strength. To be a man.

They try to maintain the illusion of control, the semblance of normality, masking their fears and behaving as if they are active participants in what is happening, rather than passive victims. Dogs barking at the end of a chain. Troops whistling as they march off to war. Many of the men have put their suit back on for the occasion and are wearing their best hat, as if they are departing on a business trip.

These are individuals who formerly had some standing in polite society. Now, here they are, powerless and completely lacking in any stature at all, packed into filthy railway boxcars built for animals.

Yet, they still try to retain a last vestige of self-respect and the mythology that they are still somebody.

Tears come. Rachel isn't crying for herself. She is crying for them all. She can picture Louis in exactly this situation, trying to do the same thing, keeping a brave face for the benefit of others, determined to be an upstanding citizen and a team player, but eaten up inside by fear and humiliation. She misses him. He was a good man. At the end of the day, these are all good men.

When there is no room in a wagon for any more people, an FK guy slams the door shut, consigning them to almost total darkness. The only light comes through tiny gaps between the wooden wall panels. A series of thuds and clunks follow as the heavy external bolt is secured.

Rachel whispers to Maurice.

"Can't have us jumping out now, can they?"

He doesn't reply. He is just staring at the closed door, lost in thought. Joseph is curled up, head on his father's lap, eyes closed. It's unlikely he is sleeping. Escaping, probably. This dark, stinking box is not what he expected. Nothing to get excited about here. Unlike Rachel's, their ride to Westerbork from Amsterdam was in a regular passenger train. They had been spared the cattle-car experience - until now.

Rachel shuts her eyes and tries to shut down her thoughts too. These days, they have a tendency to spin off at tangents. She may well be in this box for a long time. Better conserve energy for the challenges that lie ahead.

Whatever they may be.

Where are they going? How come nobody ever returns? Why are the long-term prisoners in Westerbork so resolute in their determination to stay where they are? What do they know?

No point worrying about that now. She will find out soon enough.

PART III
ANKA

WE ARE YOUR PEOPLE NOW

ONE HUNDRED AND FIFTY-FIVE DAYS. That's how long Anka has been here. There's a calendar on the wall and, each morning, she moves a chair over, clambers onto it with her pencil in hand, stands up straight and stretches to write a new number in the next empty box. Yesterday, she wrote 154. Today, she writes 155.

Her aunties applaud gently, as they always do, and compliment her on her neat writing.

"Well done, Anka. Good girl. Now, come and join us. Have your breakfast."

Her aunties were strangers and already living in this room when she was delivered. Now they are her friends.

They are Mrs C, Mrs T and Mrs J, but they have told her just to call them aunty.

Nobody talks about Mamas and Papas any more.

Her last Mama is in this place too, but Anka has only ever glimpsed her in passing and from a distance. It is clear that her last Mama does not wish to have anything to do with her and Anka understands why.

Anka is older now. At least, that is what her aunties tell her. They say she was four when she arrived. Then, one day, she woke up and her aunties all wished her happy birthday. Now she is five. Anka has no clue how they know how old she is. Maybe they know other things about her too, but if so, they don't speak of them.

Everyone is now well aware that it is not a good idea to tell Anka anything that you don't want the whole world to find out.

Which, of course, is not fair. Anka is good at keeping secrets, but you have to tell her something's a secret. If you don't do that, how is she supposed to know?

When Anka first met her aunties, she asked them, as usual, if the people might know she was there. Tears sprung into their eyes and at first they found it difficult to give her an answer. They just repeated things like:

"Oh dear…oh dear…oh dear…oh you dear girl."

Then Mrs C told her, "even if people do know you are here, sweetie, there is nothing they can do about it. But, don't you worry, we will take care of you. We are your people now."

The four of them share this room, although they don't call it a room. It's a cell, because this place is a prison. She thinks the previous place she was in was a prison too, as it also had a metal door with a small hole in it and the door was kept locked most of the time.

She wasn't in that place for long. During the night there, it was so dark that you couldn't see your hand even if you waved it in front of your face. She was alone and she was terrified. She would scream and her screams would bounce off the walls and wrap themselves around her. This made her scream even louder. The more she screamed, the more terrified she became and the more terrified she was, the more she screamed.

Her heart starts beating faster just at the memory.

Now, she has her aunties for company and they make sure there is always a small light on at night in case she wakes up.

People bring food to their cell. Sometimes it comes three times a day, sometimes only two. Nobody asks her what she wants to eat any more. Here, you eat what they give you, when they give it to you and you always eat it all, whether you like the taste or not.

Her tummy growls constantly and she has forgotten what it is like to feel full. Her aunties often complain to the people who bring the food, but whenever they ask for extra, they are told that nobody anywhere has enough to eat these days and that they should be happy with what they get.

"People are starving to death out there. This is the Hunger Winter? You're lucky you're in here. Outside it's Hell."

Anka doesn't think they are lucky at all. Before, when she was living with the various Mamas and Papas, she sometimes thought her life was as bad as life could possibly get.

She doesn't think that any more. Now, she looks back on those days as relatively comfortable and peaceful.

There is no peace in prison. The days and nights are punctuated by wailing, shouting, doors slamming, alarms ringing and the pounding of running boots.

She was afraid before, but never this afraid. Now, fear so numbs her mind that she even finds it hard to escape into her daydreams.

Before, she thought she knew a little of the world she lived in. Now, she realises she knew nothing. And she worries that she still knows almost nothing.

This can't be how life is for everyone.

Why is life like this for me?

Where are the other children?

Am I the only one?

Each day is the same as the previous day. The only change is the new number on the calendar.

———

ANKA IS A PROBLEM. The people who work here and tell everyone what to do have informed her many times that she is a problem.

She guesses this is mainly because she can't answer any of their questions.

Time after time, they ask her:

"What is your family name?"

"How old are you?"

"What is your mother's name?"

"What is your father's name?"

"Where were you born?"

"What day is your birthday?"

"Where are your papers?"

When she doesn't reply, they shout and call her names. They call her dirty, scum, cockroach, vermin, little rat. Sometimes they get so angry that they hit her. She's been knocked down so many times that she now sits on the floor, legs crossed, hands in her lap, while they question her. She refuses to use the chair. What is the point when they are only going knock her off it?

They seem to believe that if they yell at her, hit her and insult her, she will, by magic, then be able to come up with the answers to their questions.

How could that ever work?

If she had the answers, she would not hide them. She has no reason not to tell these people everything. But, all she knows is that her name is Anka.

Even that they don't believe.

"This is not your name."

"Who gave you this name?"

"What is your real name?"

Finally, there is the question that her interrogators ask each other, when yet another fruitless session has ended in frustration.

"What can we do with her?"

———

Now, it seems that they have come up with an answer to this question at least. She and her aunties will be leaving here together tomorrow.

They are going to be taken on a train to a place they refer to as "the camp". They received the news yesterday and her aunties then spent the rest of the day huddled on one of the lower bunks, muttering and whispering. There was lots of sighing too and, once or twice, tears and group hugs.

Anka was not privy to the discussion or the hugs. She didn't care then and she doesn't care now. Talking won't change anything. She is just happy that she will finally be getting out of this place. Even more exciting, she will get to ride on a train!

As for the camp, wherever it is and whatever it's like, it can't be worse than here.

Can it?

Surely not.

She's been wrong before.

FIRE ALL AROUND

IT'S DEPARTURE DAY, but the hours go by and nothing happens. No food arrives either.

The aunties aren't talking much. Each is adrift in her own thoughts. They spend a lot of time just staring at the wall and look sad and anxious, although, when they catch Anka watching them, they give her a weak smile and say something like "cheer up" or "don't worry".

Which is strange, because Anka isn't at all worried, nor does she need cheering up. They will soon be putting the prison behind them and moving on. She can't wait.

But, she has to wait. All day.

Eventually, someone comes to unlock their door and, together with many other people, they are led out of the building and into a cold, dark night. They climb into the back of a truck, which is completely covered, so they can't look out. Or is it so that nobody outside can look in?

The truck moves off.

In the back, Mrs T has managed to get a seat on one of the two benches and Anka sits on her lap. Most people have to stand and they sway back and forth with the movement of the vehicle. There is total silence. Nobody utters a word. Mrs T wraps both arms around her, pulling her close. Even through their clothing, she can feel the pulse of the woman's heart. It's beating hard and fast.

The truck stops and everybody gets out. Mrs T hands Anka out into waiting arms, then climbs down after her. She clutches Anka's shoulder as they wait in the darkness. Her grip is so tight it's painful, but Anka doesn't want to complain.

The group moves off slowly. Mrs T searches for Anka's hand and Anka curls her tiny fist around two of her plump, sausage-like fingers. Anka can sense her aunty trembling and she gives her a little squeeze. She just wants to let Mrs T know that everything is going to be all right.

Mrs T releases a brief sob, which brings her a slap on the face from one of the dark-clad figures shepherding them along.

"Stil," he hisses.

They pass through a building, which is so large that you can't see any of the walls. Even the ceiling is out of sight above them. It is like being in an enormous cave. The only light comes from the small torches carried by their uniformed escorts.

Anka and Mrs T step with great care, watching where they place each foot. They don't want to stumble. They have seen others trip and fall, then get kicked or poked with a short stick until they stand up again.

It is slow going.

A train is waiting. The wagons are just black shapes silhouetted against a sky that is only slightly less black.

A queue has formed at the door of each wagon, where there is a low set of steps. Mrs T walks Anka past one of the lines to the edge of a wagon and lifts her up so she can crawl in.

The smell is just like the prison toilets, but much worse. There is straw on the floor and the straw is damp. She lifts one hand to her nose and smells her fingers. Pee-pee! Yuck!

Anka looks for a dry spot and finds one against the wagon wall.

Eventually, the aunties appear and gather around her. A heavy door is dragged across the doorway, then comes a series of metallic clunking noises that are all too familiar. They have just exchanged one prison cell for another, except this cell is on wheels.

Yet another disappointment to add to her ever-growing catalogue.

Will the camp be like this too?

The darkness is now absolute. Anka will have no nightlight tonight. She clutches the skirt of her nearest aunty, determined not to let go. Her aunty shifts a little and raises her arm, allowing Anka to snuggle close, then folds her into a cosy embrace. In spite of this and the fact that she is wearing several layers of clothing, Anka shivers. The chill emanates from deep inside her. It's a long time since she has had anything to eat.

With a screech, the train moves off. It proceeds in a repetitive pattern of clattering that reminds Anka of the strange sounds she used to hear while she was perched on her wooden chair in the roof space all those many months ago. There's a soporific rhythm to the rolling motion of the wagon.

Her eyes close and her head begins to wobble a little. As she topples sideways, her aunty gently eases her onto her lap. Before long, Anka is asleep.

————

ONLY TO WAKE to what seems to be the end of the world.

The train is no longer moving and outside there is roaring, squealing and a succession of enormous bangs that rattle her bones and teeth. Everybody in the wagon is either wailing or shouting. For a change, it's not just Anka who is screaming in the dark.

Some light filters into the wagon from outside through tiny cracks in the wood panels, a red flickering light that looks like fire.

Then they smell the smoke.

It IS fire.

Either the train is on fire or there is fire all around the train.

The screaming gets louder. Voices rise above it.

"We are going to burn to death! Help us! Let us out!"

Anka turns to her aunty.

"What's happening?"

"We're being attacked. There are aeroplanes. They are bombing us."

The door slides back with a thunk. A man's voice:

"Get out! Get out! Run for your lives!"

His upper torso is a dark shape framed by total chaos. Dots of light skitter across the sky, where huge, fast moving objects weave back and forth, growling and spitting fire and fury.

Anka stares out through the open door. At the front of the train, flames are climbing into the night amid plumes of sparks and black smoke. The aeroplanes come again and there are more deafening bangs. The wagon rocks but remains upright.

A cry is taken up and rings through the night.

"Jump, jump, jump!"

The people in the wagon crawl to the edge, hang their legs over the side and fall out into the darkness. Anka's aunties wait their turn, then shuffle towards the gaping black mouth that is swallowing the jumpers one by one.

"Come on Anka! Come with us!"

Anka is dubious about the wisdom of this, but she tags along. By now, the wagon is almost empty.

Mrs T is the last aunty to go. She turns to Anka and says, "I'll jump now. After I drop, count to 5, then follow me. I'll be down there, ready to catch you."

Then she's gone.

The only person left in the wagon is Anka.

She wiggles forward, shifts her feet and lower legs over the side and peers down between her knees.

She doesn't want to start counting just yet. It won't take her long to get to 5 and she needs to think about it.

The metal edge of the track that the train is riding on is visible below. It reflects the glow of the fire in the sky.

Beyond that, there is emptiness.

No Mrs T.

Nobody.

Nothing.

It is a long way down.

Too far.

Did all the people who jumped out just keep falling until they hit the ground far below?

Are they all now injured and bleeding?

Are they dead?

Will Anka also get hurt if she jumps?

The aeroplanes come yet again. They pass overhead in a crescendo of raging sound, so close that Anka is buffeted by the force of their passage. Then, more thunderous booms produce blossoming flowers of fire that illuminate the night.

But no further light is shed on the yawning dark of the void below Anka's dangling feet.

She can't do it. It's too much.

She looks out at the sky, mesmerised by the noise, the horror and the destruction being wreaked around her. There must be people in those aeroplanes. People who hate Anka, her aunties and all the people on the train. How can anyone have so much hatred that they would do something like this? And to her? What could she ever have done to make someone this angry?

Finally, the aeroplanes leave. She waits, fearing that they may return, not daring for a moment to relax her guard nor relinquish the death grip she has on the rim of the wagon floor.

The fires still burn at the front of the train, but the night eventually becomes silent and still.

Anka shouts, "aunty, aunty, are you there?"

There's no reply.

She calls out again and again and again, but the darkness just takes all her words and gives nothing back.

She's wasting her breath. Nobody's out there. Or if they are, they are no longer living. Maybe Anka's the only one left alive, perched there on the edge of the world.

After a while, a breeze picks up and she moves back into the depths of the wagon, as far away from the door as possible, and waits for something to happen.

THE SLOW, GREY RISE OF DAY

SHE HEARS them for a long time before she sees them.

A distant shuffling and scrabbling of boots on loose stones, the clink of metal on metal and the call and return of voices using words she doesn't understand.

Who are these people? Where is she?

She has not slept, for fear of what might come for her out of the darkness while she was asleep.

She was also afraid of what dreams might come if she slept, although she has never had a dream anywhere near as terrifying as what has just happened in the real world.

The screaming aeroplanes, the ear bursting bangs and booms, the flickering fires, everybody jumping out of the train and disappearing, leaving her alone. This is all way beyond anything even Anka's vivid imagination has ever conjured up.

And she is cold, so very cold.

Night starts to retreat before the slow, grey rise of day and she can now see. The people who fled have left behind bits of clothing and blankets. Shivering, teeth chattering, she crawls quickly around the wagon, throwing everything into one corner. Then, she burrows into the pile like a little mouse, nestling inside with just the top of her head poking out.

That's better.

The voices approach. Men speaking in short, sharp staccato bursts. The boots crunch nearby and stop. A beam of light shines through the door space and tracks across the floor before coming to rest on Anka's face peeping out of the pile of belongings. She closes her eyes and turns her head away.

Excitement ensues.

A shout of surprise triggers a cacophony of calling and the clatter of running feet. The beam shifts away from Anka and wanders around the wagon, perhaps to find out if anyone else may be skulking in its dark recesses.

Anka wants to tell them there's no need to bother looking any further. They have all gone. The only one left is her. Little, lost Anka. Abandoned again.

More heads pop up in the door space, silhouetted against the dawn. The heads are misshapen and hairless and Anka recoils, horrified. Has she fallen into the hands of monsters?

But the smooth, rounded shapes turn out not to be heads, but hats. Shiny metal hats with the brim pulled low over the wearer's eyes and a wide chinstrap. In the low light of morning with the sun at the back, the facial features are in shadow and barely discernible.

These are no monsters. They are just men.

One hops into the wagon. Crouching, he scuttles over to Anka. He is not carrying a torch. He has another thing in his right hand, a black object connected to a thin tube. He keeps the tube directed at her head while, with his left hand, he pulls at the pile, piece by piece, until she is revealed.

He grunts, then puts the object he was carrying into a funny-shaped pocket attached to his belt. Then he says something and reaches for her. She doesn't flinch. She is not afraid of this man. It is a good thing that he is here. She is cold, hungry, weak and tired and she doesn't want to be on her own any more.

He grabs her under the armpits and stands, pulling her up with him. For a moment, he holds her at arms length, studying her as if she's a creature he's never seen before. Then he draws her towards his chest and cradles her on his left arm. It is like the man is made of wood. There is no softness to him at all. Not like Mrs K.

Ah, Mrs K. Where is she now? Does she sometimes think of Anka? What would Mrs K say if she knew where Anka was right now? But there is no point thinking about Mrs K. She is no longer part of Anka's world.

They move to the doorway and the man hands Anka down to another person with a metal hat. Quite a few have gathered. They all look the same and they are all wearing identical clothes.

She looks around. The train is resting on top of a high bank made of packed earth and big chunks of stone. The bank is topped with a thick layer of smaller stones, through which the metal tracks run. There are two sets of tracks. At the bottom is a flat, grassy plain that stretches out to the horizon.

Anka has never known anything but the city. The world has never looked as big as it does right now.

So there is no black pit after all. The people jumping from the wagon will have landed on the side of the bank and rolled down to the bottom. It is not even a very long way down.

There is nobody there now of course. No injured people or dead bodies. No sign that anyone except Anka was ever here. They have all vanished. But, the bent, blackened wreck of the train behind her is ample evidence that the events of the night were no dream.

Anka doesn't regret not following her aunties.

Nor does she blame them for not returning for her. Climbing back up to the wagon in the dead of night, with everything that was going on, would have been insane. Who in their right mind would return to a burning train being attacked by aeroplanes, after they had just escaped from it?

Her aunties would have waited there for a while, expecting her little body to come tumbling down out of the sky towards them at any moment. Then, when it became clear that this was not going to happen, they would have turned and run for their lives.

Anka doesn't miss her three aunties. They were nice to her but people are only people. Some people are nice. Some are not. The only thing that people have in common is they come and go. They never stay long. Change is the only aspect of life that Anka can count on. She moves from place to place and from face to face. Sometimes things get better, sometimes they don't.

Usually they don't.

PART IV
RACHEL

YOU'RE A DIAMOND WORKER,
ARE YOU?

AT FIRST, she thinks it's a dream. But she's not asleep. She's only just closed her eyes. The train hasn't moved. They are still at the Westerbork platform.

She waits. Seconds later, to her astonishment, she hears it again. She wasn't imagining it. It's real.

There's a man outside the wagon calling out a short list of names and one of those names is hers.

Is this good or bad?

What does she have to lose? Nothing could be worse than this.

She looks at Maurice. The glance they share suggests that the same thought has occurred to him.

He shouts out at the top of his voice. The noise reverberates around the wagon. He shouts again and again.

"Here! In here!"

Others take up the cry and start hammering on the side of the wagon.

The bolt is thrown, the door slides open and the afternoon light pours back in. Rachel stands up and gives her name.

The FK guy checks his list:

"You're a diamond worker, are you?"

Rachel nods.

"Out you come."

Maurice gives her a brief wave, as if to say, off you go, take your chance, may God be with you.

Joseph is struck dumb and can only stare at her, eyes wide open in astonishment.

His expression says, I can't believe you're leaving us.

Rachel lays her palm on the top of the boy's head as if in blessing.

"Be a good boy. I'll see you soon."

She's doing exactly what the FK guys do, but what else is there to say?

Joseph nods.

He mouths, his voice hardly perceptible.

"Bye-bye, Tante Rachel."

She makes her way through the tangle of bodies to the door, sits on the edge, makes sure her coat isn't going to get caught on anything, and drops to the platform. The FK man extends his free arm to steady her.

"Just wait here. I'll be back."

He moves off down the platform, eyes on his clipboard, calling out his list of names over and over again.

Rachel turns to catch a final glimpse of Maurice and Joseph, but is just in time to see the wagon door slam shut. On the outside of the wagon someone has scrawled "74 pers" in white chalk.

Whether it has just been written or is a relic from a previous journey, nobody comes along to change the number.

The train pulls away from the platform. Plumes of black smoke obscure the sky and a deafening screech of metal against metal makes her teeth tingle. The engine strains to move its heavy load. There must be thirty wagons or more, all packed with human cargo behind the bolted doors. She does a quick count in her head. At least two thousand souls aboard.

The FK workers and German soldiers are wandering away in the direction of the camp. Some distance away from Rachel, a large group of women is sitting together, chatting and smoking. Nobody has come back to tell her what to do, so she heads over towards them. Little Joseph's farewell echoes in her mind. It sounded so final.

As she approaches, one of the women looks up.

"Nice coat."

"Thanks."

"Left family on that train, have you?"

"Yes."

"Haven't we all. Diamond cutter?"

"I used to be. In another lifetime."

"Take a seat, love. Meet the gang."

NOT A SPY

THEY ARE KEPT WAITING on the platform for a long time and this gives Rachel a chance to learn something about the group of women she has joined. It turns out that every single one of them is a former Amsterdam diamond worker. Like her, at one time or another they have all been in "the trade", as they call it.

Some of the women sit with their arms wrapped around others, holding and comforting wives torn from husbands, daughters taken from parents, mothers separated from children. Rachel knows their pain.

Many are obviously old friends and, when Rachel remarks on this, she learns that most of them were picked up and transported out of Amsterdam over the last few days. Previously, their work was "protected", giving them immunity from deportation.

Then, the protection was withdrawn and now here they are.

Rachel recognises no one, which doesn't surprise her, as she did almost no diamond cutting at all after Johanna was born. However, she does have acquaintances and experiences in common with her new companions.

As soon as she sits down, the questions begin.

"Which company did you work for?"

"Do you know so and so?"

"Do you remember that time...?"

"Wasn't it terrible when...?"

On the surface it is all innocuous enough, but it's clear she is being tested. Everyone is wary of strangers these days. She's not offended. It would not be unusual for the Germans to place a spy in their midst. She's a stranger, that's all. You don't trust strangers.

She isn't a spy, so she has nothing to worry about. Neither is she the only outsider. She can hear others elsewhere in the pack being given a similar casual interrogation.

Rachel is not up to date on recent diamond world gossip and doesn't pretend to be. There is nothing suspicious or extraordinary in that. A lot of workers in the trade in Amsterdam lost their jobs or chose other professions when the centre of activity shifted to Antwerp just before the war. There are plenty like her who are out of touch.

It doesn't take long until the members of the little group around her all seem happy that she is genuinely one of their own and the chat moves on to other topics, with Rachel, to her relief, no longer the focus of attention.

Will her new friends be so ready to accept her when they find out that she's a Jehovah's Witness? Who knows? Anyway, that's something for later. No need to worry about it now.

Finally, a train pulls in and an FK team appears to rouse them, rush them and usher them on board.

"Come on! Come on! Let's go! Let's go! Quickly! Quickly!"

Nobody explains what's going on. Why would they? What's the point? It is not as if they have a choice. After all, you wouldn't tell a goat heading for slaughter that it's about to have its throat cut, would you?

A PRIVILEGED BUNCH

RACHEL WAKES as the train slows to a halt. She has dozed for most of the last 48 hours, wrapped up in her coat, curled up on a two-person bench seat. Each of the diamond workers has a bench to herself. What luxury!

Each time they stopped, she would rise from her slumber to look out of the window, inquisitive rather than anxious. She's more comfortable than she has been for weeks and she doesn't want the journey to end.

Her carriage could not be more different from the cattle wagon she was taken off. For a start, this is a train for human beings, not animals. There are soft seats and an actual toilet, which even has a door you can close for privacy.

The diamond workers are not the only people on board.

There are soldiers, who leap off every time the train stops and deploy in evenly spaced ranks on either side. They always face outwards, away from the train, as if they are protecting the passengers, rather than preventing them from escaping.

How strange? Where is the threat? Who do they think is going to attack a train full of Jewish people travelling through a German controlled territory?

Young women pass up and down the carriage at regular intervals, bringing them food, water and hot drinks. And, even more astonishing, a couple of people in white coats come by every few hours and stop to ask each of the diamond workers how they are feeling and if they have any medical needs.

A more gullible observer than Rachel might think that the Germans had had a change of heart, that they were genuinely concerned with their welfare, that they had decided to treat them like human beings after all.

Rachel doesn't buy it. There is an agenda behind all of this. It is a German agenda and, although she is being treated well right now, whatever is going on will definitely not be in her favour in the long term. So much is certain.

As far as she can tell, all the white coats and waitresses are Jewish too. Some are Dutch, others speak only German, but none says a word beyond the minimum necessary for them to perform their duties. Their circumstances may be different from Rachel's, but they are no less imprisoned than she is.

————

THE BILLOWING black smoke clears to reveal a long platform. In the distance lie a tall fence and several rows of long single-storey huts.

A prison camp. This must be it. They have arrived.

The sign reads Bergen-Belsen. A cry goes up.

"Out! Out! Out!"

Hours of processing follow. Queue here. Queue there. Room allocation, bunk allocation, regulations, procedures, lists of things to do, things not to do, things that might get you shot, things that are sure to get you shot.

A briefing is convened. The new arrivals gather in the canteen. Tables and chairs have been pushed back to free up space.

A young woman places a single three-legged stool in the centre of the room. She arranges Rachel and her colleagues in a semi-circle on one side of it, then stands guard, making sure nobody comes too close.

Rachel is left standing in the front row. This is not at all where she wants to be. She tries to press back into the crowd, remembering advice from her schooldays: avoid the front and back, stay in the invisible middle. But the women standing behind her are packed shoulder to shoulder and don't allow her to squeeze through. A few hisses and tut-tuts dissuade her from trying to force the issue. It is obvious that they don't want to be in the front row any more than she does. Maybe they were told the same when they were young.

An older man, short and tubby, emerges from the rear of the canteen. Has he been there all this time, waiting for a cue?

The young woman calls for hush and helps the man up onto the stool.

So that's what it's for.

He is dressed for an occasion. His brown suit is well cut and looks expensive. He is closely shaven and well groomed, his necktie is perfectly knotted, his trousers have one neat, straight crease in each leg and the yellow star pinned to his jacket looks new.

This is not someone who has spent the last two weeks sleeping in the only clothes he owns.

The man wobbles and wavers at first, struggling to find his balance. He looks uncertain about the wisdom of the stool concept and glances at the young woman, who smiles, nodding encouragement. Nevertheless, she remains nearby, just behind him, one arm slightly extended, poised to offer support if needed.

Even thus elevated, the man's head barely rises above his audience. He raises one arm, forefinger extended, and waits.

The room becomes still.

He clears his throat.

"This," he declares, "is Bergen-Belsen!"

It's a powerful first salvo and Rachel almost quails as the man's voice booms around the hut, reverberating off the walls.

His expression suggests that he is quite taken aback himself and, as he continues, he dials down the volume a little.

"If you have heard of this place, you may be fearful and this is understandable. However, I want to reassure you that you have nothing to be afraid of. If today, you have spotted unfortunates in striped pyjama-like uniforms, do not be anxious. That is not your future. We are not them. They are not us. We are special."

He waves his arms around in a vague gesture presumably meant to encompass them all, signifying that they are a team, united, pulling together, all in the same boat.

He pauses, as if for applause.

None comes. Perhaps many in his audience are sharing the same thought that has sprung into Rachel's mind.

We may be in the same storm, but, judging by the look of you, we are certainly not in the same boat.

"You will be well-fed and you will be well looked after. We have our own kitchen and our own medical staff. You will be able to keep your own clothes."

He taps his chest. "With the usual decorative feature, of course. Apparently, this is why the other," he pauses "um, residents of Bergen-Belsen call our section of the camp the Sternlager."

He hesitates again.

"At least that's what they tell me. But, maybe that's not the reason. Perhaps it is rather the case that the word has spread that we are all stars in our particular specialised trade."

Unbelievable! This horrible little man is making a joke about the Judenstern, as if it's just something quirky, an amusing idiosyncrasy.

The man again casts a glance at his assistant. She returns the smile back and claps her fingertips together quickly a couple of times. Keep going. You're doing well.

His eyes drift along the front row in search of further positive reaction to his attempt at humour.

Rachel concentrates on removing a stray piece of fluff from her coat sleeve.

If he's disappointed at the lack of response, he doesn't show it.

"Officially, we are referred to as the diamond camp. Now, most of you are mere cutters and polishers. You come in, you do your shift, you clock off. But, in this place, you will not just be rubbing shoulders with your fellows from the factory floor. Oh, no. Here, you will be hobnobbing with VIPs, captains of our industry, world-famous traders, jewellery designers, pillars of society from Amsterdam and Antwerp. People you have looked up to will be your dinner companions. Those you have admired from afar will be your roommates. There will be no standing on ceremony here, no rank pulling, no doffing of caps. In this place, we are equals, all the same, just diamond people."

The downward turn of his mouth as he completes each phrase suggests what he really thinks about these circumstances. Or, perhaps it's a facial tic. Maybe this is how he always speaks.

"Among us are men whose fame goes before them and whose faces have looked out from countless newspaper photographs. I am sure I, for example, need no introduction."

His confident gaze once again travels the room. Rachel averts her eyes. She has no idea who he is. She supposes she should. But she has been out of this world for a long time. Or maybe he is not as famous as he thinks he is.

Nevertheless, now she has something much more important on her mind. If this is a camp full of diamond people, is it possible that Louis has somehow ended up here too?

The brown-suited man's next utterance extinguishes that faint hope before it is fully formed.

"This is a new venture. None of us has been in this place for more than a few days and nobody is sure how everything is going to work. We..."

He stops. Stares at his audience. Rachel looks over her shoulder. What has he noticed? Each of her fellow workers has the same grim, stone-eyed, faraway expression. Many have just lost loved ones. All have had their lives ripped apart. Not a single one of them wants to be here. To varying degrees, they are miserable, afraid, angry and exhausted. The last thing they need is someone trying to convince them that they should think of this as just some sort of inconvenient career move.

Perhaps, it has just dawned on the man that this is not a group that will be receptive to any attempt at cheerleading or team building.

His tone changes again. He is no longer lecturing.

"Look, I am well aware that none of you volunteered for this. Trust me, it wasn't part of my life plan either. In an ideal world, we would all be at home, leading our normal lives. But, the world is far from ideal at the moment and, as I am sure I don't need to tell you, things could be much, much worse for us."

The man's assistant now looks anxious. He has evidently departed from his script. But his attempt at empathy is short-lived. He is soon back on track, hectoring them.

"So, we are a privileged bunch. I ask you to remember this and recognise that what has been given can easily be taken away. Let me make one thing crystal clear. In order to retain our privileges, we have to continue to deserve them. This applies to each and every one of us, great or small, important or..."

He hesitates. There is silence. He looks up to the ceiling as if in search of inspiration. The reason is clear to all. He has realised too late that he can't use whatever word he had in his head – insignificant? trivial? unimportant? – and is trying to find a suitable alternative.

He fails, gives up the struggle and moves on.

"Well, I'm sure you understand. If just one of us rocks the boat, we may all fall out, and we don't want that, do we?"

Fear tries to hide behind the bluster, but it is present in the desperate look in his eye, the fine sheen on his forehead, the way his hands are clasped in front of him, the knuckles shiny white.

This time, Rachel does not turn away as he surveys the crowd, searching for support. That is what this little speech is all about. He is as frightened as they are. His special status is harnessed to theirs and he is terrified that one of the little people he has always despised may pull the plug and he will go down the hole with the rest of them. The power now lies with the group, not the individual, no matter what rank in society they held before.

The man pulls a sheet of paper from the inside pocket of his jacket, unfolds it and starts to read. The story is long and involved but the gist of it is that the Germans are setting up a diamond factory here and they are the workforce. An unpaid workforce, naturally.

However, there is a problem. They don't have any actual diamonds. All the workers can do for now is prepare the equipment and make plans, so they are ready for when the diamonds arrive. Delivery is expected soon. In the meantime, none of the women will be required to do any other kind of work, in order to spare their hands for the important and delicate tasks to come.

Still reading from his script, the man finally arrives at the culmination of his tedious speech. His voice rises again.

"When this factory is established, what we do here may prove to be enormously important and absolutely critical to the national war effort. The funds we generate will help finance the final stages of this war and ensure that victory is achieved."

For one awful moment, it looks like he is thinking of closing with the words "Heil Hitler!" but thank God he doesn't.

Rachel is confused. What was that last bit all about? Who was that rallying cry aimed at? Does this peculiar man genuinely think that any of them has any interest in helping their persecutors beyond the minimum necessary for their survival? Is he that deluded? Or does he suspect that, in fact, there are spies among them? Maybe he thinks the hut is bugged and there are Germans listening in. Is he hoping that reports of his loyalty will be passed on to the camp authorities?

Nevertheless, she is well aware that she is blessed to be here among this advantaged group.

She pictures Maurice and Joseph sitting in the dark among the mass of bodies in the putrid atmosphere of the cattle car and her thoughts turn to the pathetic, gaunt-faced, emaciated creatures in their striped pyjamas beyond the fences surrounding the Sternlager. Is this the fate that was awaiting them at their destination? Is this how Louis, Sylvain and Carry have ended up too? On the verge of death, the life sucked out of them?

According to the brown-suited man, "they are not us".

The arrogance of it! They are us, you pig. What makes you think you are any different? When you are no longer needed, when they have taken everything they need from you, when they have wrung you dry, you too will get your pyjamas.

That night, she adds Maurice and Joseph to her prayers. In her dreams, she sees Joseph's mouth open wide in surprise. It continues to open wider and wider, his throat like the dark centre of a maelstrom, pulling her in. She tries to resist but the pull is too great. She begins to scream, the dark water roils around her and then all is blackness and nothing is left.

THE DOCTOR'S BIBLE

WEEKS PASS. Nothing happens. The wait for diamonds continues.

Rachel may have been saved, but this is not the kind of saved that makes her feel at all safe. She is still a prisoner and she is still in a prison camp. She is still Jewish and still being interned by people who hate Jews.

The diamond workers may be treated well in comparison with other camp inmates - who make it clear they detest them for this - but they are still malnourished and exposed to the same diseases that run rampant throughout the camp and cannot be kept out by fences and walls.

Neither do viruses and infections have any respect for status, station or reputation, as they have discovered. Many have fallen sick, even the so-called VIPs.

Rachel and her colleagues have developed a daily ritual. Each evening, lying in their bunks in the darkness of the barrack room just before they sleep, they recite a short chant together. The idea is to keep their spirits up and the spark of hope alive, to celebrate their survival of one more day and fortify them to face the next.

It was one of the diamond workers who came up with the words.

"Notwithstanding this whole day
or the disquieting information,
Still we are one day closer
To our liberation."

Rachel loves it and looks forward to it. The rhythmic murmur of all their voices speaking as one takes her back to the many times she gathered in prayer with her brothers and sisters in Amsterdam. She misses those days so much.

She has prayers of her own too, but she doesn't speak these aloud. It's not the same to pray alone. The absence of others just reinforces her loneliness.

The evening chant also makes her feel like she belongs. Through their collective background and this shared experience, the diamond workers have become a closely-knit group. However, as Rachel expected, her status as the only Jehovah's Witness makes her an outsider.

It is not that her companions object to her religion - at least nobody has ever said anything or chosen to engage her in debate over it. None of them appears to be particularly devout about their own faith and she has sensed no resentment.

They just think she's strange, that's all.

And they are right. She isn't the same as them. To her, their outlook on life is entirely alien. The things they like to gossip about - hair, make up, clothes, men, film stars, singers - are not things that occupy Rachel's mind at all, so she never has anything to offer. The general chitchat just goes on around her, but without her.

Maybe, she would have fitted in much better before she became a Jehovah's Witness, but in the last two years she has changed so much.

She soon discovered that the women have no interest at all in the things that occupy her mind, the things she wants to talk about, like what the Bible says and the life of Jesus. In the early days of their imprisonment here, whenever she introduced a biblical quote into a conversation, it would be greeted with an awkward silence and she would sense a metaphorical door being slammed in her face.

This of course is far from a novel experience. When she used to do her rounds in Amsterdam in the early days, she quickly found out what that was like. Then the slammed doors were all too real, but she learned to move on and not be disheartened. You never could tell. Behind the next door there might be someone who was ready to receive her message.

Not here, though. So now she holds her tongue and keeps her quotes inside. Nobody wants to hear them. How long is it since she last sat down and spoke of important things with like-minded friends? Just a matter of months.

But it feels like years.

Sometimes, lying in bed, the encouragement instilled by the nightly chant fades fast and Rachel slides into despair. This is when she needs a Bible to hand, With a Bible by her side, she can always find words to sustain her when she is low. But, Rachel's personal Bible was never returned to her after the Amsterdam police took it away and, in any case, prisoners are not allowed to have Bibles or religious works of any kind. The Germans know what power books have.

————

THEN, one evening, providence strikes.

Rachel is lying on her bunk, eyes closed and lost in thought, when two of her colleagues come in, sit down nearby and start to chat.

Rachel can't help overhearing.

One of the women has just returned from an appointment with the Sternlager's Jewish doctor.

"So, I knocked as usual. No reply. Then I knocked again. Still no reply. I thought maybe he didn't hear me. The door was a little ajar, so I just pushed it and poked my nose round, as you do. And there he was, sitting reading a book."

" Maybe, he just didn't hear you," says her friend.

"No, that's not what I'm talking about. I wouldn't have given it a second thought, but as soon as he saw me, he closed the book in a hurry and tucked it under a cushion. Then he looked up at me with such a guilty expression on his face. It was as if I'd caught him doing something he shouldn't have been doing."

"What would that be then?"

"Well, the book was small, black and had a floppy leather cover with gold letters on it. I couldn't make out what the words said before he hid it away, but I've got a good idea."

Her voice drops to a whisper. "I think it was a Christian Bible!"

The two women then have a little discussion about how they have always thought there was something a bit off about this doctor and speculate on how he managed to smuggle a Bible into the camp.

Rachel has caught the whispered secret and is finding it difficult to contain her excitement.

Can it be true? It is the most thrilling news she has heard since she got here. But, what can she do with this information? She has never met the doctor. She has been fortunate so far not to have needed to arrange a visit. Should she just approach him out of the blue? If she is polite, is there a chance he may allow her to share his Bible?

This is so unexpected. She worries that her enthusiasm may lead her to be foolish and impetuous. She needs to consider the potential consequences of such a move. What if he gets angry when she reveals that she knows his secret? What if he denies it and all she succeeds in doing is making an enemy of an important person in their community? What if he doesn't even need to deny it? What if the woman was mistaken? What if the book wasn't a Bible at all? Then she will have falsely accused him of being guilty of a crime.

But, what if it is indeed a Bible and he does allow her access? That would change her life.

Eventually, her desperation wins over her concerns and she makes an appointment.

What has she got to lose?

———————

WHEN THE TIME COMES, after knocking, she makes sure to wait until she hears him tell her to come in, before easing open the door and closing it behind her.

She doesn't want anyone in the queue outside to hear what she has to say.

There's a tremor in her voice as she introduces herself. This is the moment. The anxiety has kept her awake long into the night for the past few days.

"Don't worry," he says. "I won't bite you. Take a seat."

He points to an armchair facing his.

His easy manner is encouraging and Rachel abandons her plans to make small talk before disclosing the true purpose of her visit. She leans forward and says quietly, "I hear you have a Bible, doctor. Is that true?"

His eyebrows shoot up, but she can't detect any annoyance in his face. So far, so good.

He thinks for a moment, then shifts in his seat, inclines his head towards her and lowers his voice to match hers.

"I do," he says. "Would you like to see it?"

Rachel nods. She can hardly breathe, let alone speak.

He smiles, gets up, leaves the room and returns a few minutes later. He hands her a small black volume. The pages are edged in gold, matching the words on the cover.

Rachel clutches it to her chest.

"Thank you. I so miss holding a Bible. I haven't had one in my hands for such a long time. You have no idea how much this means to me."

She's babbling away, but she doesn't care. Nor, apparently, does the doctor. It is clear he is enjoying her reaction.

"I think I'm getting the idea," he says.

Encouraged, Rachel goes for the big question.

"I wonder if you would permit me to share this with you. Perhaps I may read it from time to time?"

He hesitates.

"No," he replies. "I will not share it."

His tone is abrupt. Her fragile hopes shatter and fall into pieces around her.

"But..." she stammers.

"I won't share it with you. That would be difficult. But, I will give it to you. It's yours," he continues. "I have little use for a Bible here. I thought I would, but I don't. I read it occasionally but I find that, in these difficult times, it gives me more doubt than certainty. Already, I know that it will have much more value in your hands than in mine."

Rachel can't be hearing correctly. Or, either he or she has misunderstood.

"You want to give me your Bible?"

"Yes, young lady, I do."

The doctor pauses. Again, a smile crosses his face.

"Actually, following the accepted ways of the place in which we both find ourselves, I shall not give it to you. Instead, I shall trade it with you."

"Of course! Of course! But what could I possibly give you in return that would..."

Her voice trails away and her anxiety returns. It is like she is walking along a tightrope across a gorge. Her goal lies just ahead, but every so often there is a gust of wind that threatens to blow her off.

She is still clutching the Bible to her chest. She doesn't want to let it go, ever. She racks her brain for something to offer the doctor that would even come close to equalling the importance of this precious book.

"I am quite partial to bread and butter," the doctor says. "Tomorrow, you give me your bread and butter ration and we'll be even. How's that?"

He holds out his hand.

"Deal?"

Rachel grips his hand in hers. The tears have started to run down her face but she couldn't care less.

She finally manages to get the word out.

"Deal!"

"Very good. Now pop it in the pocket of that lovely coat of yours and let me deal with some of those sick people waiting out there."

Rachel gets up.

"Thank you so much."

She catches the doctor's expression as he stands and comes around the desk. Impossible though this may be, he looks just as happy as she is.

And she is on top of the world.

Just before the door, he turns to her and lays a gentle hand on her upper arm. His eyes glisten behind his glasses.

"You know," he says. "It is a big part of my work to make sure my visitors leave this room feeling better than when they came in. Looking at you, I have the impression I have rarely done my job so well."

————

DURING THE DAYS THAT FOLLOW, Rachel spends every spare waking moment devouring her precious new Bible. Now she has spiritual sustenance, she is no longer so alone.

She is uplifted and stronger. Her troubles are lighter to bear. The doctor's kindness has touched her deeply. Rare it may be, but goodness still lives on in the hearts of men.

THE SAME NUMBER EVERY DAY

WHEN RACHEL WAS A CHILD, she had a set of 28 coloured pencils that she was extremely proud of. They were a present from her grandfather. Every day, she would wake up, open the pencil drawer and gaze at them, neatly lined up in the order of the colours of the rainbow and sub-divided by shade, dark to the left, light to the right. Before closing the drawer again, she would count them. There were always 28 and this gave her the reassurance she needed. She could then start her day with the confidence that all was right in the world.

Here in the camp, she, her colleagues and all the other diamond camp prisoners are the Germans' coloured pencils. What other explanation can there be for making them get up in the morning, long before dawn, whatever the weather, and go outside to stand in ranks, just for soldiers to walk up and down the lines and count them?

It's the same number every day.

Unless someone is so sick that they can't walk or has died.

When it's over, the prisoners troop back to their barrack rooms, cold, miserable and dispirited already before their dull, pointless day has even begun.

Maybe that's the idea. Keep them crushed and deprived of hope.
Beat them down and keep them down.

————

ONE MORNING, they are detained in the yard for much longer than
usual.

A pale light is showing in the east by the time they are released.
Only then do they find out what has been going on. Their beds, bags
and cupboards have all been dismantled, emptied out and searched.
The prisoners' meagre remaining store of personal possessions and
family photographs, tucked away in dark corners, concealed under
seams, inserted between cracks in walls or wooden furniture, all gone.
Taken away for burning is the rumour.

Rachel hunts for her Bible among the debris, but of course it's
gone, like everything else. Stupid! Why didn't she keep it in her coat?
But random body searches are common too. It wouldn't have been
safer there. At least the authorities couldn't connect it to her directly.
She had hidden it squeezed between the leg of a neighbour's bunk and
the barrack wall.

Although, it wouldn't take a genius to figure out which of the
women it belonged to.

She is devastated. That night, her despair returns, this time with
greater force. Her mood becomes darker than at any time since her
arrest.

What's the point of life when there is nothing to live for? She has
nothing to do, nothing to occupy her hands or mind and nobody to
talk to.

Yes, it's a mistake to allow your happiness to rest on physical
things, because things can always be lost, stolen or destroyed. But, for
her, right now, that's how it is. Her Bible is everything to her. Was
everything to her. Now she is bereft. Thank God she still has her coat.

Even the bedtime chants don't help. As the days pass, she withdraws deeper and deeper into herself. Nobody asks her what's

wrong. Why should they? It's just strange Rachel being strange again. Anyway, look around. What's wrong for Rachel is wrong for everyone. They all have their own problems. All of them are missing loved ones. All of them are deprived of their freedom. Any of them may fall ill and die any day. Each of them is face to face with oblivion. Who has the time or energy to be concerned with anybody else's issues?

If Rachel is going to survive, she is going to have to do it herself. If she falls, nobody will lift her up. If she abandons the struggle, there is nobody to encourage her or fight for her.

She tells herself she needs a sign to prove that life is indeed worth living. It doesn't have to be a major event, like an eclipse or an earthquake, but she'll recognise it when it comes. And if there is no sign, well then that means it is OK to give up the struggle.

There she goes again, balancing all her hopes on one thing. Except it's not a physical object this time. It's just a construct, shapeless and undefined. This is probably not a step forward.

———

A FEW DAYS LATER, Rachel is caught outside in a storm and she ducks into one of the camp administration blocks to get out of the rain. She is alone and she shouldn't be there. These blocks are out of bounds. But, this one makes for a convenient, and dry, shortcut to the canteen. She strides down the corridor trying to exude confidence, to give the impression that she is there on official business - whatever that may be. If anyone accosts her, she will think of something, but she hopes she doesn't have to.

The door to one of the offices just ahead of her is open.

She glances in as she passes...

... and stops.

There is her Bible, the doctor's old Bible, sitting on top of a cabinet just inside the door.

Oh my goodness! It's so close. It wouldn't take two seconds to

snatch it up and walk on. She glances one way, then the other. The
corridor is empty.

Her heart is pounding. Anyone for miles around must be able to
hear it.

She takes one step forward and peeks around the door.

It's quite a large office and appears to be unoccupied.

She looks back at the Bible. It is definitely hers.

Just one more step and it will be in reach.

Does she dare?

She jumps as a clattering sound comes from the furthest reaches of
the room, the distinctive tapping of typewriter keys. In the left-hand
corner, a woman sits almost hidden behind piles of files and folders.
She is hunched forward, her attention fixed on her work.

But, if she were to raise her head at any moment, Rachel would be
in full view.

Or someone may step into the corridor just as Rachel snatches up
the Bible and catch her, evidence of her theft in hand.

The consequences would be devastating. Her diamond worker
status would not prevent them putting a bullet in her head. They
would never let such an offence go unpunished. What message would
that send to the other prisoners? Privilege only goes so far. Her skills
are not unique. She's not irreplaceable.

The longer she stands there, the greater the temptation.

And the greater her fear.

It's too much.

But, it's the only way.

She makes her decision.

———

RACHEL KNOCKS. The woman looks up and notices her.

"Yes, yes. What is it?"

"That Bible." Rachel points at the cabinet.

"What about it?"

"It's mine. I lost it the other day. It's very important to me. I wonder if it would be possible for me to get it back."

"That is", she adds quickly, "if it's convenient. For you. I don't want to disturb you."

"You have already disturbed me. How did you lose it?"

The woman has pushed her chair back.

"It was in my barrack room..."

"You're a prisoner. Prisoners are not allowed Bibles, are they?"

"Yes, this is true."

"Come inside. Close the door."

Rachel takes a couple of paces forward, then shuts the door behind her. She turns back.

The woman stands up and walks over, clipping across the floorboards in her pencil skirt and high heels. She is older than Rachel. In her mid-forties, perhaps?

The woman stops, folds her arms and inspects Rachel up and down.

Rachel is immediately conscious of how pitiful and dishevelled she must look. Among the other prisoners, she never thinks about her appearance. They are all in the same situation. Their clothes are faded, old and frayed. The condition of their hair and skin reflects their inadequate nutrition and the absence of any opportunity for self-care. And, not to put too fine a point on it, they all smell terrible.

This woman, however, is smartly dressed, wears a touch of make up, has had her hair styled in the latest fashion and, even at this distance, Rachel can smell her perfume. She is from the world beyond the camp fence, a world that is so remote that it might as well lie on the far side of the moon.

"So, you were well aware that you are not allowed to have a Bible. Yet, you had a Bible. It was confiscated from you and now you want it back. Is that right?"

She raises her eyebrows, challenging Rachel to answer.

Rachel can't think of anything to say that would improve her situation. She just nods briefly and looks down at the woman's shoes.

Then, fearing that she's being rude, she adjusts her gaze so that she is staring over the woman's shoulder.

"Hmm..."

The woman hesitates. Rachel waits. It is as if she is standing at the edge of a cliff.

"Now when you passed by and saw the Bible there, you must have been so tempted to just reach in and grab it. That would have been easy. I'm sure I would not have seen a thing. I was concentrating on my work, as you may have noticed."

Rachel nods again. The woman is not asking her anything. She is just stating the facts. Rachel has nothing to say.

The woman pauses again before continuing.

"Yet, you didn't do that. Why not?"

There is no challenge in the question. The woman's tone is simply curious.

Rachel looks her in the eye for the first time, more confident now.

"It would have been wrong. I know it is mine, but taking it would have been the same as stealing. I am not a thief."

"This Bible must mean a great deal to you."

"It does. It really does. It means everything!"

The woman reaches over, picks up the Bible and hands it to Rachel.

"You treated me with respect and I feel I should return that respect."

She whispers, "hide it better next time."

———

RACHEL ALMOST BOUNCES her way out of the building. The rain has cleared. She begins to count her blessings.

She's alive. She's healthy. There are many who are much worse off than she is and now she has her Bible for company once again, she can deal with anything they throw at her. There she goes, tempting fate again.

SO MUCH TROUBLE

DAY BREAKS on an icy December morning. Together with her fellow diamond workers, Rachel is crouched on a train platform in northern Germany. They huddle naked against a bitter wind.

She can't take this much longer.

A gust slices through her, chilling her to the core. She tucks her hands deeper into her armpits. The press of icy-cold bare flesh all around does not convey any warmth at all.

What else can they do?

The clothing they arrived in is scattered on the bare concrete ground around them. Rachel's frozen feet are squeezed into one sleeve of her beloved coat. It has sustained her for so long. This may be its final act of kindness. Her Bible is stuffed into one of its deep pockets. She will lose that too. And this time it will be lost forever.

Unclothed and deprived of the two pillars of comfort on which she depends, she is defenceless and exposed.

Gathered in a loose circle around them is a group of huge female uniformed guards, wielding heavy batons. One fist curls around the grip, the other cradles the thick rounded knob at the other end. Those who were slow to obey the order to strip have already felt the force of these sticks.

The cold is numbing Rachel's brain. When they were herded off the train and told to remove their clothes, she wondered what it was all about.

Now, she doesn't have enough mental strength to try and understand anything. She doesn't care. If this goes on much longer, she is sure she will die right there on the cold stone. And, if somehow she survives, then what difference does it make?

Is this life genuinely a better alternative?

Two more guards arrive, dragging a wooden cart.

"Your new clothes. Put them on!"

The cart is full of the same blue striped dresses worn by the other women prisoners in Bergen-Belsen. The ones on the other side of the fence. She shuffles over, delves into the pile and picks one out.

Another cart appears with wooden clogs and a large basket of kerchiefs.

The dress is making her itch. She scratches. Something is moving around in the patch of hair under her arm and she squishes it hard between two fingers. When she withdraws her hand, she looks and sees a tiny carapace oozing mush, the legs and antennae still twitching. She flicks it off onto the ground.

Lice! Disgusting!

Her dress is crawling with them. They are all over her: on her neck, her back, her arms and her scalp. She tries to seek out and kill as many as she can, but this is a battle she can never win.

She is still shivering. She may never stop.

A guard addresses them in rough German, her speech peppered with insults and curses. With evident delight, she tells them that she and the other guards, who are now lined up on either side of her, are former prison inmates too. They were convicted of violent crimes, but now they have been released to help the war effort.

"They gave us this work because it suits our special set of skills," she explains.

At this, the guards break out in an explosion of laughter.

Some joke! It is obvious that their privileged Sternlager days are a thing of the past. Nobody will give them special treatment any more.

———

OF COURSE, the Germans found no diamonds for them to work on, the whole idea of a Bergen-Belsen diamond factory was scrapped and the women, all 108 of them, have been transferred here. The male prisoners in the diamond camp have been sent off somewhere else.

Their new workplace is near a town called Beendorf, where several factories have been constructed deep within an old salt mine to try to conceal their whereabouts from patrolling enemy aircraft.

They are told, "even if the British try to bomb us, they can't hurt us. We are too deep underground!"

It all sounds terrifying.

The prisoners do 12-hour shifts and commute to and fro between factory and surface in a tiny cage that runs up and down the mineshaft.

It doesn't take much imagination to work out that if this single avenue to the surface is blocked or damaged, then they will all be buried alive.

So much for "they can't hurt us!"

Rachel's first ride to work is the most traumatising experience of her life. She clings on to the rough, rusty metal frame with both hands as they drop fast down the unlit rock chimney.

The cage rattles, shakes and lurches back and forth. She imagines that it's hanging from a hook and that, at any moment, one extravagant lurch may cast it loose and send them all plunging to the bottom of the shaft in the bowels of the earth.

The deeper they go, the darker it gets and Rachel is seized by absolute terror. Her mind goes blank. She opens her mouth but she doesn't even have the mental strength to fashion a scream.

Then, a faint light from below rises slowly up to meet them. The rough-hewn rock they are descending through is close enough that, if she wanted, she could reach an arm out through the frame and touch it.

She doesn't want to do that.

She has just decided that this torture will never end when the cage hits the base of the shaft with a thump. They are no longer moving. The rattling has stopped, but it is still quite a while before she is brave enough to loosen her grasp on the frame. Its sharp edges have scored lines in the puffy flesh of her palms and, as the blood returns, small trickles appear, tracing the course of her lifelines.

She crosses her arms and tucks her hands under her armpits to staunch the flow and so that nobody can see the damage. Then, she hurries to catch up. The briefing has already begun.

She learns that it is not by chance that they have been chosen for Beendorf. The factories produce essential parts for rockets and fighter planes and assembling these parts requires skilled and nimble fingers. The diamond workers are used to working fast and carefully with small tools on intricate jobs, so they are well suited to this work.

Rachel waits, She is sure there is a pep talk coming.

Yes, here it is.

They are fortunate. They have a workplace that is safe, warm and dry. They will find this job rewarding and inspiring. The machines they will be helping to build are the secret weapons that will win the war for the Fatherland. The work they do will bring them glory. One day, the whole world will thank them for their contribution to the victory that is certain to come.

Blah, blah, blah...they've heard all this before. The same sort of claptrap they were given in the diamond camp.

As if they care.

And then it dawns on her.

She does care.

She cares a lot.

Not about the Fatherland, though.

Something completely different.

She can't do this.

It's wrong.

Oh no! She's going to be in so much trouble.

The thought had first occurred to her after she was arrested. There was a moral choice she might have to make at some point, depending what sort of work she was asked to do at whichever labour camp she was sent to.

But after she arrived at Bergen-Belsen and found out that she would just be cutting or polishing diamonds - a job that presented no moral dilemma at all - she hadn't given the matter any further thought and it had slipped from her mind.

It has her full attention now and there is no question in her mind as to the choice she has to make.

It's going to be painful.

The guard delivering the briefing motions them all forward to take turns trying their hand with the machines.

Rachel hangs back. She steels herself.

"Come on!"

The guard is beckoning her. It's her turn.

"No."

"Come on!"

"No, I can't. I can't do this. I will not do this work."

Her colleagues are staring at her as if she has lost her mind.

The guard moves fast. She marches over and slaps Rachel across the face. The blow causes her to stagger, but she stays on her feet.

The guard puts her face close to Rachel's and screams, "what is your problem, you little bitch?"

Rachel flinches. Splats of spittle fleck her cheeks. She is afraid, but she won't change her mind. She must be resolute. She raises her chin.

"I will not contribute to the fabrication of weapons of war."

"What?"

The guard screeches again. Her large nose has turned a furious purple.

"Who do you think you are? Are you mad? Are you stupid?"

"My faith will not permit me to do this."

"What faith? What are you talking about, Jew?"

The guard slaps her again. This time, it turns into more of a punch and catches Rachel on the point of the jaw. Her head snaps back. She's on the verge of blacking out.

"What does your faith think of that, bitch?"

She manages somehow to stay upright and just shakes her head. She can't get her mouth to move but she will not back down.

The guard hits her again. This time it's an almost casual gesture with the back of the hand to the head, as if she's just moving Rachel out of the way. Knuckles connect with bone and there's a cracking sound that ricochets around Rachel's skull. She hears it before she feels it and collapses to the floor like a puppet with its strings cut.

The guard stands over her. There is not an ounce of pity in her voice, just pure contempt.

"Get over yourself. You had better be ready to work tomorrow or there will be consequences. This is a party game compared to what I'll do to you if you try and pull this kind of trick again."

She stalks away. The women follow. The familiarisation programme must continue. Rachel is left alone, ignored, bruised and bleeding. Her lips are moving but the sound she makes is almost inaudible. Which doesn't matter, because nobody's listening.

"I will not do this work."

———

SHE LIES IN BED, fully dressed, blanket pulled up against the cold, staring up at the slats in the overhead bunk. She's trying to work out what to do. Her fellow workers have all ignored her since the events in the factory. Like her, they know this is far from over and they fear her antics may get them all into trouble.

They are quite right. Everyone has heard the stories of how fond the Germans are of punishing the many for the sins of the few. But

Rachel is determined. She will not betray her values. If only she can come up with a plan that will not betray her colleagues as well.

She will not sleep tonight. What's the point? This may be the last night of her life.

PART V
ANKA

THE WOMEN IN WHITE

ANKA IS in hospital in a town called Zwolle. She has been told not to get out of bed without a grown-up to accompany her. All the grown-ups here are women and they all have clean white dresses and pretty white hats.

Anka has slept a lot since she arrived. She has also had some hot food. Best of all, when she asked for more, they gave her more. What a treat!

The women in white have explained where she is and why she is here. She has to get stronger. When the men in metal hats took her away, she was too weak to walk by herself and they had to carry her. They found another child in the train too, a baby boy only 6 months old. He is here with her, sleeping in a cot on the other side of the room.

They tell her they are waiting for the next transport. Then she will be released. These are the words they use. This probably means that she will soon have to go on another train. This is not something she is looking forward to. She never wants even to see another train, let alone ride in one.

There is no sign of her aunties. Maybe they are already at the camp.

Night falls and the hospital becomes quiet. Having been asleep all day, Anka is now wide awake. A window next to her bed gives onto a larger room, which is almost in darkness. The only light comes from a lamp placed on a desk, where one of the women in white is sitting. She looks very proper. She is sitting up straight, her shoulders are pushed back and her neck is bent slightly forward. The lamp directs a perfect circle of light onto the pile of documents in front of her. She has a pen in one hand. The other hand, fingers splayed, is resting on the sheet of paper she is writing on.

A man appears at the other end of the room. He is very tall and he is wearing a hat with a wide brim and a long coat that flares out behind him as he strides with purpose towards the desk. A woman follows behind. She is much shorter and almost has to break into a run to keep up with him.

The woman in white is concentrating on her work and doesn't notice the tall man until he says something. Then she looks up. His voice is brusque and loud. It sounds out of place amid the peace of sleeping sick people.

The tall man speaks just like the men in the metal hats. The woman in white jumps to her feet and bows slightly, with just a small tilt of the head. The man hands her a piece of paper. She glances at it, then points to Anka's room.

Uh-oh!

OVER MY DEAD BODY!

THE MAN BURSTS into her room, snaps his fingers first towards Anka, then towards the baby in the cot, and barks out something that sounds like, "Schnell! Schnell!"

The woman in white helps Anka dress in the clothes she arrived in. The woman's hands are shaking and she keeps making mistakes, missing a buttonhole or getting Anka's little finger snagged in her cardigan. Meanwhile the woman who arrived with the tall man gathers up the baby and swaddles it in blankets. The man hurries them both along with short, sharp instructions.

In minutes they are on their way, rushing down several flights of stairs, the tall man in the lead. Anka is holding the hand of the woman in white and trying not to trip and fall. The other woman brings up the rear, moving more slowly. She's carrying the baby as if it's something precious that might break if she drops it.

A car is waiting. Someone is at the wheel, smoking a cigarette. The burning red tip is the only light in the car and illuminates his face briefly as he takes a puff.

Anka has spent plenty of time watching various Papas smoking.

She knows how it works, although she can't understand the point of it. Mamas never smoke.

The tall man grabs Anka and pushes her - almost throws her - into the back of the car. She scrabbles across the silky-smooth seat to the other side and, after a short delay, the woman's head pops through the open door. She reaches in, places the pile of bedclothes with the baby inside next to Anka, then hops in and pulls the door closed with a click. The baby is making no sound. Perhaps it's sleeping.

Anka stays silent too. Her mind is reeling. Her life, once again, has been transformed in a flash. A moment ago, she was lying in a nice warm bed in a room that smelt of the ointment that Mamas usually put on cuts and scratches. Now here she is, squashed into the corner of a cold, dark car full of cigarette smoke.

The tall man leaps into the front seat next to the driver and slams his door shut. The driver flicks his cigarette out of the window and they take off at speed. Anka clings on to the door handle so she doesn't go flying. The woman next to her grabs the baby and cradles it in her arms. The car sways from side to side as they swing this way and that. Anka doesn't dare let go of the handle.

In the front, the tall man takes off his hat, turns to Anka and extends a hand. He is holding something between his long slender fingers.

"Sorry I had to be a little rough there. How are you doing? OK? Here, have a chocolate bar."

It is most peculiar. She can now understand every word the tall man says. He is a different person altogether. Not only has he changed the way he speaks, he now seems gentle and kind, rather than cruel and annoyed.

"We've got you," he says, "you're safe now."

Anka's not sure about this definition of safe. It is dark and cold, the car is going very fast and the only reason she is not being thrown around in the back is that she is clinging on to the door. She doesn't know who these three grown-ups are and they are not behaving like any other people she has ever met before. She definitely felt safer in the warm hospital with the kind, gentle women in white.

However, the tall man has given her a chocolate bar, so she'll accord him the benefit of the doubt, for now.

A thought crosses her mind.

"Am I going to the camp?" She asks.

"Ha-ha!" the tall man replies. But he's not laughing. His face is deadly serious. He looks her straight in the eye.

"You? The camp? Hell, no! Over my dead body!"

Is that a good thing or a bad thing? Whatever it is, it shuts her up and she turns her attention to the chocolate bar instead. It is wonderful. The best thing she has EVER tasted.

The tall man starts laughing and joking with the driver and slapping him on the shoulder. The woman next to Anka is laughing along with them. They are all extremely happy. They are acting as if they have won a prize or something.

Anka wonders if they are the prize. She and the baby.

Now that would be something.

THE LADY

ANKA HAS YET ANOTHER MAMA. In fact, she has a whole new family. The tall man delivered her to her new house, but he didn't stay long.

As he left, he turned to Anka, picked her up in his arms and whispered, "no camp for you. I promise."

Then he kissed her on the cheek and handed her back to her new Mama.

"Here you go, Mrs S, all yours. She's special, this one."

Special.

Anka has never been called special before.

She guesses the tall man is special too.

———

TODAY, Anka feels special again.

A Lady has arrived. She is the most beautiful Lady Anka has ever set eyes on. Her hair is perfectly styled, arranged with an assortment of clips so that not a single wisp is out of place. A simple row of pearls decorates her long, elegant neck and she has small gold studs in her ears. Her skin is unblemished and seems to glow from within. Is that even possible? She is wearing a dark jacket that matches her tight skirt and, when she sits and crosses her legs, her movement is as fluid and effortless as flowing water.

This Lady is so glamorous that Anka suspects she may be a princess. She is not wearing a crown or a tiara, but maybe that is because she is in disguise. She supposes that real princesses reveal themselves in other ways. She will have to look out for signs.

The Lady notices Anka watching her.

"Who is this little girl?" She asks.

A brief discussion ensues, then the Lady and her Mama get up and walk into another room, leaving Anka behind.

They are gone for quite a while. Anka can hear the murmur of conversation in the distance. It's all quite unusual. Her Mama is run off her feet all day every day. She has so much to do that she is often quite impatient with people who call in and interrupt her daily routine. She is short with Anka too, sometimes.

"You ask too many questions," she tells her, "and you are always under my feet."

The second thing isn't fair but the first may be true. There are so many things Anka doesn't understand.

However, her Mama is giving this Lady plenty of her time. She is relaxed and unhurried. She even smiled when they met at the door. The Lady must be important. Princesses are important people. Is this a sign?

Anka waits. She hopes they will be back soon.

————

HERE THEY COME!

The Lady who may be a princess arranges herself on the sofa, taps the empty cushion beside her and invites Anka to come and sit.

Anka doesn't need to be asked twice. Close up, the Lady is even more beautiful and she smells magical. Is this another sign?

She says she lives in Amsterdam. She has a big house, where she has previously looked after many people, but they have all moved on to other places and now she is alone.

The Lady tells Anka that her Mama here in Zwolle works hard, has no free time and is afraid that she cannot care for Anka as well as she would like.

Anka nods. She knows. However, this Mama is still much better than some Mamas she has had, so she has no complaints. Anka has learned not to sacrifice the good in pursuit of the perfect.

She wonders where this conversation is leading. She has an idea but experience has also taught her not to get her hopes up. Oh no, she remembers all too clearly where that can lead.

The Lady asks if Anka would like to come to live with her and keep her company. Her cheeks have turned pink. Her voice has a slight tremor in it. Is the Lady nervous? Is she worried that Anka may say no?

Of course, she won't say no. Turn down the opportunity to live with a Lady who may be a princess? Not a chance!

So Anka says "Yes, please" in her best voice.

The Lady tells her that she has only ever had grown-ups living with her. She has never shared her home with a child. She is worried that she may make mistakes and asks Anka to tell her if she does anything wrong. She wants to be a good Mama.

Anka pauses for a moment. This is an important issue and merits consideration. In fact, Anka knows quite a bit about Mamas and the things they often get wrong, as well as what the good ones get right.

In her most serious voice, Anka informs the Lady that she can help her be a good Mama.

The Lady laughs out loud and claps her hands.

"How precious! I can tell we are going to have a great time together, you and me".

PART VI
RACHEL

SHE WILL LET YOU BEAT HER TO DEATH

RACHEL HASN'T TURNED up for her shift.

In the middle of the night, she crawled underneath an unoccupied bunk at one end of the hut and pressed herself against the wall.

There she stayed until, several hours later, the others all got up and headed out for roll call. Nobody noticed she wasn't with them. As she had hoped. Sometimes it is useful to have no friends.

She hadn't wanted them to look for her and find her, because then they would have tried to force her to go out with them, for fear of being punished for turning up without her.

She would not have been able to resist their pleas.

————

So, here she is, still under the bunk.

Part one of her plan has worked. Now for part two.

Her absence at roll call will of course be noted and the guards will send a team to search for her, while they keep everyone else standing in the yard.

They will find her.

And they will hurt her.

She may even be shot.

However, she will be on her own when the confrontation with the guards takes place.

This is important.

The Germans are fond of enforcing group responsibility, but there is another tactic they are notorious for too. If she restates her refusal to work at a time when she and her colleagues are all together, whether in the barracks or the factory or anywhere else, there is a good chance that the guards will try to change her mind by harming one of her colleagues, chosen at random.

At all costs, she wants to avoid the risk of this happening. The plan she has set in train now is designed to make sure that she is the only one who is punished.

She hears the sound of heavy boots moving fast and coming closer. They go past the barrack room without stopping.

They're going to the toilet block. They must think she's sick.

The prisoners' toilet is an open pit, covered with planks for the prisoners to squat on while they do their business. The planks are covered in blood and faeces. Many of the women have dysentery. The toilet block is somewhere you spend the minimum amount of time possible.

It's not long before the boots return.

Rachel is quivering. She has anticipated this moment for hours, but she still can't prevent the terror consuming her.

One of the guards calls out in a singsong voice.

"Come out, come out, wherever you are. We know you're here."

Rachel can't move. Frozen in fear, she faces the wall, eyes wide. The footsteps come closer. There's the noise of furniture being scraped across the floor.

"Come on, out you come."

The footsteps stop. Some heavy breathing is followed by a loud sigh. Then silence.

Rachel holds her breath.

"Ah, there you are. You stupid bitch."

A hand grasps the back of her dress and drags her out from under the bunk.

She is now lying on her back staring up at the ceiling.

The guard is leaning over her. It's the same one who beat her up yesterday. Perfect! This will be over quickly.

The guard pokes Rachel with her thick, knob-ended baton.

"Up!"

Rachel gets to her knees and bows her head. She waits, shoulders hunched, eyes on the floor. She knows what's coming. It doesn't help to know.

Just get it over with.

The baton comes down hard on her left shoulder. She cries out and crashes back to the ground.

Next, a boot connects with her ribs, almost lifting her off the ground, and sends her skidding across the room. She cracks her head against the leg of a bunk and nearly passes out.

The guard shouts at her.

"Why won't you work?"

Rachel gasps. She can hardly get the words out.

"It… is not… allowed."

"What?"

"Not allowed."

"Who doesn't allow it."

"God. It is forbidden."

"On your feet!"

Rachel stays where she is. She will die there. She can do this. Once they knock her unconscious, there will be no more pain. She closes her eyes and begins to pray.

She is struck on the thigh, then again on the back. After that, she just loses track of where the blows fall and how many there are.

The guard continues to scream.

"Get up!"

"You stupid bitch!"

"Get up!"

Through the fog enveloping her brain, Rachel is aware of a new voice. It must be another guard.

"You might as well stop hitting her. Unless you want to kill her. If that happens, there will be all that damn paperwork to do and you can count me out. I'm not sharing the blame. You can see it's useless. She's a damn Bibelforscher. They are completely impossible to deal with. I've had them before. She will let you beat her to death for her God."

The hitting stops. The guard standing over Rachel is panting hard.

"So, what do we do?"

"Get her up."

Together, they lift Rachel into a sitting position, her back to one of the bunks.

She is in agony but she is still alive. For now.

She has been steadfast in her determination and she has survived. Again, for now.

But, this still qualifies as a victory, albeit temporary. Pride pulses inside her, although she can't let it show on her face.

The guard who was beating her slots her baton back under her belt. She is red-faced, sweating and scowling.

The other guard pokes Rachel with her boot.

"What are we going to do with you? Do you want to die here, now, like this? Is this your plan?"

Rachel is ready to die but she doesn't want to. Her children are out there somewhere. One day they may need her.

A flash of inspiration comes out of nowhere.

In a quiet voice, she says, "let me clean the toilets."

"What did you say, bitch?" The first guard spits at her, still furious and out of breath.

Louder, Rachel repeats, "I'll clean the toilets. Every day. That will be my job. Instead of going to the factory. I will do this. Only if you allow me, of course."

This is the worst job of all. Nobody wants to do it, because it is almost guaranteed to make you sick. In Bergen-Belsen, it was a punishment task.

Even as she speaks, though, she is congratulating herself. This is an ingenious solution. Not only will cleaning the barrack toilets mean that she never has to go to the factory, it also ensures that nobody, neither her fellow prisoners nor the guards, can claim that she is seeking to gain an advantage because of her faith.

If only these guards will go along with the idea.

They exchange a long look. She can guess what they are thinking.

Of course, they can't be perceived to accede to the wishes of a prisoner, especially a Jew prisoner. Despite the paperwork, they would still kill her rather than risk being accused of that and, usually, they wouldn't think twice about killing a Jew.

But, these are not normal times. The guards are not bullet proof either. They are not soldiers, protected by their status and their superiors. They are just criminals who have been given a uniform. They only have their jobs because anybody who has had any military training at all has been sent to fight at the Front.

If they kill a Jew, they may find themselves accused of bringing harm to the war effort. With the acute labour shortage, the factories are under-staffed.

This works for them too. The commandant might even compliment them on their unexpected display of diplomacy.

A thought that, in spite of the intense pain coursing through every single part of her body, almost makes Rachel want to smile.

The second guard, the one who stopped the beating, squats down and puts her face close to Rachel's. Her breath smells of rotting cabbage.

"We'll think about this. But remember, this is our idea, not yours. If you blab to your friends and go around acting like you're happy about cleaning the toilets, then you can forget it. You'll go back to the factory and, if you won't work, we'll keep hitting you until you come to your senses."

She pauses. A thought has obviously just crossed her mind.

"And if that doesn't matter to you, then we'll see how you feel when we start whacking one of your friends around the head, all because of your stupidity."

She pulls her baton out and brings it down hard onto the side of the bunk inches from Rachel's head.

She flinches.

No doubt, the second guard is keen not to leave the impression that she is any more kindly disposed to Rachel than her colleague.

Not wanting to be left out, the other guard chimes in.

"And not just the toilets. You will also be in charge of keeping the barrack rooms clean and tidy at all times. You will scrub and sweep from the moment you wake until the moment you collapse onto your bunk exhausted at the end of the day. You will have no help. You will work alone. The responsibility will be entirely yours. Do you understand?"

Rachel nods. Keeps her eyes fixed on the floor. To all appearances, she is defeated. Inside, she is elated.

In Bergen-Belsen, the barrack room job was another punishment post. It's almost certainly the same here.

Nobody wants to do it because, if there's an inspection and the barracks are not entirely spotless and well-ordered, the blame doesn't just fall on the person responsible for their upkeep. Each person who occupies the barrack room in question pays the penalty, usually in the form of a reduction in rations or a missed meal.

This makes everyone very unhappy and they usually take their anger out on the designated cleaner. The prospect of that doesn't worry Rachel in the slightest. It isn't as if she ranks high in the popularity stakes anyway.

DOUBLE RATIONS

Rachel's new role is unpleasant and tiring but, through her efforts, she makes a positive contribution to the quality of life of her group.

That's how she likes to view it, anyway. Of course, nobody has approached her to tell her this. After the incident in the factory, she is even more of an outsider.

So far, she has avoided coming down with one of the many diseases that incubate in the toilet areas, but the job has brought an entirely different potential threat from an unexpected quarter.

————

She works in the barracks while the inmates are doing their shift in the factory and is mostly left on her own. She enjoys the solitude. It allows her to indulge in prayer and reflection, and this prevents her dwelling on the squalor and misery that surround her and the degrading work she is doing.

Every so often, a guard will come by on her rounds and check on her. Usually, the guard just puts her head around the door, sees that Rachel is there and moves on.

One day, Rachel is on her hands and knees, scrubbing a toilet block floor, when she senses that she is no longer alone. She sits back on her heels and looks behind her. A guard is standing there, lounging against the frame of the open door, legs crossed, a hand on one hip, as if she is posing.

Rachel doesn't recognise the guard. Maybe she's been assigned from elsewhere.

Why is she standing there, anyway?

The guard is watching her intently. There's a hint of a smile on her lips. Which is an unusual thing in itself. The guards normally look at the prisoners with one of three expressions, anger, disgust or disdain.

"Hi!" Says the guard. "Tough job you've got there."

Rachel nods in acknowledgement. She is not sure what to do. Does she ignore the guard and get back to work or does she stand up to face whatever abuse is sure to be coming her way.

Why else would a guard initiate a conversation with her? Perhaps something bad has just happened in her life, so she wants to take out her frustrations on someone and today that someone is Rachel.

The relatively benign expression on the guard's face doesn't fool her for a second. They are all the same. These are vicious, violent, vindictive women and it's best to keep them at a distance.

If you can. Here, she's trapped.

So she just stays where she is on the floor and returns the guard's gaze, waiting to find out where this is all going.

The guard is looking Rachel over as if sizing her up for a dress or inspecting her for flaws.

The smile hasn't left her face.

"I've been watching you. Most times you don't even notice I'm here."

She chuckles. No doubt enjoying Rachel's confusion.

"You work hard. It keeps you in good shape."

Rachel should say something, but she has no idea what. She just wishes the guard would go away and leave her alone.

Unfortunately, that is not going to happen.

"What's your name?" asks the guard.

Rachel tells her.

"That's a nice name. It suits you."

This is unbearable. What Rachel would give for someone - anyone - to walk in to use the toilet right now.

The guard introduces herself and tells Rachel where she's from. She tells her she's single.

"I'm not like the others," she says. "I'm one of the good girls."

She laughs.

Evidently this is meant to be a joke, but Rachel has no idea what she is talking about.

"Anyway, I have to get going on my rounds," says the guard. "Can't stand here chatting all day."

She is half way out of the door and Rachel is just about to expel a sigh of relief, when the guard turns back.

"Hey, I've got an idea..."

What now?

"Why don't I ask the kitchen to give you double rations today, in view of how hard you're working? Would that be nice?"

Rachel manages to squeeze out a quiet thank you.

With a friendly wave, the guard strolls off, humming to herself.

Sure enough, at meal time, there are double rations for Rachel. She doesn't need the extra food and hates having more on her plate than the other prisoners. What will they think? When nobody is watching, she slips some inside a fold of her dress and takes it back to the barrack room to give to one of her colleagues who has been sick.

That night, instead of passing out as soon as her head touches the mattress as she normally does, she can't sleep. She keeps running the whole exchange through her mind.

What on earth is going on?

Whatever it is, it can't be good.

––––––––

A FEW DAYS LATER, the guard is back. She marches briskly into the barrack room where Rachel is mopping.

"Hi, Rachel, nice to see you again. How are things?"

How do you think things are? I'm a prisoner, my skin and my hair crawl with lice and I have to mop up shit all day. I'm probably going to get dysentery or typhoid, die in this dump and have my body thrown into a furnace.

"Fine," she says.

The guard plonks herself down on a bunk.

"These beds are like concrete. Can't imagine how you can sleep on them. Still, it's nice to get off my feet for a few minutes. Hope nobody comes in and catches us."

Us? What's that about?

The guard waves her over.

"Why don't you take a break too?" she says. "Come and sit over here with me."

She taps the bunk she is sitting on as if to indicate that Rachel should sit beside her.

Compliant but wary, Rachel takes a seat instead on the opposite bunk. She perches on the edge, torso straight, hands in her lap. The bunks are so close together, however, that their knees almost touch.

The guard starts chatting about herself. She tells Rachel she is lonely and that she doesn't get on well with her colleagues.

"They don't like me because I'm different."

She reaches over, places a hand on Rachel's thigh. Squeezes.

"I have a feeling you might understand me, though."

Rachel's attention is fixed on the guard's hand. It's a heavy, fat, meaty hand. A powerful hand. A farm-worker's hand.

And her grip is threatening rather than friendly.

Rachel remains still. She tries not to flinch, not to let her fear show.

The guard tilts her head to one side.

"How about you? Don't you ever get lonely?"

"I have my friends," she murmurs.

The guard will not be put off.

"Maybe it might be useful to have another friend. A friend who can help you from time to time. Do little favours for you. Give you protection. What do you think?"

"My God protects me," says Rachel, daring now to raise her head and look the guard in the eye.

"Not doing a great job so far, your God, is he?"

After squeezing her thigh one last time, the guard takes her hand away. Rachel's going to have bruises.

"Anyway, think about it. Work it out. We can do things for each other. I give you what you need. You give me..."

Her voice trails away, the sentence unfinished.

"You know what I mean."

The guard gets to her feet. She towers over Rachel and smiles down at her.

Rachel looks up. This is not the smile of someone who wants to be her friend. This is the smile of a cat playing with a mouse, teasing it and tossing it up in the air from time to time, confident that it can trap and kill the mouse any time it wishes.

"See you soon," says the guard. "There'll be extra rations for you again today. Need to fatten you up."

She giggles and walks out. Her laughter continues to echo down the corridor until a door slams and the barracks are silent once again.

Rachel is being drawn into a situation over which she has no control.

The guard has all the power. Rachel has none.

She can't escape.

She can't complain.

Who would listen to her anyway? Who would believe her? Who would care?

Her fellow prisoners might sympathise with her if they knew. But what good would that do?

THE JEW THAT DOESN'T WANT
TO WORK

ONE MORNING, soon afterwards, Rachel is mopping the barrack room floor when the camp commandant arrives on one of his rare tours of inspection. She recognises him. He is always there at the morning roll-call, being saluted by everybody. He reminds her of a wrestler, short, stocky and broad-shouldered. His head is round and completely hairless, like a bowling ball.

Rachel used to love to go bowling with Louis.

As usual, the commandant is flanked by a small cohort of guards and, today, his escort includes the guard who has taken a shine to Rachel.

He wanders through the room, running gloved fingers over the wooden rims of the bunks, peering underneath them and examining the floorboards, his face radiating a combination of disgust and boredom. Rachel continues to mop. She has no idea what he is looking for. She just wants this over and done with as fast as possible. If she pretends he isn't there, maybe he'll return the favour and ignore her.

No such luck.

He stops right in front of her, standing so close that she has no alternative but to stop what she is doing and lift her eyes to meet his.

The guards are gathered behind him, their faces eager. They are expecting a show.

"So, you are the Jew that doesn't want to work."

It's not funny, but the guards all laugh as if the commandant has cracked the funniest joke in the world.

He ignores them.

He is not accusing her and he doesn't sound angry or bitter. He is just stating a fact.

"As you can see, I am working right now," Rachel replies.

Or, at least, she was working, until the commandant and his cronies interrupted her.

"But you will not work for the war effort?"

Again, he doesn't appear to be upset.

"No," she answers. "God does not want that."

"But, your work in the factory will not actually kill anybody, will it?"

"God does not permit me to work on weapons of destruction."

The commandant points to her mop.

"Give me that."

The guards snicker. A little action: this is more like it. Much better than boring chitchat about God.

Rachel hands her mop over. The commandant takes it in both hands and raises it above his head. Instinctively, Rachel cowers before him.

"Isn't this a potential weapon of destruction too? If I wanted to, I could use it to kill you right here, right now."

The guards watch on with eager eyes, enthralled, waiting to see what he's going to do next. This is great. Better than they expected.

"Yes, you could kill me with that." Rachel answers in a small voice. "But a weapon is something made for killing, while a mop is not."

The commandant holds his pose for a few seconds and then he does something that amazes both Rachel and the guards.

He smiles, lowers the mop and hands it back to Rachel with unexpected gentleness.

"You are frightened. I apologise. Sometimes my fondness for the melodramatic gesture makes me forget my manners. You are a Jehovah's Witness, I believe?"

Rachel nods.

"Tell me a little about your beliefs."

Rachel guesses that her own expression mirrors the astonishment she sees on the faces of the guards.

But she recovers quickly. This is her pet subject after all. She starts explaining her faith and the commandant listens with interest, interspersing her remarks with a few of his own, such as:

"Yes, sometimes we need to remember that Jesus was indeed Jewish."

After several minutes, he tells Rachel that he must leave to continue his inspection, thanks her for the conversation and clicks his heels before marching away. The guards follow in his wake, still looking slightly stunned at what they have just witnessed.

As she's walking out of the room, the guard who has been flirting with Rachel turns back and stares at her. It looks like something is bothering her. She doesn't smile.

Rachel returns her gaze without flinching. If the guard is feeling uneasy, then this suits Rachel just fine.

She's not the powerless, defenceless, friendless little mouse the guard thought she was, is she? Does the guard now suspect that she might not have the upper hand, after all?

————

LATER, reflecting on the exchange, Rachel considers the commandant's interest as validating her decision to stand up for herself and her faith. This gives her enormous confidence.

A side-benefit is that the flirtatious guard subsequently stays away from her. Which means no more double rations, but no more disturbing chats either.

HOW MANY DEAD?

THIS WARM SPRING day began like any other, but has now taken a unique turn.

In early morning darkness, Rachel and her colleagues lined up in the courtyard to be counted as usual. It is now mid-afternoon and they are still there. The first woman swayed then collapsed to the ground a few hours ago and subsequently three more have fainted and been dragged off into the shade.

Nobody has gone to the factory today. Nor, as usual, has anyone told them what is happening.

Rachel looks around. Are they still going be in this courtyard when the time comes around for tomorrow's roll call? If so, there won't be many left on their feet by then.

The amazing thing is that they are all still alive. There were exactly 108 of them on the Westerbork platform all those months ago and, today there are still 108. There have been illnesses, injuries, fights, beatings, close calls and near misses. But, they have all survived.

So far.

Today has shown just how weak some of them are. Their perfect record may not last much longer.

Suddenly, there is some activity among the guards, who, like the prisoners, have mostly just been hanging around, waiting to be told what to do.

An announcement is made. It's brief and to the point. They are all leaving Beendorf. They have to move fast. The train that will take them away is going to be here soon.

Nobody says where the train is going. Nobody asks. What does it matter?

They have permission to go and grab anything they want to take with them and they rush towards the barracks to gather the meagre possessions accumulated over the last few weeks. Some have secret food stocks that they have saved from daily rations and defended from rats and other prisoners. Others have little treasures in the form of trinkets, tools or scraps of this and that, stolen from guards or the factory floor. Valueless in themselves, but priceless as symbols of rebellion.

A crowd has gathered around the entrance to a small building Rachel has never noticed before. She approaches. The door has been smashed open and is hanging off one hinge. Women are filing in and out. Rachel joins the queue.

No guards are in sight. They probably have more pressing concerns at this point than watching over the prisoners. Whatever emergency is causing Rachel and her colleagues to be moved on in such a hurry will be affecting the guards too.

The building consists of just one room and in the middle of the room is a mountain of clothes and bags.

One woman is kneeling, half buried, in the midst of the mound. She is flinging articles of clothing left and right and shouting to nobody in particular.

"Take what you can. This is all our stuff."

Rachel's heart leaps. Is it possible?

She scans the pile. There it is, near the top, poking out, the distinctive collar of her much-mourned and much-missed coat. She last saw it on the morning of their arrival, lying among the mass of discarded clothing on the platform. She scrabbles her way over and pulls it out. It is creased and now smells of mould rather than perfume, but it is no less welcome and wonderful a find.

She has another thought and thrusts her hand into one of the pockets. Nothing there. The other pocket? Her hand closes around the small volume nestling in its depths.

Hallelujah!

THE WOMEN reassemble and are herded towards the platform, where they wait again. They have had no food all day. The only people who have had water are the ones who fainted.

Good tactic, thinks Rachel. She should have thought of that. Maybe she should give it a try now. But where would anyone find water out here?

Eventually, a train arrives. The engine crawls into the station as if it is dragging the weight of the world behind it.

Cattle wagons again. The guards unbolt the doors and drag them back. It's clear that Beendorf is not the train's first stop by any means. Each wagon bulges with bodies. Live bodies. Inmates from other camps and all women, by the look of things.

The Beendorf workers are divided into small groups and pushed up into wagons wherever there is space - even where there is no space.

Rachel climbs in to her assigned cattle car and looks around. She has barely seconds to get her bearings before the door slams shut behind her, extinguishing light and closing off the only source of fresh air.

On taking her first breath, she chokes. The atmosphere is thick with the collective fumes of filth and faeces.

Welcome to Hell!

Inside this dark hole, strangers are pressed against strangers. Some snarl, some whimper, some cry out for air, others cry out for water. Many just cry out, using words she doesn't understand.

Rachel lifts her coat tails up - she has not lost the habit - and wraps them around her waist, then settles to the floor, easing those already seated there aside, being gentle yet insistent. She has no choice. She is there now. She needs her space too.

Wetness seeps through her thin striped prison dress. She puts a hand down and raises her fingers to her face. Evidently, in this wagon, if you want to piss, you piss where you sit.

She lifts her bottom up slightly, untucks her coat and spreads it out beneath her like a mat.

Not great, but better. She will worry about her coat later.

If that time ever comes.

Her eyes get more accustomed to the dim light and she begins to examine her situation and her new companions.

It is hard to find any positives.

Before, in circumstances such as these, she has been at least a little encouraged by the unspoken sense of unity, the common bond forged by shared suffering.

Here, there is no such sentiment. Many of the pale, pinched faces around her display fear or resignation, but she also spies malevolence, watchfulness, eyes alive for opportunity. There is evil as well as desperation in the air.

Here, jungle rules will apply. The strong will prey on the weak. It's every woman for herself. This is not a time to be alone.

Those among Rachel's fellow diamond workers who have been assigned to this wagon appear to have reached the same conclusion: there is value in solidarity. Within a couple of hours, she and they manage to manoeuvre themselves into a block in one corner, all huddled together in a small pocket of security.

They establish an impromptu rota to ensure that at least two of them are awake and alert at all times, although deep sleep seems unlikely for anyone. The air is so dense, it is hard even to breathe.

Night falls and, in the depths of darkness around them, women sob and wail, fights break out and, on more than one occasion, agonised screaming is cut short with brutal finality.

On the first morning, the train stops. The wagon door slides open and a voice calls out:

"How many dead?"

Rachel watches open-mouthed in disbelief as hands go up and fingers point. During the night, in their wagon alone, six women have lost their lives.

Their limp bodies are passed via raised arms over the heads of the living to the doorway and dropped onto the platform. After a few minutes, they are picked up and carried away.

While the door is open, Rachel cranes her neck to get a better view of her fellow passengers. She casts her eye over a mass of mostly recumbent, dark-dressed forms. Not all are dull, drugged drones staring into space. More than a few meet her gaze with their own sharp-eyed challenge.

How did the six women die? Did they just abandon their struggle for life? She remembers the truncated screaming. Or did their vulnerability allow the more powerful to smother them in the darkness, simply to get more living space and air to breathe?

The door is slammed shut again, the engine rumbles and the train rattles into movement once more. Night runs into day, then runs into night again. Rachel scratches a mark for each new dawn on the wooden panel she's leaning on.

Every morning, the train stops for the soldiers to separate the dead from the living. Only the dead can leave the wagons. The living must remain.

One of Rachel's fellow diamond workers dies on the third night, without any of them noticing. When last they were conscious of her, she was still a living, breathing human being, sleeping peacefully among them. But, by the time feeble slivers of daylight relieve the gloom, she has become just a cold and lifeless body.

She has left them with no fuss and no farewell. Rachel says prayers under her breath for the woman's soul and her corpse is taken away when the train next stops. They are no longer 108.

They rarely receive food or water. Their daily ration usually amounts to no more than a handful of macaroni and some sugar. The deprivation turns some into beasts and makes others despair. The crying and moaning is incessant.

Having little to eat is something Rachel finds she can manage, but the thirst is driving her to the brink of insanity. It is worse, almost unbearable, just after they have been given their food. Maybe it's the sugar? The macaroni fills her stomach but the sugar is useless. It may be giving her energy, but what does she need that for?

She decides not to eat the sugar and this turns out to be a good move. Her manic urge to drink is not so acute after that.

She prays a lot, but is frustrated that there is hardly ever enough light to read her Bible by. She consoles herself by turning the book over and over in her pocket with her fingers as she recites memorised passages in her head.

At one point, the train stops at a railway station and the doors are opened as usual. The platform is curved and, from her vantage point, the back of the train is visible. She watches as villagers with carts line up at the rearmost wagon to unload and take away the many bodies that have been stored there over the past few days.

No doubt, to make room for more. This journey is far from over. How many will still be alive when it does end? Everyone is becoming weaker. Some appear strong, then fade fast and are suddenly gone. Others seem to be on the cusp of death but, by some miracle, they keep hanging on, clinging to life by a thread.

The train isn't moving but, despite the open doors, the prisoners stay put in their wagons. Nobody has told them not to go out. They don't have to. None of them has the will to even move, let alone try to escape. Where would they run? They don't even know which country they are in.

The next day, the doors are opened again and, this time, a few of the healthier prisoners are selected from each wagon, handed buckets and sent to fetch water from a nearby men's prison camp.

Rachel is one of the designated water carriers.

When she reaches the tap, she kneels, turns her head and allows the water to pour all over her face. Then she opens her mouth and takes gulp after gulp after gulp, until she can drink no more. She stands and looks down. Her stomach is distended. She looks four months pregnant.

She fills her buckets and waddles back towards the train platform, concentrating hard, trying not to spill even one drop. She thinks back to Joseph, all those months ago, in Westerbork. Where is he now? Where are the others? Have any of them survived? It is hard to imagine they are still alive. Even for her, it must just be a matter of time before her luck runs out.

A noise interrupts her reverie and she looks up.

Limping and staggering towards her are a pack of her fellow prisoners. They can't wait any longer. As they reach her, they fall on her like hyenas on a gazelle and her buckets and their life-giving contents go flying.

Roars of laughter erupt from further down the platform. The guards think this is hilarious. It's the best entertainment they've had all week. Utter bastards!

The women who bundled her over are now lapping like cats at the puddles of water on the platform. A couple take the empty buckets, invert them over their heads and try to catch the few drops of water that fall from them on their parched tongues.

Many of the women have already died. More will die. If this journey continues long enough, they will all die.

So much is certain.

SOMETHING IS GOING ON

RACHEL HAS JUST SCRATCHED an eleventh line on the panel next to her head, when the train stops again.

The doors are thrown open.

"Out! Out! Out! All of you, out!"

Wherever it is, they've finally arrived.

She crawls out of the wagon and drops onto the platform, blinking into the light of day. She is the Count of Monte Cristo escaping his crowded windowless cell in the Chateau d'If. Like him, she has committed no crime but, unlike him, she is still a prisoner. Neither is it likely that she will ever exact revenge on her captors.

Her body is bent. Her bones ache. Her legs can hardly hold her up. She is alive, though, while many are not. When the Beendorf women reassemble, they find they have lost almost half their number.

All those months of suffering, all that effort to survive, the struggle to stay well, the battles against illness, the nightly chants, the quest to keep the spark alive - the whole edifice of their resistance demolished in just 11 days.

———

THEIR NEW HOME is a camp called Eidelstedt, near Hamburg. The camp is unoccupied, but it is obvious that people have been living here, even up until quite recently. Clothing lies abandoned on bunks, pots and plates sit on canteen tables.

Where have they gone? Why did they leave their things behind?

Rachel doesn't have the energy to pursue the thought. She has never felt so weak and helpless.

Her strength of mind, her faith and her obstinate spirit have sustained her so far, but how much longer she can keep this up? How many more challenges can she survive? If she were subjected to another train journey like the last one, would she have the fortitude to resist the temptation to abandon the quest to live? She has observed so many women succumb in this way over the past few days. Would the light fade in her eyes too? One day, would she also just give up the fight?

Here, at least for now, there is food to eat and time to recover, but this camp's only purpose seems to be to keep them fenced in. They are given occasional pointless tasks, but the camp officials and prison guards are just going through the motions. Their minds are on other things. They can't even be bothered to be cruel.

One morning, Rachel is sitting on her bunk reading her Bible, when she spots an officer peering in through the window.

She always tries to be alert for such moments, but she did not see him coming. She swiftly slips the Bible under her blanket.

Did he notice?

How long was he there?

He marches in.

"What's that you were reading?"

He did notice. She was too slow.

She pulls her Bible out and shows it to him.

"Hand it over."

He reaches out and takes it from her hand.

She has lost it. Again! Why is she so stupid and careless? She braces herself for the beating that is sure to be coming her way.

The officer flicks through the Bible, taking his time. He even pauses occasionally, as if to read something.

Rachel is not fooled. He is just pretending, drawing out the moment, building tension, playing with her head.

Then, to her astonishment, he closes the Bible with exaggerated care, wipes the cover on his sleeve and holds it out towards her.

He's giving it back? This has to be a trick. She's not going to fall for it.

She looks straight ahead, silent, still, hands folded in her lap.

The officer sighs and throws the Bible onto the bunk.

"Keep it. You'll need it. Women are dying here every day. You might want to read something out for the next one that kicks the bucket."

He clicks his heels, turns smartly and strides out.

Rachel sits stunned. Another sign that the Germans don't care. They can't even be bothered to bully them any more.

Or maybe they have started to care. Which would be still more surprising.

Whatever it is, something is going on.

Have they decided it's pointless keeping them all prisoner? If so, if they are no longer of value, if they have just become useless mouths…

…Well, perhaps this is it.

That would explain what happened to the people here before them. Now, it is their turn.

They all know how it goes. They have all listened to the horror stories whispered from bunk to bunk at night in the barracks. They'll stand in line at morning roll call and concealed machine guns will open up, tearing them to shreds. Then, teeth will be pulled, hair chopped off and whatever's left thrown into a lime pit.

One good thing: at least then it will all be over.

PART VII
ANKA

REBORN

IT'S A WONDERFUL LIFE!

Anka has good food to eat and plenty of it. She has a comfortable bed. She has toys to play with. Best of all, she has someone she loves who obviously loves her back.

She and the Lady ARE indeed having a great time together.

And Anka is truly happy for the first time she can remember.

Of course, the Lady is not a princess. Her house is grand and lovely, but it is not a palace and she has no servants. This doesn't matter at all, though. To Anka, looking and behaving like a princess is just as good as actually being one.

On her first morning, the Lady took Anka into a bedroom and showed her a hidden room behind what the Lady called a false wall. Anka was amazed. If you didn't know the room was there, you would never find it. The Lady said if Anka ever needed to hide, then this was where she would bring her.

But, she's never needed to hide there and now she never will.

Today, so the Lady tells her, the war is over and nobody ever needs to hide again.

There is going to be a parade in the streets and a party, which the whole city will attend.

The Lady is happy so Anka is happy too, although she has no idea what a war is, nor a parade or a party for that matter.

The Lady tries to explain, but most of what she says makes little sense. Anka understands that the war is something that has been going on throughout Anka's whole life and that it is to blame for a lot of her problems. But why the war chose Anka to be the victim of so much suffering and pain remains a mystery.

Anyway, if it is finished and her troubles are behind her, that is all that matters. Already, memories of bad times and dark dreams are fast receding and being replaced by the lightness and brightness of the days spent with the Lady.

She is reborn.

To her delight, on this day, the universe is in tune with her mood and is bidding her welcome. When she pokes her head out of the front door and steps into a world in daylight for the first time - at least the first time she can remember - the sun is shining, the sky is bright blue, soft white clouds are floating slowly past, changing shape as they go, and the air is warm on her pale skin.

There is no yellow island and the trees in Amsterdam are a little different but it all brings to mind the picture in that book, where the child was looking out of the round window.

She wants to spin around and jump and dance and asks the Lady if she may.

The Lady smiles.

"Go ahead. It's a free world."

Then laughs out loud and keeps chuckling to herself, as if she has just made a big joke.

The two of them walk through the city and find more laughter and happiness everywhere they go. Anka holds the Lady's hand whenever she is not spinning, jumping and dancing.

In places, it is so crowded that, if she didn't have the Lady's hand as an anchor, she would be terrified of getting carried away on the tide of people flowing through the streets and the squares. Sometimes, the throng is so thick it blocks out the sky from down where she is, her head at the same level as all the flying feet and swirling skirts.

The Lady bends down, scoops Anka up and holds her high above her head so that she can watch what is going on.

And what a scene it is!

Hundreds of men sit, stand or just hang on to the side of a column of slow-moving vehicles. Engines throb and roar and the ground shakes as they pass but just as loud is the clamour emanating from the mass of people that divides as the vehicles inch forward and reforms behind them.

The people on the street call out, wave or hand flowers to the men on the trucks. In return, the men are throwing things up and over the crowd. A small forest of uplifted arms reaches up to catch them as they fall to the ground.

Something lands on the ground close by. It's a chocolate bar. Anka is just about to direct the Lady's attention to it, when a passing teenage girl picks it up. The girl turns and notices Anka looking at her. Correctly interpreting the expression on her face, the girl laughs and holds out the chocolate bar.

"Here, I think this is yours!"

It is all quite exhausting and they don't stay long before heading back home.

PART VIII
RACHEL

A WHOLE NEW WORLD

EXACTLY TWO WEEKS after their arrival in Eidelstedt, according the marks on the wall next to her bunk. Rachel finally learns the secret behind the Germans' bizarre behaviour.

She wakes, splashes a little water on her face, puts her clogs on, walks out of the barrack room…

…and enters a whole new world.

The guards are gone. All of them.

The gates are open.

Prisoners are wandering around aimlessly. Some have gathered by the main entrance, but no one has yet taken a step beyond. It is as if some invisible force is preventing them from leaving.

Rachel is lost. For the first time in a long, long time, nobody is telling her what to do.

So she does nothing. She sits on the kerb and waits. She has nowhere to go. Even if she did have somewhere to go, she would have no way of getting there.

There is a sudden burst of activity at the gate. Rachel stands to see what is happening. The group of women gathered there is now much larger and something that is happening outside is making them almost giddy with excitement. Many of them have their faces pressed to the fence. Some are waving and shouting and jumping up and down.

There are soldiers sauntering down the dusty road towards them, rifles hanging from shoulder straps, baggy trousers tucked into boots.

They don't look like Germans. As they get closer, they call out to the women at the fence. They don't sound like Germans either.

YOUR BROTHERS AND SISTERS
ARE HERE

IN EARLY MAY 1945, Rachel boards a Red Cross train bound for Sweden.

She is placed in a school near Malmö, which has been turned into a refugee camp, where she will be quarantined for six weeks. The world is not yet ready to welcome her back, not because of who she is but because of the diseases she may be carrying.

Her filthy, lice - ridden clothing is taken away for burning. Rachel thinks of objecting when the reception staff add her coat to the pile, but it has to go. It has performed its function. It has sustained her and made an enormous contribution to bringing her to this point in time, alive and well.

She closes her eyes and offers a prayer of thanks for the miracle of its arrival in her cell all those months ago.

She adds a further prayer for her anonymous benefactor. She hopes that she too has survived.

Rachel can keep her Bible, but not before it's been sprayed with a foul-smelling liquid.

She has new clothes. Of course, they are second-hand clothes, but they are hers and they mark a huge step up in quality from what she's been wearing for the last few months.

As the pile is handed to her, she catches the fresh smell of clean laundry and, on a whim, buries her nose in the light blue woollen cardigan that lies on top. It is soft and ever-so-lightly perfumed.

One of the camp people is watching her. Rachel catches her eye and returns her smile.

"Heaven!" she says. "Thank you so much."

————

EARLY ON IN HER STAY, Rachel asks the camp personnel if there may be any Jehovah's Witnesses living nearby.

"Thursday is market day," one of the men tells her, "and there are always a few people in the square handing out leaflets. I'm sure they are Jehovah's Witnesses. I'll let them know you are here."

A few days later, Rachel is having lunch when a member of staff comes in and calls out her name. She is escorted to a point on the fence line surrounding the camp and is instructed to stand at least five metres away from the fence.

"No closer, OK?" admonishes her escort. "Don't forget you are in quarantine."

"What's happening?" Rachel asks.

"It's a surprise. Just wait here. You'll see. Anyway, I'll leave you to it. Have fun!"

Her escort strides away. Rachel waits. After a while, a woman appears on the other side of the fence. She appears to have been told to remain some distance away from it as well. Or maybe she is just being cautious.

The woman waves. Rachel waves back.

The woman points to herself and says something that sounds like "vitne".

Rachel shakes her head.

"I don't speak Swedish."

The woman tries again.

"Jehovah!"

Now, Rachel understands all too clearly. She points to herself, repeats "Jehovah", then bursts into tears.

As does the other woman.

It takes a while before they are both calm again. There is much sniffling. The woman uses a large handkerchief. Rachel, who has no handkerchief, uses her sleeve.

The woman extends both arms towards Rachel and gives her a beaming smile.

They exchange further signals of gratitude and affection, then the woman falls to her knees and adopts a position of prayer. Rachel does the same.

Finally, they get back to their feet and the woman points to her watch, then to the ground and says:

"Sondag!"

"Sunday?" asks Rachel.

"Ja, Sondag!"

The woman blows her a kiss and turns to go. Rachel stays where she is, watching her new friend walk away, not wanting to miss a thing. She will never forget this moment. The woman looks over her shoulder, waves one last time, then disappears around the corner.

Rachel sits down on the grass. The tears flow again.

On Sunday, the woman returns and this time she is accompanied by a few other people, one of whom speaks some German.

Her visitors have brought her cake. They tell Rachel that, for the last few years, they have prayed every day for their brothers and sisters in the prison camps.

After that, they visit her frequently. Whenever they reappear at their special place behind the fence, someone comes to find Rachel and says: "hey, your brothers and sisters are here again."

———

FINALLY, Rachel's quarantine is over and she is allowed to go outside the camp. Her new friends are all waiting for her at the gate.

They have organised an elaborate afternoon gathering to welcome her back into the world. Even though she can't understand much of what they say, it warms her heart to be surrounded once again by the loving smiles of people like her.

She has been on her own for such a long time.

Now, she is alone no more.

SHE IS NOBODY AND SHE HAS NOTHING

FOR THE PAST YEAR, Rachel's sole purpose in life has been to survive. Each day, she has woken and wondered if this might be the last day of her life and her ambition has been to make it through to the next day. On occasion, she has opened her eyes at dawn, convinced that she would not see nightfall.

Now, the burden has been lifted and she no longer has such concerns. She is in a place where she can eat, bathe and sleep in peace. She is among people who view her as a human being, not an animal: people from whom she has nothing to fear.

Her mind turns at last to the future, something that, for such a long, long time, she has not even dared contemplate.

Some avenues are closed to her. News has filtered through. Louis, Carry and Sylvain are dead. Maurice and Joseph are dead too. Rachel now knows that the sole purpose of Auschwitz was to murder Jewish people in great numbers. She shudders each time she dwells on the thought of how close she came to being one of the many that will never see home again.

Although Rachel actually has no home to return to, at some point she will go back to Amsterdam and begin a new life.

She hopes that this life will include her baby Johanna, although, if she is still alive, Johanna is of course no longer a baby.

Rachel has no idea if Johanna managed to stay hidden or if she was taken. She doesn't know where she is, what name she is known by or if she remembers she was once Johanna.

Some sixth sense, and Rachel hopes it is not just foolish optimism, tells her that Johanna has survived. She has written a letter to a Jehovah's Witness friend in Amsterdam to try to find out.

It has, of course, crossed Rachel's mind that it might be better for Johanna if Rachel just leaves her to the life she has now, rather than disturbing, confusing and uprooting her again.

After all, who is Rachel? She is nobody and she has nothing. She has lost everything. She has no control over her own life and she has no idea what the future holds. What can she offer Johanna? She worries that, if she finds her and takes her back, all she will be doing is tearing her away from a good life with somebody she loves, just to become another nobody with nothing like Rachel.

But, on the other hand, perhaps Johanna has not fared well. Perhaps she is hurt and unloved and waiting for Rachel to return and rescue her.

Rachel also needs to prepare for the possibility that far from having forgotten about her, Johanna may remember her all to well. Perhaps she has harboured hatred over the years for the mother who didn't want her and gave her away. People may have told Johanna lies, not necessarily out of malicious intent but in order to protect Johanna. Maybe she thinks Rachel is dead.

It would be better if Johanna is ignorant of everything that happened before and Rachel just appears in her life as someone new. In that case, there will only be rebuilding to do. She won't have to tear down a wall first.

Time passes.

A letter arrives.

By a miracle, Johanna is alive, healthy and in good hands. Rachel does not recognise the name of the person who is caring for her, nor has she ever even visited the part of Amsterdam where Johanna is now living. What strange sequence of events has brought her baby there?

No matter. All will be revealed in time. Sooner or later, they will be reunited.

And they will spend the rest of their lives together.

PART IX
ANKA

SANCTUARY

ONE DAY, a visitor arrives.

It's a woman. She is thin. Anka has never seen a person so thin. Her forearms and fingers are just bones with blotchy skin stretched over them. Her face looks like someone with strong thumbs has gripped it and pushed her cheeks deep into her skull. Her eyes are black and have dark circles around them. Her hair is short, stubbly and the same length all over her head. There are patches of grey in the black.

The woman's clothes are worn and look like they used to belong to someone else. They are mismatched and don't fit her properly.

She is not elegant like the Lady. She is not beautiful like the Lady.

Anka watches the Lady greet the visitor and welcome her inside. They exchange a few words, then, to Anka's astonishment, the Lady and the visitor both start to cry. The visitor looks like she may collapse and the Lady takes her in her arms.

The two of them stand there for a long time, the visitor sobbing and shaking, the Lady holding her and rubbing her back and shoulders with gentle strokes, like she does when Anka becomes upset. Which doesn't happen as much as it used to.

The visitor's face is buried in the Lady's thick jumper. She will be inhaling the Lady's scent, the scent that makes Anka feel so happy, so loved and so safe.

After a while, the Lady eases the poor woman gently away from her and holds her at arms length, looking into her eyes with her kind, encouraging smile, the same way she gazes at Anka, whenever Anka is sad. It's a look that says:

"That was then. This is now. The bad times are behind you. The good times are coming. Don't worry about what is past. I am here. I can fix this. I have what you need."

The Lady brings the visitor into the front room, beams at Anka through teary eyes and says something completely and utterly unexpected, something that turns Anka's world upside down.

"Anka, I have a wonderful surprise for you. This is your real Mama. We have found her."

The Lady's expression suggests she thinks Anka will be overjoyed.

Anka is far from overjoyed: quite the contrary. The last thing Anka needs right now is a new Mama, real or otherwise.

It's too much. Anka can't hold it in. She begins screeching at the Lady, her small fists clenched in rage.

"Why? Why did you find her? I didn't want you to find her. I never asked you to find her. I don't want another Mama. I just want you!"

Anka has never spoken to the Lady in this way. Even as she is screaming, part of her is wondering where this is all coming from. She is behaving disgracefully, but she can't control herself. It is as if a dam that has been holding back years of despair has finally burst and a torrent of emotion is flooding out.

Anka throws herself to the floor, her face pressed into the carpet. She erupts in enormous, gulping sobs of bitterness. She is bereft, her fury directed at a universe that can always be relied upon to deliver disappointment.

The Lady and the visitor are now crying again. Anka can hear their sniffles in the gaps between her own outbursts.

It takes a while before Anka runs out of sobs.

She utters one last sigh, then looks up. The two women are now seated on the sofa, side-by-side, silent, patient, waiting. The visitor stretches her arms out wide and beckons Anka towards her. New tears run down her cheeks. She tilts her chin up and closes her eyes. Her lips move slightly but without sound. Anka examines the visitor's face in more detail. Her sunken cheeks and lips are raw and dry, her skin has a yellowish tinge, her teeth are chipped, her arms are bruised.

It makes her sad. Like her, this woman has known pain. She must have experienced difficult times too.

Stil, Anka will not go to her.

The Lady is looking at Anka with sad, understanding eyes. Her gentle, loving Lady, the best Mama she has ever had, the one she hoped would be her last Mama.

Anka says nothing. She is exhausted after her fit of anger. She has no fight left in her. She just stares at the Lady, hoping that the Lady will tell her she doesn't have to do this, that she'll send the visitor away and that she wants to keep Anka for herself, for always, just the two of them.

But the Lady shakes her head almost imperceptibly - of course she knows what Anka is thinking, as always - and nods towards the visitor, still sitting there in her mismatched clothes, eyes shut tight and arms outstretched.

The visitor is going to smell bad. This is so unfair. Her days with the Lady have been the happiest she can remember. She adores being in this house. Now she is going to have to leave. To yet another home. With yet another Mama.

Is this how her life is always going to be? Forever changing? Forever moving on. Never allowed to settle.

It is true, this time it does seem different. No new Mama has ever acted like this before. No new Mama has started crying just on catching sight of Anka for the first time. This is novel behaviour.

However, just because something is different doesn't mean that it's good. How many times has she found that out the hard way?

Anka edges towards the visitor, who sensing movement, opens her eyes and smiles. Her face is transformed. Her eyes radiate happiness. She invites Anka forward into her embrace and Anka keeps moving in her direction, although she sets her face in a frown to make sure the Lady and the woman are both quite clear that she is doing this against her will.

Anka is only indulging the woman with a hug because the Lady wants her to and Anka will do anything to make the Lady happy.

Even if the Lady has betrayed her! Anyway, she can analyse that aspect of things later.

Anka is now so close to the visitor that she can't take another step. She stops. The visitor wraps her arms around her and folds her into her chest.

Anka takes a tentative sniff. As it turns out, the visitor doesn't smell bad at all.

Anka is ashamed. She has done the visitor a complete injustice. She was about as wrong as she could have been.

It's not that the visitor smells of special soap or expensive perfume, of something artificial or applied. No, this is more essential, more fulfilling and entirely unprecedented. Of their own volition, her arms curl over the woman's shoulders and she presses her face into the space between the woman's neck and her prominent shoulder bone. It's a perfect fit.

Anka breathes deep and is immediately immersed: buffeted by wave after wave of intense, inexplicable yet familiar sensations.

She senses origins. She senses warmth. She senses eternity. She senses belonging and she senses sanctuary.

And that deep pain that Anka has always felt, the pain that was always there, the pain of some indefinable loss…

…It starts to fade.

———

THE VISITOR'S mouth is close to Anka's ear. She is whispering, her voice softer than a sigh. She is repeating the same three words over and over again.

"My darling Johanna…"

"My darling Johanna…"

"My darling Johanna…"

…

…

Johanna?

…

Who's Johanna?

PART X
JOHANNA

LEGACY

I OFTEN SIT LOOKING out of my upstairs bay window at the drizzle of Europe in springtime and cast my mind back almost 80 years to when I was Anka. I run my finger back and forth along the old scar on my left calf. It's been there forever. I can't remember how I came by it but I am always reminded of it whenever the weather turns damp and it starts to itch.

The sky is the same shade of grey as it was on the days when I would glance out of the attic window, perched on the wooden dining chair, surrounded by sheets of newspaper, lonely and in pain.

It was as if I was a shipwrecked sailor, marooned on a desert island, and the sheets of newspaper arranged so carefully about me were shark-filled waters, trapping me.

Although at that time, as Anka, I knew nothing of sharks, shipwrecks or sailors.

MY MOTHER RACHEL passed away several years ago. Throughout her life, she was sustained by the same faith and inner strength that helped her survive the war years.

I have often wished that I had her mental fortitude. Perhaps, as a young child, I shared a similar spirit, but after the war, I don't remember ever feeling particularly strong, mentally or physically.

As my son, now a strapping man in his late fifties, sometimes says:

"Ma, they broke your character".

I was Anka for only a comparatively short time, but I now consider those years to have been possibly the most significant of my long life. Not only did they form the world I came to live in, they formed me and they formed how I look at the world and interact with people.

Since those tumultuous years, I have known only peace. It is as if the winds of war raged so ferociously in Europe in the first half of the last century that they blew themselves out. The fires in the hearts of even the most warlike of men were extinguished, leaving not even embers. No wonder the subsequent conflict was referred to as cold.

How strange it is that, the older you get, the further into the past your thoughts turn. Your mind casts back deeper and deeper into the well of your life and you seek to understand more, to penetrate the darkness, to allow light in, to see more clearly.

These days, I know much more about the time when Europe was on fire and I was trapped in the flames.

The memories have been recorded. The crimes have been exposed. The figures have been tallied. A few accounts were settled. The remaining accounts will never be settled. Too much time has passed.

In the beginning after the war, the world wanted to look forward to the future. People said: why look back on pain and hardship? Why overturn rocks to find the truth, only at the risk of finding more pain? Just look ahead. Move on.

Which is what my mother and I did. We had lives to build and daily challenges to face. There was no time to reflect or wonder.

But, recently, I've started to spend more time looking back to the events of my childhood. Maybe my mother's death was the catalyst?

Or maybe it is that I have more time on my hands these days?

Perhaps it is just because I'm getting old and this is what old people do?

The things I have learned enable me now to travel back in my mind to when I was very young. Now I can picture the world beyond Anka's walls. Many of the holes in my fragmented memories have been filled. Things that were inexplicable then have been explained.

At that time, nobody knew.

No, that's not right. At that time, few people knew.

Now there is no excuse for anyone not to know.

———

I WAS NOT the only child in Holland to be given away so that I might have a better chance of survival.

I was one of hundreds.

Many of my fellow hideaways never saw their parents again. Some, like me, were reunited, but even that process was rarely happy and never straightforward.

Again, like me, the very young soon forgot everything about life before the hidden times.

Older children remembered the old days all too well, but, in many cases, they reacted to the transition by switching off all feelings for their birth parents. The experts say this may have been an instinctive, subconscious response that enabled them to avoid sinking into grief and despair at their loss and to focus instead on their new life.

Some parents similarly mourned the loss of their children immediately following their separation, knowing that there was a high chance that they would never meet again.

After the war, when they were reunited, the children, now older and hardened by experience, often found it difficult to turn their feelings back on. Nor were many mothers and fathers able to cope with their children's unexpected resurrection.

If it was traumatic for birth parents and children to rebuild their life together, the trauma was no less severe for the temporary mamas and papas, when they had to hand back a child they had been looking after for so long, had grown to love and had expected to be theirs forever.

This presented yet another hurdle for returning biological parents to overcome. Now, they had to deal with the fact that their own child had a closer filial bond with someone else than with them.

This was how it was for my mother and me. When we were first reunited, my mother, recently rescued from the concentration camp, was traumatised by her experiences and felt inferior in every way to the Lady, my last and best war-time Mama, whom I had come to adore.

My mother wouldn't allow me to spend any time with the Lady after she found a place for us to live and took me away - amid floods of tears - from the Lady's home.

That was the last time I saw the Lady.

I later learned that she was a genuine heroine of the Dutch Resistance, a courier and a safe-house keeper who saved the lives of countless Jewish people, enabling them to escape from Holland to safety in Spain and beyond.

My mother kept the Lady at a distance because she wanted me to grow to love her instead. And I guess the Lady may not have insisted on staying in touch with me out of respect for my mother's wishes.

Of course, I am also well aware that, while the Lady stands as a towering beacon in my life, I was just one of many refugees to pass through her caring hands.

Nevertheless, I am proud to have been the only child who ever got to call the Lady my Mama.

When, far too many years afterwards, I finally did try to find the Lady, it was too late. She had died two years earlier.

This remains a source of enormous regret for me today.

I still hold the Lady in my heart.

———

My mother often said that, when she found me again, I was no longer the same child she had handed over three years earlier. I was scared of strangers and had no self-confidence. I also tended to get occasional fits of terror, when I would crouch down on the floor and start screaming uncontrollably.

For years afterwards, when anybody rang the doorbell, I would cower, look at my mother with fear in my eyes and ask:

"May the people know I'm here?"

Physically, I was a wreck of a child. I walked bent over and had to have treatments to straighten my back. My mother cared for me almost like a doctor until I was 16 years old.

Even as a teenager, I was inhibited in my relationships with other people. It was only once I got into my twenties that I began to open up more. Even now, I am often too accommodating and over-tolerant of the opinions and the behaviour of others. I rarely argue or pick fights.

One aspect of Anka's legacy that has never left me is a permanent sense of insecurity. In life, you are never completely safe. Something bad can always be waiting around the next corner.

MAMAS AND PAPAS

THINKING BACK, I can't picture in detail the faces of any of the many Mamas and Papas I had as Anka. My vision is blurry.

But I owe my life to them all: those who treated me kindly, those who neglected me and even the ones who cruelly abused me.

They spared me from the certain death that I would have faced, had I been found and taken away earlier than I was. Thanks to them, I have had a life.

I frequently ponder over the astonishing courage of the people who took me in. They were not Jewish, but, in concealing me, they risked arrest, imprisonment and torture. They could have even been taken out and executed on the spot, in order to discourage others from doing the same thing.

Nobody forced them to put their lives on the line. When they were asked if they would take on the responsibility, they stepped up and accepted the danger. Nobody would ever blame anyone for refusing to do something like this for a stranger. The potential consequences were enormous.

Yet, they did not refuse.

For every moment of every day I was living with them, these

Mamas and Papas must have feared the knock on the door or the careless word of a malevolent nosey neighbour that would destroy their lives. Maybe this is why I was moved from house to house so often. The pressure and stress on those hiding me must have increased the longer I stayed with them. At some point, it must have become unbearable.

Or, perhaps I was a difficult child and that is the reason I had so many temporary homes. Maybe I had my mother's wilfulness in those days. If so, it had disappeared by the time my mother reappeared. A casualty of everything that happened to me, perhaps?

I still find it difficult to understand or forgive the cruelty I suffered at the hands of that one couple, the physical and psychological consequences of which have followed me through the last eighty years - years filled with doctor's visits, surgical procedures, psychologists, painkillers and pick-me-ups.

Yes, they took me in, and yes, like the others, they helped save my life. But, even so...

Why would anyone ever agree to take in and conceal a small child in the first place, if they have no affinity for children?

Why would anyone risk their life to do this if they cared so little for the child that they would beat her viciously, over and over again?

Why would anyone agree to hide a stranger's little girl and then treat her like an unloved pet?

Was I just unlucky to fall into the hands of a child abuser and his enabling spouse? Did they just seize the opportunity to look after a child to enable them to satisfy some violent urge? Was I the only child who passed through their hands?

These are questions that have always haunted me. I will never have the answers.

I only know that child abuse existed then, just as it exists now, and that it is an indelible function of the human condition.

I also know that, just as I did, victims tend to question the reasons for the abuse and try to find the answers inside themselves. They assume that the abuse has been triggered by something they did or by some quality they possess or lack.

I am now well aware that the answers to the questions lie within the abuser, rather than the abused.

My mother somehow found out about the childless couple and what they did to me, but she rarely mentioned it and we never discussed it in any detail.

I suppose she felt guilty, even though, of course, it was not in any way her fault. Crimes like these are carried out all the time in the shadows, in secret, unseen. The victims have no voice. The perpetrators are friends, neighbours, co-workers, fellow worshippers, even pillars of the community. They are clever and aware. They know how unspeakable their acts are. That is why they take every measure possible to conceal them.

Such crimes are rarely detected. And even when they are, it is rarely by someone with the courage, determination and strength of character to do something to stop them.

Such people are rare treasures.

Thank God for Mrs K!

————

A THING that used to worry me greatly was what became of all the people who were arrested with me - and because of me - in the big house with the secret cupboard.

Judging from what I now know, I have concluded that it is unlikely that the Jewish people in that house ended up in the gas chambers.

I hope this is not just wishful thinking.

I can't be completely certain, but I believe that the day I was distracted by the shiny black boots, fell for the smiling blue eyes and uttered the fateful words "My real Mama is hiding somewhere" was September 2, 1944.

Records show that the final deportation train out of Westerbork Camp departed for Auschwitz the following day, September 3. The

Dutch police were efficient, but, even so, it seems impossible that a person arrested in Amsterdam on one day could have been processed, sent to Westerbork and put on an Auschwitz train less than 24 hours later.

After that, following the allied seizure of Antwerp on September 4, rail traffic across the country was disrupted by attacks like the one that disabled the train I was put on.

It then took eight long months of fighting to liberate Holland from the Germans entirely: a period that included the countrywide famine that became known as the Hunger Winter.

Westerbork Camp continued to function until April 1945, when the Canadian forces arrived and freed the 876 prisoners who remained. But, after September 1944, no trains carried Dutch Jews from Westerbork to Auschwitz. Indeed, Auschwitz itself was destroyed and abandoned in January 1945, as the Soviet army was approaching.

I dearly hope that among those prisoners freed from Westerbork by the Canadians were the people I betrayed and that, while I may have been the cause of significant trauma and hardship for them, I was not responsible for any of them being murdered in the gas chambers.

As for my aunties, the ladies with whom I shared the Amsterdam prison cell and who were with me on that interrupted train journey to Westerbork, I know for a fact that they all survived the war.

In the 1960s, I made contact with them and we exchanged letters. They already knew that the Germans had picked me up again after the train was stopped, but they didn't know that I was subsequently rescued by the brave folk of the Dutch resistance.

When I wrote to them, I always used my real name, but they still began their replies with the words, "Dear Anka".

After all, in their minds, that is who I still was.

———

AND WHAT OF my mother Rachel?

I have no doubt what an enormous debt I owe her. I remain in awe of her courage in taking the almost impossible decisions that probably saved both our lives.

Had we been arrested simultaneously, which is almost certainly what would have happened if she had kept me with her, then we would have been sent to Westerbork at the same time.

Even if the timing had still coincided with the Bergen Belsen diamond project, would the Germans have taken her off the Auschwitz train to join the diamond workers with a small child in her arms?

Unlikely. When she spoke of the time she spent with the women at Bergen-Belsen and Beendorf, she never mentioned any children being there.

I find it inconceivable that she would have abandoned me on the Auschwitz train when her name was called.

Come to think of it, would her name have been called at all? Would she have given diamond worker as her occupation when she checked in if I had been with her? I think she would just have told them she was a housewife and mother.

Then, we would have stayed on the train to Auschwitz and shared the same destiny as Maurice, Joseph and almost every other member of our family.

DEATH OF A FAMILY

ONCE IT BECAME clear that Germany would lose the war, pyramids of corpses were burned and dissolved in lime, while buildings were demolished and their foundations buried in order to try and conceal the evidence of the mass murder of Jewish people.

However, at the same time, at the other end of the process, following the example of a Führer who, at least outside his innermost circle, would not allow any action that even vaguely hinted at the possibility of defeat, paper pushers in offices all over occupied Europe continued their painstaking efforts to document the events.

The Dutch Railways and Nazi institutions were immensely proud of the efficiency of their bureaucracy. They collected and stored away mountains of paper, files and index cards, thus providing future investigators with incontrovertible and astonishingly detailed proof of the most horrific crime the world has known.

They even recorded the events on film and kept multiple copies.

Thanks to this evidence and the work carried out by historians and archaeologists over the last seven decades, I have a complete picture of the fate that befell my family.

Over and over again, in my darkest moments, I visualise the

murders of loved ones I hardly knew. I know them better in death than I ever did in life, but the pain I feel at their loss is no less severe for that.

————

It is autumn 1942 and my half-sister Carry is being held under arrest in Westerbork. She is 9 years old and attends the camp school. Whoever she is living with in the camp, it is not someone from our immediate family.

Perhaps she has an aunty or aunties with her, like I had.

On the evening of October 29, Carry's name is read out and, the next day, carrying a small suitcase containing everything she owns in the world, she is taken to a train and packed into a closed freight car together with 70 or more other people.

The bolts on the outside of the heavy wagon doors are slammed into place and the iron wheels screech as they are forced into motion. Then, the train and its cargo pull slowly away to begin their three-day journey across Europe.

On arrival at Auschwitz, all the passengers descend in silence to the platform. There they stand and wait. It is bitterly cold. Instructions are bellowed in German. Carry doesn't understand. She watches what the grown-ups do and copies them.

Eventually, it is her turn to join the line of people walking slowly past a German officer in a peaked cap, positioned in the centre of a ramp leading from the platform, flanked by helmeted soldiers with guns held across their chest. Other soldiers, ushering the queue along, use their guns to jab and stab those who move too slowly, stop to ask questions or walk the wrong way.

The officer directs Carry towards a large group composed of young children like her and their parents, as well as older people, fat people, people with glasses and people who have difficulty walking. Some in this group are sobbing. Others look very ill. Some need help to walk. Others can't even stand up unaided.

A much smaller group, made up mostly of young adult men, has assembled on the other side of the platform.

Then, there is another announcement. Carry asks one of the grown-ups what is happening and she is told that they all have to be disinfected before they can enter the labour camp.

Again, following the example of the others, she leaves her case behind on the platform and joins the throng of people shuffling along a pathway.

Their destination is a red brick farmhouse. When they get there, they are not allowed to go in until they have taken off all the clothes they are wearing. While they undress, the soldiers keep shouting at them. It's all hurry, hurry, hurry. There is no time to think about what is happening. Finally, they are herded, poked and prodded through the single narrow doorway into the farmhouse, crouched, cringing, shivering, hands attempting pointlessly to conceal their nakedness.

Inside there are two windowless rooms. More and more people follow until it is no longer possible for them to avoid contact with each other. Naked stranger is forced to rub against naked stranger. Still the crush increases as more bodies are shoved in from behind to press on those already there.

Then, there is the sound of a heavy door closing and bolts being thrown.

Carry stands in the darkness. She senses the shame around her. She smells the fear. There is almost total silence. Being smaller, she can move around a little among the legs of the adults, but this also means she gets splashed by streams of urine as fear releases bowels. She manages to crawl towards the edge of the room. She sits on the ground with her back to the wall. All of a sudden, a wooden shutter is removed and a hole opens right above her head.

A shaft of light illuminates the mass of white flesh that fills every available space and a collective gasp is accompanied by a panicked shift away from the source of light, leaving a small empty section of floor beneath the opening.

A head pokes through the hole, wearing a gas mask.

Then the head withdraws and a canister is positioned on the edge of the hole, held in hands protected by thick gloves. The hands shake the canister for a few seconds and a small pile of pellets appears on the ground. Then, the hole is closed and the room is plunged once more into total darkness.

And the dying begins.

———

CARRY WAS MURDERED on November 2, 1942, poisoned by Zyklon B hydrogen cyanide, in the Auschwitz gas chamber known as the Little Red House, a repurposed farmhouse capable of holding 800 people standing squeezed tightly together.

Carry was selected to be gassed immediately on arrival because, as a 9-year old child, in the eyes of the Nazis, she was deemed to be not worth even feeding.

The records show that, between July 15, 1942 and February 23, 1943, a total of 42,915 Jewish people were transported by train from Westerbork to Auschwitz.

Only 85 of them survived beyond the end of the war.

———

ON JULY 6, 1943, my half-brother Sylvain boards a train at Westerbork Camp with his father, my mother's first husband.

Their destination is another extermination camp in German-occupied Poland called Sobibor. Their journey is surprisingly comfortable. There is no shortage of food or medicine on board. They are even accompanied by Jewish nurses.

On July 9, the train arrives at a railway siding with a large platform. Sylvain and his father disembark and a man wearing a white coat addresses them. Although he is dressed like a doctor, this is no doctor. He is the Camp Commandant, an SS officer, amusing himself with a little role-play.

He tells his audience that this is a transit camp. They are all going to be sent off to join work units, but before this, it is necessary for them to go through a disinfection process.

The male passengers are separated from the female passengers. They are all instructed to undress.

Leaving their clothing and possessions on the platform, together with a group of other naked men and boys, Sylvain and his father are led along a 100-metre pathway that runs between two rows of saplings.

They are ushered into a building and, once they are all inside, the door is locked behind them. An engine taken from an old battle tank is switched on and the exhaust fumes from the engine are piped into the building. After a short time, the door is opened again and the bodies are removed. After teeth have been extracted and jewellery removed, the corpses are thrown into a communal pit with thousands of others and covered with lime in the hope that they will never be found and what happened to them will never be known.

———

SYLVAIN WAS 12 YEARS OLD. He was a talented piano player, as was his father. My mother never discovered how it was that they came to be on the train together. Nor did she ever find out how Carry came to be picked up alone.

Of the 34,314 Jewish people transported from Westerbork to the Sobibor death camp between 1942 and 1944, only eighteen survived.

———

MY FATHER LOUIS was also taken from Camp Westerbork to Auschwitz.

As a fit 29-year-old man, he was selected for forced labour, instead of the gas. His hair was shaved off before he was disinfected and deloused. Then he was tattooed with his registration number and issued with a striped uniform, hat and clogs.

His reprieve was brief. Whether through starvation, disease, torture or a bullet in the head for not working hard enough, he died three months later.

———

BETWEEN AUGUST 24, 1943 and September 3, 1944, 11,985 Jewish people were deported from Westerbork to Auschwitz. Only 588 lived. The dead included Maurice and Joseph.

My mother's fortuitous removal from the train to Auschwitz saved her life. But, even with this stroke of luck, she still had to use her wits and strength of character to survive.

In 1944, 3,751 Jewish people were deported from Westerbork to Bergen-Belsen. Despite the relatively favourable conditions many of them were held in, nevertheless, over 1,700 of them died.

My mother lived.

———

MY MOTHER'S younger sister Elsje was one of the very few who was sent to Auschwitz and walked away.

She and her husband went into hiding in Amsterdam separately but were arrested after about eight months, one shortly after the other, and transported to Auschwitz, via Westerbork. Elsje's husband was murdered in the gas chamber on arrival.

Elsje, however, was selected to be a test subject in medical experiments that were conducted in Block 10 of the Auschwitz Birkenau Camp. These experiments included forced sterilisation by injection.

At war's end, when she was rescued from the camp, she weighed only 36 kilos and was suffering from tuberculosis. Because of the experiments, she was never able to have children. Although her health was poor throughout the rest of her life, she still managed to live into her nineties.

In the case of my mother's elder sister Lina, who was murdered along with her husband and daughter while trying to escape from Holland early on during the German occupation, there was to be no retribution for the Dutch neighbours who betrayed them and stole their house and possessions.

My mother filed a complaint after the war, but the complaint failed. The neighbours produced documents purporting to show that, before their departure, Lina and her husband had signed the house and all its contents over to them should they not return.

The court adjudicated in the neighbours' favour. The only thing my mother ever recovered was a violin. Today, I have it here on the mantelpiece in my apartment. I look at it often. It is an eternal reminder of those dark times and symbolic of a largely unrecognised truth.

The German invaders were not the only enemies that Holland's Jewish people had to deal with during the occupation.

CAREFULLY ORCHESTRATED CRUELTY

I KNOW EXACTLY when and how my siblings died, because the record-keepers were so dedicated and because the extermination processes at Auschwitz and Sobibor were so carefully thought-out, precise and predictable.

The systems were an exercise in carefully orchestrated cruelty cloaked in an inspired and vicious web of deceit, designed as much for the satisfaction and amusement of the captors as for the operational goal of keeping the victims as quiescent and obedient as possible for as long as possible.

Today, I view the whole sequence, from arrest to execution, as an elaborate drama, leading to an inexorable conclusion. The actors who played their parts in the drama, in all its various scenes, knew their roles and played them perfectly.

In Holland, these actors consisted of:

The Dutch civil servants who designed the registration process.

The Dutch policemen who made the arrests and pocketed the tips.

The Dutch mayors and their staff, who ran the human collection system.

The railway bosses who made sure the trains were well maintained and ran on time.

The thieves who stole property, land and possessions from deported Jewish people or acquired them from the authorities for a cheap under the table price.

The Jewish collaborators at Westerbork, who sent others to the death camps so that they could remain safe.

The German officers and soldiers, for whom it was all just a dull sideshow enlivened by moments of brutality.

And, finally, the millions of extras - the bit-players who adopted occasional walk-on roles and were never responsible, yet remained silent, never speaking up against what was happening.

———

To my mind, one of these actors deserves special mention in any analysis of events.

The Dutch state train company Nederlandse Spoorwegen, or NS as it is popularly known, made a great deal of profit from the carriage of Jewish deportees. Over a two-year period the NS transported over a hundred thousand Dutch Jewish people to their death, often in cattle wagons like beasts to a slaughterhouse.

The NS raised no objection nor did it manifest any resistance to working with the Nazis on the project. On the contrary, it actively facilitated the process by building, at its own expense, a branch line, where none had previously existed, out to Westerbork transit camp, specifically to make the transportation process more efficient.

The NS sent the German authorities an invoice for each train journey and the invoices were paid promptly, although not from official German coffers. The payments were made out of money confiscated from the prisoners. The Jewish passengers were forced to pay in cash for their tickets on one-way trains to oblivion.

It was sixty years before an NS director issued a formal apology on behalf of the company, but it was only in 2017, 72 years after the end of the war, that a Dutch prime minister for the first time expressed regret for the conduct of the Dutch authorities during the German occupation, saying that they:

"Failed in their responsibility as a provider of justice and security."

Compensation for the victims of the death camp deportations was not offered until 2019, by which time almost everyone involved, whether NS collaborators or survivors like my mother, was dead.

I was one of the very few victims still alive to hear the prime minister's belated apology. It left me cold. I found it totally meaningless.

I applied for compensation. Not because I needed the money. The amount was relatively insubstantial. No, it was just a question of principle. My application was rejected. My name was not in the records. There were plenty of travel records for unidentified children. Was I able to prove one of these was me? Of course not.

The decades have rolled by. Generations of company officers have come and gone. Times have changed. But the heartless culture of company bureaucracy evidently remains as it ever was.

————

THE DEPORTATION PROGRAMME in Holland was the most efficient and effective example of its kind anywhere in Nazi-occupied Europe - and that includes Germany itself.

Adolf Eichmann, the Nazi leader who ran the entire programme from his headquarters in Berlin, was effusive in his praise, describing the work of the Dutch NS as "quite wonderful".

This was a significant accolade coming from a man who, following his arrest in 1945, was quoted as saying:

"I will leap into my grave laughing because the feeling that I have five million human beings on my conscience is for me a source of extraordinary satisfaction."

NOT UNIQUE

THE KNOWLEDGE that my terrifying and scarring experiences as Anka were not unique gives me no solace - quite the opposite. Awareness of the scale of the suffering still gives me sleepless nights.

In September 1939, there were about 1.6 million Jewish children living in the territories that the Germans would eventually occupy.

Less than six years later, when the war in Europe ended, more than 1 million of those children were dead.

Many who survived faced a future without parents, grandparents or siblings.

The Nazi machine targeted Jewish people of all ages, but the youngest were the most likely to die. Not only could they not perform any useful function, the Germans feared that, if they left any children alive, they would one day exact revenge for their parents' death.

When Germany occupied Holland in May 1940, there were about 140,000 Jewish people in the country. Of these, only 38,000 were still alive five years later.

If you were a Jewish person living in Holland in 1940, you had around a 1 in 4 chance of surviving the next five years.

———

Do I blame my mother for giving me up?

No, I do not.

At the time, everyone had their own idea of the best thing to do. Escape, go into hiding, obey the rules, register for the so-called labour camps, give your children to their grandparents, send your children away or keep your children with you.

No solution was guaranteed to succeed. The odds were stacked against you, whatever you chose to do. It is impossible to say that anyone got it right or got it wrong.

My mother did not live because of the choices she made for herself, nor did I survive because of the choices my mother made for me. We both avoided being murdered thanks to a succession of chance events, combined, in my case, with the intervention of brave strangers.

TODAY'S RACHELS AND ANKAS

TODAY, when I watch the international news, I can't help but identify with the mothers and children that I watch being separated, going into hiding, fleeing from war and being persecuted, all over the world.

Beyond the words and images, I know their pain, I share their misery and I despair that the suffering I experienced as a child must be replayed incessantly in a world that seems to be unable to learn from its mistakes.

In the Americas, in Eastern Europe, in the Middle East, in Asia and in North Africa, millions of people are on the move or living in refugee camps.

The concept of people in power following a political ideology that considers certain individuals in society as worthless did not die with the defeat of the Nazis in 1945.

People are still isolated, hounded, banished, expelled, deported, incarcerated and murdered simply on the basis of their ancestry, culture, upbringing and religion.

I know that, right now:

Other Ankas are sitting in empty rooms in strange places, alone and unloved.

Other Ankas are spending their lives confused, abused, hungry and fearful.

Other Ankas are in prison.

Other Ankas have been abandoned by their parents in a desperate attempt to keep them from harm.

Just like my mother, women are giving up their children, leaving everything behind and fighting to survive each day, in the hope that one day they may find their children again.

People like my mother are being rounded up and put in detention camps and many of these camps are as inaccessible to the outside world as the German death camps were.

Our story is not ancient history.

Our story is now.

PART XI
PHOTOGRAPHS

Baby Johanna before she was Anka

Johanna after she was Anka

Johanna dressed up

Rachel with Carry

Sylvain and Carry

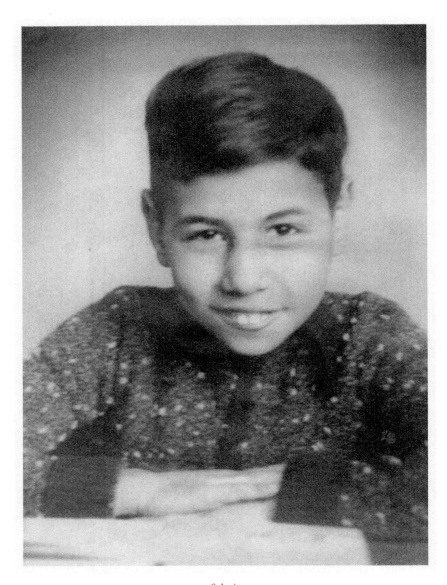

Sylvain

Johanna as a teenager

Rachel with grown-up Johanna

Rachel in 1943

Aunt Lina with husband Jaap 1931

Aunt Elsje (Adelaide) (centre) 1935

Aunt Elsje with second husband 1947

The Lady

AUTHOR'S NOTE

This is a work of narrative nonfiction, based on the extraordinary real-life experiences of two extraordinary people caught up in extraordinary times.

Johanna Marianna Sacksioni (Anka) is still alive and I am grateful for her approval to publish this book. Her memories, first recounted to me at the dinner table one evening in a conversation that began: "I haven't told you my story, have I?" were what prompted me to start writing it. I sat open mouthed in astonishment while the rest of her family exchanged here-we-go-again glances. They had heard it all before.

But it was new to me and I was rapt.

Then she told me her mother's story too and I realised that theirs was a tale that deserved to be shared with a wider audience.

Rachel passed away some years ago, but she left written and video-taped accounts of her war years and I have used these as my guide for her sections of the narrative.

Any errors in this book, however, are completely mine.

I have used very few family names in order to preserve the privacy of individuals and their families.

For the same reason, I do not include copies of the actual documents that record when and how members of Rachel and Johanna's family were transported to Westerbork then on to Auschwitz and Sobibor.

I am most grateful to Fernand Hostyn for his research and insights relating to the historical context of these events, as well as the wonderful cover image, and to Tracy, Jacqueline, Karen, Amy and Sofie for being stringent, yet kind, early readers.

While writing this book, I was inspired and informed by the following:

Amis, Martin. The Zone of Interest. Vintage 2015

Bregman, Rutger. Humankind: A Hopeful History. Bloomsbury Publishing, 2020.

Carey, M.R. The Girl with all the Gifts. Orbit, 2014.

Gronowski, Simon. L'enfant du XXe convoi: La Renaissance du Livre 2005

Hitler Adolf, Mein Kampf, James Murphy translation, 1939

Kershaw Ian. Hitler 1889 to 1936: Hubris. Penguin, 2001.

Kershaw Ian. Hitler 1936 to 1945: Nemesis. Penguin, 2001.

Reiss, Johanna. The Upstairs Room. Graymalkin Media, 2011.

Van Es, Bart. The Cut Out Girl. Penguin, 2018

PART XII
BACKGROUND READING

A few brief notes for readers who may wish to know a little more about the background to what happened to Anka and Rachel.

THE GREAT WAR AND CORPORAL HITLER

NOT EVERYONE in Europe wanted war in 1914. However, for some, it was a useful diversion or a convenient means to an end.

In Germany, there was some fear that a war would disrupt the progress being made by the country's spectacularly successful economy, but there was also ambition that war might bring further gains.

Great Britain was finding it hard to cope with Germany's economic miracle as Germany adopted protectionist policies at home, yet demanded free trade elsewhere.

France was still struggling with the consequences of its heavy defeat by Prussia and the loss of Alsace-Lorraine in 1870. It did not have the strength to go to war alone, but found an unlikely partner in Russia.

Russia, the largest country in the world at the time, had suffered its own defeat against tiny Japan in 1905 and was simultaneously dealing with internal social upheaval that would eventually erupt in revolution.

Serbia dreamed of bringing all Serb peoples in the Balkans under its control, despite the inevitable clash with Austria-Hungary that this would bring.

On June 28, 1914, Franz-Ferdinand, the heir to the Austria-Hungary throne, visited the Bosnian capital Sarajevo. He was being driven through the city in an open wagon with his wife Sophie, when Gravilo Princip, a young Serb nationalist, jumped out of the crowd and shot them both.

In response, with Germany's support, Austria-Hungary declared war on Serbia. Later they were joined by the Ottoman Empire and Bulgaria. This group of nations was referred to as the Central Powers.

Russia and France came in on the side of Serbia, as did Great Britain and, later, Romania. In 1917, the USA entered the war too. These countries were referred to as the Allies.

Over 70 million soldiers ended up fighting in one of the biggest wars in history. More than 9 million of them lost their lives.

This was the first war that featured machine guns, poison gas, barbed wire, tanks and planes.

————

AUSTRIAN ADOLF HITLER volunteered for service as an infantryman in the 1st Company of the 16th Bavarian Reserve Infantry Regiment of the German Army and became a courier. The first surviving photograph of infantryman Hitler shows him with his rifle hung over his shoulder in Flanders in May 1915.

He was promoted to the rank of Gefreiter (similar to corporal), wounded in action and awarded the Iron Cross. At Ypres on October 13, 1918, he was temporarily blinded in a poison gas attack and hospitalised.

In later life, Hitler rarely mentioned that he had been a courier and had spent most of the war away from the front lines. He preferred to suggest that he was an ordinary soldier who risked his life every day side by side in the trenches with his comrades.

Corporal Hitler served under two Jewish officers. One, lieutenant Hugo Gutmann, left Germany for the United States in 1939. Another,

Ernst Hess, was sent to a concentration camp in 1941 but survived the war.

DEFEAT

IN EARLY NOVEMBER 1918, a military rebellion and the flight of the German Emperor to neutral Holland led to Germany requesting an armistice. A ceasefire was declared on November 11, 1918 and this marked the end of hostilities.

The Great War changed the world. Four major European imperial dynasties collapsed as a direct result. The Hapsburgs of Austria-Hungary, the Turkish Ottoman Empire, the Russian Romanovs and the Hohenzollern Empire in Germany – they all disappeared, never to return.

Meanwhile, the United States of America emerged for the first time as a world power.

Germany was blamed for starting the war and, in victory, the Allies insisted that Germany should therefore be billed for the costs incurred. The various penalties were set out in the Treaty of Versailles.

By the terms of this treaty, Germany lost large parts of its territory to neighbouring countries. It also had to pay the Allies a lot of money over a long period of time. This was a debt that eventually proved impossible to meet.

Economic and social devastation followed. Hundreds of thousands of men, women and children in Germany died from hunger and disease as a post-war blockade continued for months after the armistice. Then, enormous levels of inflation brought widespread poverty and unemployment.

The winners of the Great War wanted the losers to suffer, and they did.

The misery that followed was felt throughout Germany and produced social conditions that were ripe for manipulation by extreme political parties on the right and left. Meanwhile, the Treaty of Versailles had considerably reduced the size of the German army and many soldiers were demobilised.

With the empire gone, a democratic republic was proclaimed in the German city of Weimar and new parties were formed all across the political spectrum.

The early years of the republic were characterised by violence on the streets between political parties of the left and the right.

On the left were the Communists, who were supported by the newly established Soviet Union. Between 1919 and 1923, they tried and failed repeatedly to seize power.

On the right were several Nationalist parties, some of which combined to execute a coup against the democratic republic in 1920. This failed too.

The violence was made worse by the fact that parties on both sides had well-trained, well-armed paramilitary divisions, manned by the former soldiers who had returned home in 1918, taking their weapons with them.

Germany descended into chaos. There were mass strikes, unrest, armed street battles, uprisings and rampant inflation. At one point, a single US dollar was the equivalent of one trillion German marks.

GENESIS

SHORTLY AFTER THE Great War ended, Adolf Hitler joined the newly-formed right-wing Deutsche Arbeiterpartei or German Workers Party. This was a minor, extreme right-wing racist political party, based in Munich in southern Germany.

It was 1919 and he was 30 years old.

He rose quickly in the ranks and was instrumental in the party changing its name to the National Sozialistische Deutsche Arbeiter-partei (NSDAP). Party members were commonly referred to as National Socialists.

Hitler's first public speech was delivered on October 16, 1919 in the Münchener Hofbräukeller. He soon discovered he had a gift for oratory and was a natural actor. He had an actor's sense for the mood of the crowd and for adjusting his delivery and his script to what he felt his audience, large or small, private or public, wanted to hear.

In 1921, two years after he joined the party, Hitler became its leader.

He presented himself as a man of the people. When he spoke of redemption for the German people, his message fell on eager ears.

Many Germans wanted a return to greatness after the humiliation that had followed their country's defeat in 1918.

When he blamed what he called a Jewish-Bolshevik global conspiracy for delivering the "dagger punch in the back" which had undermined the will, confidence and capabilities of the German Army and the German Emperor, he also struck a powerful chord.

Using a phrase linking his left-wing political enemies with Jewish people was a masterstroke.

Jewish people were easily recognisable targets. For almost 100 years, a tide of murderous Anti-Semitism had swept across Europe, spreading racist theories that Jewish people were treacherous, degenerate and biologically inferior. The National Socialists and other extreme right wing parties, all of which had anti-Semitic policies and espoused political terrorism, hammered these messages home with incessant propaganda.

In November 1923, Hitler and his followers attempted a coup in a Munich beer hall. They captured a few regional dignitaries and occupied a police station. Hitler declared himself Germany's new leader and proclaimed a National Revolution. The plan was to march on Berlin.

The police and the army crushed the rebellion almost instantly. Fourteen of the rebels and three police officers lost their lives.

Hitler was arrested, sentenced to five years in jail and incarcerated in Landsberg prison. While there, he wrote his political autobiography *Mein Kampf*, in which he revealed his racist world view and promoted racial purity and the expansion of the homeland to acquire more Lebensraum (living space) as the recipe for Germany's renaissance.

In his speeches and in *Mein Kampf*, Hitler made no attempt to conceal his hatred of Jewish people. It was there for all to see and hear. He stated clearly that, in his opinion, Jewish people should be wiped from the face of the Earth.

Many came to consider Hitler as the saviour Germany needed to restore the country to greatness and had no objection to the means by which he proposed to achieve this.

After all, was extermination not what Jewish people deserved in return for bringing Germany to its knees? They were the enemy within. They had to be vanquished. And anyway, Jewish people were not real people. They were filthy, thieving, corrupt, perverted sub-humans.

Thus, the kindling was set and the fire was laid so it would catch easily once the National Socialists came to power.

RISE

THE BIERKELLER COUP may not have succeeded, but it turned Adolf
Hitler from a provincial loud-mouthed bumpkin into a national
celebrity and a household name. He emerged from jail reinvented,
after serving less than a year of his sentence, and with a political
manifesto in hand.

An episode that might have marked the end of his short political
career instead proved to be just the beginning.

The NSDAP did not enter the German national parliament until
1924, but by 1932 it was the most popular political party in the
country.

Ten years later, on January 30, 1933, when he was 43, Hitler
became Reich Chancellor (Prime Minister). He acted quickly to turn
Germany from a democracy into a dictatorship under his leadership.
Other political parties were banned, parliament was annulled and, on
the death of Paul von Hindenburg in August 1934, Hitler assumed the
Presidency and became the undisputed leader of the nation.

In a matter of 14 years, a small regional party of extremists and its
Austrian-born leader, a former German Army corporal, had risen
from nowhere to rule the entire country.

Hitler personified German ambition and dreams of national glory and he carried millions of Germans in the palm of his hand. Credit for any victories was his and his alone. Blame for any mis-steps was placed on other senior Party leaders. Extreme violence in the streets targeted at Jewish people and the NSDAP's political enemies was attributed to an over-enthusiastic Party apparatus.

Hitler was untouchable. Nothing was his fault. He could do no wrong.

He now had the means to transform the promises and threats set out in *Mein Kampf* and reinforced in his many rabble-rousing speeches into direct action.

———

MEIN KAMPF HAD ALREADY HIGHLIGHTED Hitler's faith in the power of propaganda and this was a tool that would prove to be an enormous factor in convincing the German people to follow him and support the actions he and his Party carried out, no matter how heinous or appalling they were.

"In the big lie there is always a certain force of credibility; because the broad masses of a nation are always more easily corrupted in the deeper strata of their emotional nature than consciously or voluntarily; and thus in the primitive simplicity of their minds they more readily fall victims to the big lie than the small lie, since they themselves often tell small lies in little matters but would be ashamed to resort to large-scale falsehoods.

It would never come into their heads to fabricate colossal untruths, and they would not believe that others could have the impudence to distort the truth so infamously. Even though the facts which prove this to be so may be brought clearly to their minds, they will still doubt and waver and will continue to think that there may be some other explanation." — Adolf Hitler, Mein Kampf, Vol 1, Ch 10

His propaganda chief Joseph Goebbels also had plenty to say about the concept of the big lie.

"If you tell a lie big enough and keep repeating it, people will eventually come to believe it. The lie can be maintained only for such time as the State can shield the people from the ... consequences of the lie. It thus becomes vitally important for the State to use all of its powers to repress dissent, for the truth is the mortal enemy of the lie, and thus by extension, the truth is the greatest enemy of the State."

Hitler also wrote that propaganda should be "only aimed at the masses" and that "*it must be popular and must adapt its mental level to the comprehension of the most limited of those it targets*".

Following this concept, the National Socialists appealed to poor, disgruntled working German people with simple slogans like "*get rid of those responsible for our decline*" and "*freedom and bread*".

They were highly effective.

Hitler surrounded himself with devoted followers who would do as he wished. What he wished was well known. Publicly at least, he had been obsessed with little else for many years.

FLIGHT

WHEN HITLER CAME to power in 1933, victimisation of Jewish people became national policy. The propaganda used to foster and stoke hatred presented them as non-human rodents and parasites on the population. Cartoons and caricatures cemented these prejudices in the national consciousness.

The NSDAP had nationality and citizenship legislation ready to roll from day one. This was evidently the first thing on the mind of the new regime. With the introduction of the Nuremberg Race laws, Jewish people were placed outside the community of German people. They had no rights, no voice and no social status whatsoever,

Much effort was applied to the task of quantifying what constituted "Jewishness", in order to make sure that the net was cast as widely as possible. Jewishness was portrayed as a virus and if a person's ancestry suggested that they had enough of the virus in their blood, they were considered a threat to the purity of the Nation.

There was no room for the impure in Hitler's Germany. Nor was there any room for the dissenters that Goebbels most feared. Opponents of National Socialist policy were intimidated, expelled, persecuted or imprisoned in concentration camps.

Undefended and powerless to defend themselves, between 1933 and 1937, a total of 130,000 Jewish people left National Socialist Germany. Many ended up in South Africa, Palestine and Latin America. Families who had previously immigrated to Germany from Eastern Europe returned whence they came.

Others fled to other countries in Northern and Western Europe. However, not everyone who wanted to leave was able to do so. The international community developed refugee fatigue and countries began to limit admissions, just as conditions for Jewish people in Germany deteriorated further. Immigration became increasingly difficult almost everywhere.

Even so, desperate times encourage desperate measures. Even in 1938 and 1939, 120,000 people managed to escape from Germany.

They still left hundreds of thousands behind. Also, of course, many of those that had escaped the frying pan soon found themselves in the fire, as the Second World War began and the countries to which they had escaped or returned fell under German rule.

LEBENSRAUM

IN *MEIN KAMPF*, Hitler identified the German need for Lebensraum and this became a key feature of his campaign speeches.

He began by demanding that the humiliation of the Treaty of Versailles be redressed. Many German people viewed the forced surrender of territory to its neighbours as an intolerable insult, so the NSDAP's promise to recover these lost regions for the Fatherland was a significant vote getter.

But dressing the Lebensraum concept up as simply a repudiation of Versailles was a deception. The quest for Lebensraum was effectively a call for war. After all, the only way Germany could expand its territory in order to acquire more living space for its people was to invade its neighbours.

Just as the mass murder of Europe's Jewish population was predictable to anyone who read and took seriously what Hitler had written in his manifesto, so the Second World War was inevitable from the moment Adolf Hitler and his Party assumed overall leadership of Germany.

To fulfil his desire for Lebensraum, Hitler needed large and modern forces. The Versailles Treaty forbade German military expansion, but Hitler ignored this and nobody stepped in to enforce the treaty and stop the build-up. The ensuing manufacturing boom led to Germany accumulating massive financial debt, but also solved the country's unemployment problem. German workers became much better off. The only way to keep the people happy and repay the debt was to go to war - and win.

Hitler constantly lied and bluffed about his plans for war. The story of the invasion of Poland is a good example.

In 1935 Germany signed a non-aggression pact with Poland, which, at the time, had one of Europe's largest armies, although it was old-fashioned. Many units even still used horses. The pact allowed Germany to continue its own military build-up without having to worry about aggression from a concerned eastern neighbour.

The Treaty of Versailles had transferred control over a large part of eastern Prussia from Germany to Poland. However, a German enclave was preserved around the majority German-speaking city of Danzig (present-day Gdansk).

Hitler wanted to build a rail and road corridor through Poland from the German border to Danzig and have Poland pay for the cost of the work. Poland refused.

So Hitler started making plans to invade Poland instead. Before he did so, Germany and the Soviet Union signed the Molotov-Ribbentrop Pact, a secret agreement to divide a defeated Poland in two, one half for Germany and one half for the Soviet Union, in return for the Soviet Union not interfering with or objecting to Germany's planned invasion.

Meanwhile, Hitler had the SS invent a series of border incidents designed to suggest that Poland was planning to attack Germany. During the final incident, at Gleiwitz, twelve prisoners from the Büchenwald concentration camp were dressed in Polish military uniform, poisoned, shot and photographed. Then the Germans announced that there had been a gunfight following a Polish attack on an SS border post and Hitler used this as justification for a declaration of war.

Within a month the Poles surrendered, overwhelmed by the speed and fury of the assault by German forces, which possessed far superior technology, as well as the advantage of advance preparation.

Hitler subsequently tore up the Molotov-Ribbentrop pact too.

Holland was invaded and quickly occupied despite its declared neutrality. The invasion was simply a device to facilitate the conquest of France.

It was supposed to be a surprise but the Dutch became aware of the plans several days in advance. Not that it made much difference. They put up some initial resistance but after a night during which German bombers laid waste to Rotterdam and Utrecht, it was all over.

Hitler perceived an affinity between the two nations. He considered Holland and the Dutch people to be suitable for incorporation into Germany itself, rather than ruled over as a colony of a German empire. He admired the tall, white, blond Dutch stereotype and spoke of them as fellow members of the Aryan race.

A PROBLEM AND A SOLUTION

FIRST, Hitler and the National Socialists took away the legal status of Jewish Germans, then they took away their jobs, stole their businesses and removed them from general society.

These actions were followed by beatings, looting, the destruction of synagogues and, eventually, when all this didn't achieve the objective of getting rid of Jewish people fast enough, mass murder.

The people who had put Hitler in power continued to support and enable him once he became overall leader. His appointed officials adopted a strategy they called "working to the leader": that is: coming up with initiatives that they knew were guaranteed to please Hitler.

Developing strategies that would fulfil Hitler's oft-expressed desires regarding the fate of Jewish people was a sure-fire way of pleasing him.

——————

ACTION against Jewish people in Holland was gradual at first, then, towards the end of 1941, it accelerated.

The reasons for this were both specific and general.

During the first couple of years of the Dutch occupation, the Germans were wary of stirring social unrest in a country that they hoped to assimilate. So, action against Jewish people in Holland was pursued slowly, in order to allow time for propaganda measures to take effect and for acceptance to build among the non-Jewish population. This was a similar tactic to the one the National Socialists had deployed in Germany between 1933 and 1938.

The Germans also felt that time was on their side. They assumed that their eventual victory in the war in Europe was assured and that they would therefore have plenty of time to deal with "the Jewish problem".

Everything turned around events on the Eastern Front in 1941 and 1942.

When the Soviet Red Army launched its devastating counteroffensive in Moscow on December 5, 1941, Hitler realised for the first time that Germany might lose the war. Of course, he was not prepared to let the German people know that. Publicly, the defeat was portrayed merely as a temporary setback. Blame was placed variously on the unexpected early arrival of winter and the incompetence and cowardice of certain German Army commanders.

Even so, it proved impossible to keep the potential consequences of the events in Moscow a secret. That same month, reports were already filtering back to foreign diplomats in Berlin that the soldiers at the front no longer believed that Germany could win.

With eventual defeat now a possibility, time suddenly became more of a factor. Greater focus, therefore, was directed at the one key aspect of the National Socialists' mission that they considered still to be achievable. Accomplishing this goal would vindicate and validate their efforts, even if all else failed.

The goal was the elimination of the Jewish people.

It was around this time that the death camps were established and the deportations from Holland began.

———

On January 20, 1942, a conference took place in the Villa Marlier in the Berlin suburb of Wannsee.

The strategy that the conference was convened to address had actually been set in motion several months earlier, before events in Russia added urgency to the process.

In mid-1941, senior Nazi leader Hermann Göring instructed top SS official Reinhard Heydrich as follows:

"In addition to your assignment of January 24, 1939 to solve the Jewish problem in the form of emigration or evacuation in a way that does justice to the current era, I hereby order you to make all organisational and material preparations for a total solution to the Jewish problem."

It was this "total solution" that the conference was to discuss. Heydrich chaired the meeting and fifteen senior officials were in attendance. It started at noon and lasted less than two hours. That is how long it took to agree to put in place a system for murdering every Jewish person in Europe. At the conference, the stated estimate of the number of people to be murdered was 11 million.

———

The method for the total solution was easy to choose. It was something that the National Socialists had already deployed effectively to rid Germany of what they referred to as "useless eaters": that is, members of the German population who did not contribute to the State but just consumed its resources: people such as the mentally ill and the physically handicapped.

The phrase "useless eater" was subsequently also applied to Jewish prisoners, such as children and the elderly, who could perform no useful function and therefore might as well be murdered immediately.

In 1939, dedicated facilities were established all over Germany. The facilities were attached to psychiatric centres and their initial purpose was to kill any babies born with physical or mental defects.

This initiative was a follow-up to a pre-existing enforced sterilisation programme, which began in 1933 and was designed to ensure that the mentally handicapped, the physically handicapped and "social deviants" would never produce children and pollute the German gene pool.

In 1940, the facilities began to use gas as a quicker and more effective way of murdering the handicapped babies and, as this now enabled the staff at the facilities to fit more murders into a working day, the programme's net was widened to include adult patients in asylums and hospitals.

As capacity increased still further and as the target population dwindled, mentally sound Jewish people and other prisoners from concentration camps were also sent to the facilities to be gassed.

An estimated 300,000 people were killed by these facilities during the war years, mostly in the period from 1939 to 1941.

So by time of the Wannsee meeting in January 1942, the technology had been tried and tested. Teams of experts were available to be deployed to the new death camps being established at Auschwitz, Sobibor and elsewhere to set up similar, although much expanded, facilities there.

In fact, a month before the conference, Heydrich had already authorised the mass gassing of Jewish detainees at a camp in Chelmno, Poland to test the new process.

The attendees at the Wannsee Conference were no doubt presented with a report on the Chelmno experiment, demonstrating how effective it would be as a means of achieving the total solution.

Then, they approved the plan and adjourned for a late lunch.

That evening, according to Adolf Eichmann:

"Heydrich, Müller and myself sat cosily around the fireplace. We had drinks. We had brandy. We sang songs. After a while, we got up on chairs and drank a toast. Then we got up on the tables and went round and round. On the chairs. On the tables. Then we sat around peacefully, giving ourselves a rest after so many exhausting hours."

DUTCH NAZIS

THERE WAS a National Socialist Party in Holland too.

The Nationaal Socialistische Beweging or NSB was founded in Utrecht in 1931. It modelled itself and its policies on Germany's NSDAP.

When the Dutch Government realised that Germany was planning to ignore Holland's declaration of neutrality and invade in May 1940, the 800 members of the NSB were rounded up and imprisoned, for fear that they might act to help the invaders.

Two weeks later, victorious German troops released them all. The Germans then outlawed all political parties except the NSB and its membership grew to about 100,000. Every new mayor appointed throughout the country had to be an NSB member.

NSB leader and co-founder Anton Mussert expected that he would be appointed to rule a quasi-independent Dutch state under German sovereignty, but this never came to pass. Occupied Holland was ruled instead by an administration led by Austrian National Socialist Arthur Seyss-Inquart.

This meant that, during the occupation, the NSB enjoyed a great deal of local power but had very little influence at national level.

In September 1944, when it appeared inevitable that the Allies would soon take Holland, most of the NSB leadership fled to Germany and the party's organisation fell apart. When war ended on May 6, 1945, the NSB was outlawed and many of its members were arrested. Mussert was one of very few who were subsequently executed.

Most NSB members escaped execution and returned to normal life after a spell in prison. Among them was Edward Voûte, Mayor of Amsterdam from 1941 to 1945. He was sentenced to 6 years imprisonment, later reduced to 3.5 years. He died a year after his release from prison, at the age of 62.

THE BACKGROUND TO BEENDORF

In February 1944, male prisoners from Neuengamme concentration camp were despatched to Beendorf to excavate underground factories in two salt mines there. From August 1944 onwards, 2,500 female prisoners arrived from various camps to work for the Ministry of Armaments and War Production.

They produced munitions for the air force as well as other aircraft parts, such as autopilots, controls and steering gear for Messerschmidt Me 262 aircraft and V1 and V2 rockets. The prisoners worked in daily 12 hour shifts, at depths of between 425 and 465 metres. They were lowered up and down the mineshaft in small cages.

SS-Obersturmführer Gerhard Poppenhagen was the commander of the women's prison camp.

On April 10, 1945, the camp was evacuated and the women loaded onto goods cars. They were taken to Magdeburg, then on to Stendal, Wittenberge and Wöbbelin. The train stopped for three days at the railway station in Sülstorf in Mecklenburg and the bodies of the large number of women who had died during the journey were taken away by villagers and buried there.

On April 20 or 21, the train reached Hamburg and the prisoners were distributed to the largely empty Hamburg satellite camps of Eidelstedt, Langenhorn, Sasel and Wandsbek.

Most left Hamburg on May 1, 1945 aboard a Swedish Red Cross train, which took them via Denmark to Sweden.

HOW MUCH DID THEY KNOW?

TODAY, the facts of the Holocaust are clear and incontrovertible, although new information continues to be unearthed by researchers and earlier assumptions are always being called into question.

Several sections of Dutch society were complicit in the crimes committed against Holland's Jewish population.

But, in what were they complicit?

How much did the facilitators and bystanders know about what was happening?

How much might they reasonably have guessed?

———

BY 1942, when the mass round ups began, even the most casual and uninvolved person in Holland would have been aware that Jewish people were being arrested, deprived of their possessions and incarcerated.

They also certainly knew that Jewish people were then being transported to camps in Eastern Europe. This was not a secret, by any means. They may not have believed the Germans' definition of these places as "labour camps", but nobody expected the deportees ever to return.

Those who acquired formerly Jewish-owned homes, businesses and other assets via the widespread official looting, did not anticipate that the previous owners or occupants would ever come back to reclaim them.

They were right. Most didn't.

Those who informed on Jewish people or facilitated the crimes against them in some way, never expected to be held accountable for what they did or omitted to do.

They were also right. Most weren't.

So, it is hard to claim that certain individuals and certain sectors of Dutch society at the time were not complicit in the segregation, arrest, imprisonment and deportation of Jewish people, as well as the deprivation of their rights and the enforced sequestration of their wealth.

———

But, how much did anyone know about the "total solution"? How complicit were Dutch people in the genocide that was perpetrated in the death camps in Eastern Europe?

As early as 1942, radio transmissions and occasional eyewitnesses, such as Jehovah's Witnesses who had been arrested but then recanted their faith and returned to Holland, were talking about the "extermination" of the Jewish people.

Hitler had even referred to his plans for Jewish people using this very word in multiple speeches over the years and in *Mein Kampf*.

But, people always assumed that the term extermination was Hitler hyperbole. They took it as a code word for elimination by imprisonment or deportation, possibly because accepting this word at its face value was too difficult to contemplate.

Indeed, for a long time, even the German leadership appeared to have that definition in mind. They even came up with a bizarre idea to send all Jewish people to Madagascar as the answer to the "Jewish problem" and, strange as it may seem, this plan was given lengthy consideration.

When the German leadership eventually adopted the systematic strategy to murder 11 million Jewish people in the death camps, they were all too aware of what a horrific act this was and they tried to keep it a closely-held secret. Only those who were directly involved and therefore implicated in the crime were supposed to know about it. And the victims of course.

But they could not prevent rumours spreading. People living in neighbouring villages were asphyxiated daily by the dreadful smoke pouring out of chimneys and the constant smell of death in the air when the wind turned in their direction. Nor could they stop soldiers and camp workers gossiping in village bars nor silence those few non-Jews who were imprisoned in the camps, then released.

When it became apparent that Germany would lose the war and the Soviet Army advanced towards the camps, the Germans destroyed the gas chambers and attempted to cover the traces.

But, they had no time or lacked the will to murder all the Jewish prisoners in all the camps, so when the guards fled and liberating army units arrived, they found plenty of evidence as well as thousands of surviving eye-witnesses. And, of course, nobody destroyed the files constructed with such care by the bureaucrats and paper pushers of the Third Reich.

———

A THOROUGH STUDY of diaries kept by people, both Jewish and non-Jewish, in various sectors of Dutch society during the war years suggests that no one in Holland knew the true nature and extent of the slaughter that was being carried out. None of the diarists even came close to guessing that in excess of three out of every four Jewish people deported from Holland were being murdered and that the rapid extermination of an entire people was taking place.

Another indication that those in Holland genuinely had no idea is that many people, both Jewish and non-Jewish, believed that anyone going into hiding and thereby incurring the wrath of the authorities would suffer a worse fate than those who obeyed the summons to turn up and be deported.

Even in 1944, when the Soviet Army began liberating the concentration camps and undeniable evidence of the gas chambers emerged, the initial reaction, in Holland and elsewhere, was disbelief. It was all simply unimaginable.

However, just because you can't imagine something, doesn't mean it can't happen.

ABOUT THE AUTHOR

Author S.J. Pridmore lives on Peng Chau, one of Hong Kong's tiny outlying islands.

Writing as Simon Pridmore, he has written many books about travel and scuba diving.

Anka's story sent him into a completely new literary universe.

Made in the USA
Las Vegas, NV
16 November 2021